A CUT ABOVE

A Crime Novel by

Thomas Cox

This book is a work of fiction. Places, events, and situations in this story are purely fictional. Any resemblance to actual persons, living or dead, is coincidental.

ISBN: 1-4140-0222-X (e-book)
ISBN: 1-4140-0223-8 (Paperback)

Library of Congress Control Number: 2003112391

This book is printed on acid free paper.

Printed in the United States of America
Bloomington, IN

1stBooks - rev. 09/15/03

1

The son of the school district's assistant superintendent Lawrence Voight had been missing for six days. It was now Thursday.

Nick Cotton looked at the assistant superintendent seated across the desk from him. Ten seconds of silence had passed between them. Finally, Nick said, "Larry, I can't find your son. I wouldn't know where to begin."

"Where he was last seen," said Dr. Larry Voight.

They were seated opposite each other in the confined space of Nick Cotton's office which until recently had been a supply closet for the custodial crew. A few seconds inside and you could still inhale the aroma of mop oil. Faculty members with hay fever would occasionally stick their heads inside just to clear their sinuses. The closet had been converted to Nick's office to coincide with his official appointment as high school Chief of Security, whatever that was. Nick hadn't the faintest idea.

Nick asked, "Did you contact the police?"

"Yes." Dr. Larry Voight's head bobbed up and down. "A Sergeant Melton in Pinellas County. He sounded sympathetic enough, but—" Voight paused to shrug. "I faxed him a picture of Mark, and he said he'd check around. I don't know what that means."

"It means he'll check police records, hospitals, halfway houses," Nick said. Even unidentified bodies, he thought, but didn't say it. "You did the right thing."

"It's not enough. Nick, you've got to help me."

Nick was shaking his head. "Let the police handle it, Larry. They're qualified and equipped. I'm not."

"You were a cop in the army."

"Briefly, with the military police," Nick said. "That was a different lifetime. I haven't shined my shoes since." He saw that Voight was waiting for more. "Larry, you got it wrong. I wasn't an investigator. Most of the time I stood around like every other soldier with his finger up his ass. You don't need a gate guard or traffic control."

"You owe me, Nick," Voight said.

Nick Cotton sighed. Yes. He wouldn't have retained his teaching position in the school district now if it hadn't been for the assistant superintendent. Nick had been afraid it would come down to this.

For seven years Nick Cotton had been the head football coach of the S.O.B. Beavers. Three times he had won the Marion County championship, and two years ago had come within a point-after-touchdown of winning the Class-Five Indiana state championship. The stadium overflowed with students, parents, and alumni, and everyone rocked to the school band and the perky female cheerleaders who led with their favorite cheer: "There are no Beavers like our Beavers." But then, for Nick Cotton, as they say in the Middle East, that was when the fit hit the shan.

This past fall, third game of the season, tough loss, Nick had found himself confronted by an obnoxious, newly elected, school board member who not only wanted to tell Nick how to coach his team but also insisted on his son getting more playing time. The board member made the mistake of getting physical and grabbing Nick's jacket and sticking his snarly face squarely into Nick's. Nick promptly put an armlock on the man, marched him into the men's restroom, kicked his legs out from under him and pushed his face into the commode. It took two assistant coaches to haul

Nick away from the blubbering, sputtering board member. The team trainer, reluctant to administer mouth-to-mouth resusitation because of where the board member's lips had been, resorted to the conventional means of body pressure to save the nearly drowned man.

The board member, of course, wanted Nick fired. A special closed-door meeting, in violation of the state's open-door policy, was convened. The victimized board member ranted that Nick Cotton had to go. When reminded that the kids liked Coach Cotton, the board member thrust his fist into the air and made his most succinct pontification: "Fuck the kids! I was the one who had to swallow toilet water!"

"Look," said the president of the board and a close friend of his aggrieved peer, "it really doesn't matter whether the guy's a good teacher or well liked. Hell, teachers are a dime a dozen and only important when we say they're important. My concern is, will he go to the media? He did damn near win a state championship. Suppose the criticism is turned on us? That would be embarrassing."

To save the district embarrassment, Dr. Voight had interceded and suggested an alternative. Nick was given a new title, Chief of High School Security, along with this tiny office and told to keep his nose clean. The cruelest blow of all had been his removal as coach. Had it not been after the start of school, Nick would have resigned on the spot and sought a coaching position somewhere else. But the timing had done him in. Dr. Voight had been the only man to come to Nick's defense and, at least, keep him employed. So, did he owe Dr. Voight? Yes, he did. Did he like it? Dippity-double fuck—No!

"You do owe me," Dr. Voight repeated.

Nick made a feeble gesture with one hand. "I know—I know."

Dr. Voight sighed. He was a man of slight stature, not skinny, not given to weight gain, simply vertically challenged at about five-seven, sort of V-faced, and had finger-like streaks of gray angling up from his sideburns into his dark hair. His job, in addition to being an assistant superintendent, was curriculum director for this north Indianapolis school district. Today, he wore brown slacks, white shirt, brown-and-yellow striped necktie, and brown-speckled sports coat. His desperation showed in every line in his face. His chin quivered when he drew his breath.

He said, "Mark's not this inconsiderate to his mother and me. Two short phone messages in five days. Something's drastically wrong."

"Don't jump to conclusions yet," Nick said. "You don't know anything, Larry. Mark did tell you he's okay."

"Unless he was forced to say that." Voight shook his head, his brow creased. "Why didn't he want to speak to Marilyn or me? He knows our schedules. Why call on Monday afternoon, and again yesterday afternoon, and talk to a machine? Both times he said exactly the same thing. He said, 'Mom, don't worry. I'm okay.' And that was it. Nothing to me or Monica. It's like he didn't want to talk to somebody directly."

"Could be he's embarrassed to give you a reason just now."

"He knows he can discuss anything with his family. We've always been open." Voight furrowed his brows deeper. "This is not like Mark. You know him. You've watched him grow up."

Nick Cotton nodded guardedly. True, this behavior was definitely unlike young Mark Voight.

Mark was seventeen, his eighteenth birthday would be next month in mid-May, a senior at Sylvester Overton Barton High School on the north side of Indianapolis, the school commonly called S.O.B. by faculty, kids, and patrons, and had everything going for him. His resume included his being a high honor roll student with straight A's, handsome with his crinkly smile and raven-dark hair inherited from his mother, one of the top prep golfers in the state of Indiana and captain of his school's golf team, on the fall soccer and cross-country teams, president of the senior class council, editor-in-chief of the yearbook, co-editor of the bi-monthly school paper, recipient of a scholarship to Northwestern University for next fall, going steady with one of the prettiest girls at S.O.B., and possessing, for over three and a half years, a perfect attendance record. That was until this week.

Two weeks ago this past Saturday, at the start of spring break, Mark Voight had departed for Clearwater, Florida, with his friends Rob McKay and Jerry Lett in Rob's car. They had checked into The Blue Swan Motel and spent most of the week, along with the usual mob of other tourists and kids, on Clearwater Beach. Last Saturday they were to check out and start the drive home, scheduled to arrive back in Indianapolis sometime Sunday afternoon or evening. It was an annual spring trip for the boys together, but the first time without parental accompaniment. They had made their reservation at the motel almost a year in advance. Rob now had a car and was reputed to be a decent driver, so no one was unduly concerned—except for the parental cautions to "drive carefully," "take your time," and "don't get into any trouble," and one or two whispered phrases of advice from the fathers "not to get the clap" or "knock anybody up."

The trouble was that, when they checked out of the motel on Saturday, Mark Voight refused to come home with his friends. No explanation. Flat refusal. Rob and Jerry had thought he was joking at first. They drove around awhile and went back to the motel to get him. Mark and his suitcases were nowhere to be found.

It had been two devastated boys who came home on Sunday.

Nick Cotton reflected on this as he clenched his teeth, trying to think of something to say that wouldn't sound too patronizing or totally hopeless. For the past two days he had avoided the assistant superintendent and had not returned his phone messages.

After a few seconds, spacing his words carefully, Nick said, "I can't do it, Larry. Work with that Sergeant Melton."

"No." Voight made a nervous motion with one hand, closed his fingers and put his knuckles to his lower lip, his elbow resting on the desktop. "Marilyn and I've discussed it. We want a friend, somebody who knows Mark personally. Look, I'm sure Melton means well, but it's a job to him. Melton said he's got two cabinets full of reports on missing kids. Some they find, most they don't. He couldn't express much optimism. I need somebody who cares, who knows Mark. I want you to go there for me."

Nick drew a long breath of his own, letting more seconds elapse. "What you need to do, Larry, is find a private detective who knows the Tampa, St. Pete, Clearwater area. Sergeant Melton can refer someone. Contact that man and let him work for you."

Voight kept shaking his head. "A private eye might go through the motions for a fee. I won't know him, I won't know how serious he is. Nick, it's not the money. I'll pay you, not just your expenses but whatever you think's appropriate."

"Larry—"

"A couple of days, that's all I'm asking. I'll cover your absence. You know how to talk to people. You know how to ask questions. I trust you, Nick. Marilyn trusts you. I want somebody I can trust."

"Nobody knows why Mark's doing this," Nick said. "He might be home right now waiting for you guys."

"Marilyn would call me. She didn't go to work today. She's staying by the phone. Even Monica's worried, and you know how brothers and sisters squabble."

"Mark left you two messages and told you not to worry," Nick said. "I know that's not easy for you and Marilyn, but it sounds like he's got an agenda. Right now he doesn't want to let you in on it. Anything else is guesswork, Larry, and naturally you're guessing worst-case scenarios. What can I say? Don't worry? That's condescending and dumb on my part. He said he's okay. Long as you're sure it was Mark."

"It was Mark's voice, no doubt about it," Voight said. "But he might be in serious trouble. Maybe they won't let him say more than that."

"They?" Nick raised his brows. "Kidnappers? Larry, you're not rich. A kidnapper would've contacted you before now with demands. Nobody else would have a reason to hold Mark against his will. You've got to assume he's doing this on his own."

Voight's shoulders slumped lower. "It doesn't make sense."

Nick ran a hand over his crew-cut hair, looked down, looked up, and studied his friend. "How's Marilyn handling this?"

"She's calmer than I am," Voight said. "But you know Marilyn. She's always strong in a crisis. I told her I was going to ask you, and she thinks it's a good idea."

"Maybe Kelly Moore has heard from Mark," Nick suggested.

"No, he hasn't contacted Kelly. Not a single word to her. She's in touch with us every day. She can't believe it either. Mark's missing school. He's his golf team captain. He hasn't contacted his coach or anybody. I talk to Rob and Jerry every day, and they haven't heard from him."

"Waiting's the hard part," Nick said, then regretted saying it because it sounded patronizing. He looked down to pick at a speck of lint above his left breast pocket, wanting to look anywhere except at the other man's face. Today, Nick had on a salmon-colored, open-necked shirt, dark trousers and a navy-blue sports-coat. He took longer than necessary with the lint. Gradually, he rolled his eyes up to look at the other man. "I'm sorry. I'm not much help."

Voight, looking at him, spoke again. "Nick," he said, "I've counted you my friend ever since you came to this school. I need my friend now." Voight stuck a finger inside his shirt collar and tugged against his necktie. "A couple of days in Florida, that's what I'm asking. Even if it's a chance in a million—"

"More like one in ten million. What's Florida's population now?"

"Whatever," Voight said, getting almost animated, his eyes shiny.

"Larry, I can't find Mark if he doesn't want to be found, and that's the truth."

"You'll be away from here," Voight went on. "Someplace sunny and warm. When's the last time you saw a palm tree or a beach? Girls in bikinis, they're all over the place. Or an alligator. Hell, visit Busch Gardens."

Nick smiled wryly. “Don’t they shoot tourists in Florida?”

“That’s a bad rap.”

“Larry, I don’t know a dammed thing about Florida. I’ve been there exactly twice in my life. Somebody told me I ought to see the Everglades. I spent a whole day burning, swatting mosquitoes, and being overall fucking miserable. Then, in Miami, I got accosted by three hookers and a coked-up kid with a gun. I think I sent a postcard back saying ‘I wish you were here, and I were there.’ That’s what I know about Florida.”

“Okay. Skip the postcard stuff. Bottom line is, you owe me, Nick.”

Outside the tiny office, they could hear sounds of kids moving, bustling, and talking in the hallway. It was an early-morning passing period for the students and faculty at Sylvester Overton Barton High School. When Nick had arrived, Voight had been waiting at his classroom door and promptly steered him to this office. Voight had even arranged for a substitute teacher to be in Nick’s room.

Voight broke the silence between them. “Two days, Nick.” He held up two fingers for emphasis. “If you go,

Marilyn won't go. I'm afraid she'll do something crazy." Voight choked a small sob, then squeezed the bridge of his nose with thumb and forefinger, then touched the puffiness beneath his eye. "Right now, I wish I had a drink."

That, Nick could handle for him. He opened a bottom desk drawer and lifted out two permanently-stained, but clean, coffee mugs and set them on the bare desk. From the same drawer he brought out a half-pint bottle of bourbon about two-thirds full, opened it, and poured healthy slugs into each mug.

Voight's eyes opened in astonishment. "Jesus Christ, Nick! You keep liquor here in the school? We both could be fired for this."

"You said you needed a drink." Nick recapped the bottle and put it away. "I took it from a fourteen-year-old kid who thought she was all grown up. She was drinking at her locker. I reported it to her parents. Her father was so interested in her welfare that he laughed and hung up on me. The girl is now a runaway."

"Mark's not a runaway," Voight said. He didn't hesitate to lift the mug and drink. "I don't know. Hell, maybe he is."

At least some color was returning to the man's face, Nick noted.

Dr. Larry Voight drank more bourbon and looked at him. "It's killing us, Nick," Voight said. "We can't eat—we don't sleep. Even Monica's lost her appetite. There was no argument, no fight, before he left. He was happy as could be. You know he's been accepted to Northwestern, a full scholarship to study journalism. Looking forward to it. That's where Kelly's going, too. It's all Mark talked about for the past two months."

"Are you sure Kelly hasn't heard from him?" Nick asked. Watch out!—he was getting drawn in.

"I believe her. She calls our house morning and night. Last night she broke down and cried to Marilyn on the phone."

Nick looked at the bare wall. He wished he had a picture or something to stare at. He'd have to remember to hang some kind of stupid picture. Damn, he wanted to distance himself from this problem.

Voight said, "I'm concerned about Marilyn. Some strange, dark mood has come over her. Depression—fear—I suppose. Nick, I'm letting her down. I should be doing something. But what? I'm scared Marilyn might jump in her car and start racing to Florida on some wild notion of finding him. I think it's in her mind."

"You have to talk her out of that," Nick said.

"Am I procrastinating?" Voight asked. "Is that what I'm doing?" He drained his mug and wiped his mouth with his hand. His eyes had more shine in them now, but it was the drink working and not optimism. "Right now I'm in charge of this goddam school district while our superintendent's in the hospital getting his ass reamed. I'm butt-deep in contract negotiations with the teachers' union, I got a school board meeting tonight, and I'm preparing two court cases. I'd chuck all this shit in an instant if it would bring Mark back. When he didn't come home Sunday, I should've grabbed the first available transportation and got down there. But then what?"

"Larry, he might show up any minute wondering what all the fuss is about."

"If he does, he'll get his first spanking." Voight reached over and took Nick's mug. "I can't talk to Marilyn. Whatever happens, and this is hard as hell for me to say, whatever happens regarding Mark, I don't want to lose my wife."

Nick watched Voight down the remaining bourbon in the second mug and take a deep breath.

"Do it for me, Nick. Just—just follow your instincts. You always have. You might come up with something Sergeant Melton's missing. If you don't go, I'll have to. You'll be more objective."

Nick started shaking his head. "Where should I look? Mark could be anyplace in Florida or anywhere in-between there and here. That's a lot of the U. S. of A. Think about it."

Voight leaned forward. "I'm buying time for both Marilyn and me. I'm praying. I'm hoping, like you said, Mark simply comes home. You'll do it for us. I know you will."

From an inside coat pocket, Voight brought out a sheet of blue stationery with his wife's initials at the top and spread it on the desk, turning it so that Nick could read. There was a name: Blue Swan Motel with an address and phone number beneath. Below that was information on an ATA flight and the time 6:55.

He said, "ATA had a cancellation on a morning flight tomorrow, and no waiting list. Six-fifty-five a.m. Straight to Tampa. You pick up the ticket at the airport. I've got you booked back Sunday night at nine-fifteen. See? And you pick up a car at Alamo. I'll cover all your expenses and pay you extra. Name what you want."

"I don't want your money," Nick said, feeling a pressure behind his eyes like a sinus headache. He massaged his temples with his fingertips. "Why did they select that particular motel?"

"It was available and cheap. They tried at the Buccaneer Lodge and Peg Leg Park, but those places were booked during spring break even further in advance."

"I guess you called the motel. Did you talk to the owner?"

"I talked to somebody. All he could tell me was that Mark was there with two other boys and they all checked out last Saturday. Listen, I'm sorry I couldn't arrange a place for you to stay. It's still their tourist season. But you'll find something." Voight tapped his finger on the sheet of paper. "Two and a half days, Nick. That's all I'm asking. If you can't find Mark by then, come home. Nick—?" He waited for Nick

Cotton to look at him. "You don't know it's hopeless until you try. How many times did you tell your football squad that? They never quit on you because you wouldn't quit. I'll tell you what. If you think it's necessary, after you have a look around, you hire a private eye for me. I'll accept that."

Now Nick had to massage above his eyebrows. "Marilyn wants this?"

"She jumped on it when I mentioned it. She thinks it's a good idea."

"Ichabod won't go for it." Nick was referring to S.O.B.'s principal, Sanford Wilcox, a man called "Ichabod" behind his back by students and faculty because of his scrawny body, prominent Adam's apple, narrow face and hooked nose. "He thinks I'm a loose cannon."

"Maybe a loose cannon's what I need. Don't worry, I'll handle Ichabod. As for the Blob—" Voight was referring to the township's three-hundred-plus-pound superintendent, currently in the hospital, "—he won't even know you're gone, or care, the way he's feeling. If we need an excuse, I'll say I'm sending you to a seminar."

"I bet you checked into that," Nick said. "There probably is a seminar going on."

"Nick, there's always an education seminar someplace. You can spit out of an airplane and hit one. I'll make one up if I have to." Voight shoved another item around to face Nick. It was a four-set of Mark Voight's senior picture, cut from a larger sheet. Each photo measured about three by five inches. It showed the smiling, handsome, young man in his blue suit, white shirt, and striped necktie. Nothing but cheerfulness showed in Mark Voight's expression, but, of course, the senior picture had been taken during the fall semester. Much could change in a few months. "I figured you might need these," Voight went on. "Anything else you can think of?"

Slowly, Nick took the materials from the desk, leaned to one side, and put them in his jacket pocket. He repeated the itinerary. "Leave in the morning and back on Sunday, right? That's all there is, Larry. This won't drag on."

Voight nodded eagerly.

Nick asked, "Why did they pick Clearwater as their vacation spot? Most of our kids head for the east coast. Palm Beach, or Fort Lauderdale."

"I think it was Mark's idea. He knows his mother is from that area originally. We never took him there, even as a kid. Last time we took the boys, we went to the Keys and visited the 'Glades. I used to go to Clearwater when I was a kid. It's where Marilyn and I met."

"Does Marilyn still have family there?"

Voight shook his head. "Last one of her family died about ten years ago. Marilyn never wanted to go back. She didn't have a happy childhood. I met Marilyn's mother maybe twice in my life. The woman was crabby and suspicious of Marilyn's friends. That's why Marilyn ran away and came to me. We were married here in Indiana. I was finishing my first degree then."

"How much money did Mark take with him?" asked Nick.

"Four hundred dollars. Each boy took the same. That's not counting the cost of their motel room, which they paid for in advance. It's not a money thing, Nick. Mark knows if that became a problem he could simply call or wire me."

"Has he access to more?" Nick asked. "Credit cards? Checking account?"

"His account's at Bank One, in both our names. He hasn't requested any more. He has no plastic of his own. He left his checkbook at home."

"Might be he spent everything, is too embarrassed to ask for more, and is working to make enough to come home on."

"No," Voight said firmly. "Mark's always taken a lot of pride in his academic record, his attendance, and his extra-curricular activities. Besides, there's Kelly. She hasn't heard from him. There has to be some—bigger—reason behind this, Nick. Something in Mark's mind."

Which triggered another question for Nick. "Has Mark been seeing a doctor? Psychologist?—psychiatrist?—even an M.D. about anything?"

"No, I wouldn't keep it from you. There simply is no plausible reason for his action."

Nick realized that he wasn't going to massage away the headache Voight had handed to him. He thought some more and asked, "What will you and Marilyn do if I come back and say, 'no luck'?"

"I don't know," Voight said. "I honest to God don't know."

2

Beth Zellmer, one of the administrative secretaries, looked up from her desk at Nick Cotton and said, "Mark's not a runaway."

"Stranger things have happened, Beth." Nick tapped the pink pad of hallway passes on her desk. "Send for Rob McKay, Jerry Lett, and Kelly Moore. I'll use the conference room and see them one at a time."

While Beth was writing, she said, "Dr. Voight just left the principal's office. Mr. Wilcox wants to see you. This is not a good day for him, Nick, so go easy on him. He spilled coffee on his pants this morning. I took his pants across the street to the cleaners. Try not to make jokes about his bony knees." She tore off one slip and began writing on another. "How long will you need a substitute teacher?"

"The rest of today and tomorrow. I'll be back Sunday. Then I'll have to explain to Dr. Voight how hopeless his idea was."

"Maybe it's not." Beth tilted her head and smiled in a "who knows?" fashion. "As a parent, I can guess how he feels. I'm glad you're going. I'd want you to go if it was one of mine."

When Nick went into the principal's office, Sanford Wilcox, behind his desk, straightened up abruptly. From Nick's immediate perspective, Wilcox looked relatively normal with his black suit coat on over his white shirt and black necktie. From the waist down, Wilcox was hidden from view.

"Dr. Voight's sending you," Wilcox said. "He informed me."

"Rest of the week." Nick shrugged. "I couldn't think of a way to gracefully refuse."

On a small table by the office window was a hot plate with a carafe of steaming black coffee, one of the perks for occupying the principal's office. Nick reached to the middle of Wilcox's desk and picked up the man's personal coffee mug. It was white and had the word PRINCIPAL stenciled on it in bold blue caps. He started to turn toward the carafe.

"Wait!" Wilcox scrambled up from his chair. "Wait, Nick! Don't use that." He flung open a desk drawer. "I got another cup here."

Wilcox rushed around the desk with a plain brown mug. Nick smiled because it was true. Wilcox wore no pants. He had on red, white, and blue striped boxer-shorts and gartered socks that disappeared into very shiny black shoes. He thrust the plain mug at Nick and retrieved his own, cradling it in both hands, breathing what sounded like a sigh of relief. Smiling, trying not to laugh at the principal's skinny legs, Nick poured coffee for both of them. Even though he loved to torment Wilcox, he actually liked the man.

Wilcox, his panic dissipated, returned to his chair and sat. Nick haunched onto the corner of the desk, tasted the coffee, and looked down at a stack of wet, coffee-stained papers that had been pushed to one corner. He said, "Sanford, have you picked up on anything about Mark? Something you didn't share with Dr. Voight? A rumor?"

Wilcox drank and shook his head. "No, nothing. He's giving you two days, Nick. That's not much time."

"Too long, or not long enough. I'm coming home Sunday night. Maybe we'll get lucky by then, and Mark will show up."

"Everything I've heard about Mark Voight has been positive," Wilcox said. "You might check with his other teachers. Talk to Kaycee. Mark works on the newspaper for her. What about those boys that went with him?"

"I'll meet with them. Kelly Moore, too." Nick saw that Wilcox was in the dark about it. "His girlfriend. They've been close a couple of years. Supposed to go to Northwestern together."

"Oh, she's the pretty one. The cheerleader. I talked to McKay and Lett. They couldn't add anything."

Nick smiled. "Nobody likes to talk to the school principal, Sanford. I'll see them one at a time. Compare their versions of what happened. Together, they might overlook a detail or let something slide, thinking if one or the other didn't mention it, it couldn't be important."

"Honestly, do you have any hope?" Wilcox asked.

"Only if you believe in miracles."

Wilcox drank more coffee and apparently had a sudden thought. "I wonder what Dr. Yablod will think of this. What will he say?"

"Probably 'ouch.' The Blob's getting a knife up his ass this morning."

"I wish," Wilcox grumbled, "that you would stop referring to our superintendent as 'the Blob.' It's disrespectful. You wouldn't be laughing if you were in the hospital for hemorrhoids."

"I'd hate to be his proctologist," Nick said. "I wouldn't know where to poke. But if you want to give him a call at St. Vincent's, go ahead. He left Dr. Voight in charge."

Hal Ryerson, the senior assistant principal at S.O.B., came into the office and stopped. Wilcox stood and motioned him on inside. Ryerson saw that the principal was without trousers. He looked at Wilcox, then at Nick, and crinkled his broad face in a little smile. "Sorry, guys," he said. "I can come back later if you want to be alone."

"I had an accident with my coffee," Wilcox said, irritably, "so get that smirk off your face. Guess what our chief of security will be doing the next few days."

"Going to Florida to look for Mark," Ryerson said. "I heard. But will it do any good?"

"That's a point I tried to make," Nick told him.

"You won't get the school in trouble, will you?"

Nick stood up and finished his coffee. "Hal, I don't think anybody in Florida has heard of S.O.B. High School or gives a shit."

"Yeah, right. I wish somebody would send <u>me</u> to Florida."

Wilcox looked at his assistant principal. "You couldn't find Florida with a road map and a compass." He turned to Nick. "What if you don't find the kid?"

"Odds are a million to one against," Nick agreed. "Unless Mark is standing on the runway, waving his arms and shouting 'Mr. Cotton, here I am,' I don't have a prayer. I'll try to hire a detective who might give it some attention."

Ryerson went around and helped himself to another spare coffee mug in Wilcox's drawer. He walked over to pour coffee and said, "I've got a theory about Mark's absence. Want to hear it?"

"No," Wilcox and Nick said in unison.

Ryerson poured and set down the carafe. "My theory is, Mark's getting himself laid and don't want to come home. You know how seniors are."

Nick smiled at him. "Is that what you did when you were a senior, Hal? Get yourself laid all the time?"

"Actually, no," Ryerson said, without a hint of embarrassment. "I missed out on a lot of the fun things. I was a virgin until I got married. But I see what you mean.

Would Mark give up everything he's worked for? Hey, I've known guys who ruined their whole lives over a little pussy." He shrugged. "Sometimes a big one."

"You guys are vulgar," Wilcox grumbled.

"Honestly," Nick said, "I hope that's all it is."

He left the principal's office, retraced his steps toward the administrative conference room, and stopped outside another administrative office, this one belonging to Kaycee Tucker, one of the two, junior, assistant principals. The door was ajar, so Nick pushed on it and walked in.

Kaycee, a perky brunette with short, curly hair, was alone at her desk under the two monstrous hanging-plants that were sending voracious-looking runners down the back wall. Her eyes popped wide open when Nick walked in on her. She had been leaning back in her chair with her shoes off and her shapely, stockinged legs crossed at the ankles and propped up on the desk blotter. Nick got the tiniest glimpse of her white lace panties when she swung her legs to the floor and sat up staight.

"Make my day, Kaycee," he said with a smile.

She laughed. "I wasn't expecting company, Nick. My feet hurt."

Nick leaned over her desk, resting on his knuckles. "Kaycee, you're in charge of school publications. You work closely with Mark Voight. Did the kid seem okay to you before he left?"

"Same as I told his father. Mark has never given me the slightest problem, and I have no inkling why he hasn't come home. You're going after him, right?"

"I'm going to Florida for a couple of days. I won't find him."

"Maybe you will." Kaycee rocked forward and traced with her index finger a little circle on the back of one of Nick's fists. "This screws up our Saturday plans. After I worked so hard to get you to ask me out."

"Simple. Keep next Saturday open. Hal Ryerson's got a theory that Mark found a girl there and just hasn't come home yet."

"Anything's possible," she said. "But in the short time I've been here, I think I got to know Mark. The kid's not only smart, but happy. He's got Kelly Moore."

"Maybe Kelly's not giving him what he wants?"

Kaycee shrugged. “Bet she is. Mark doesn’t strike me as the hormonal-driven, frustrated, male adolescent. You’re worried about him now, aren’t you?”

Nick nodded and straightened up. “Concerned—curious. But I still don’t know what I can do. I couldn’t find a good way to refuse Larry Voight.”

“Nick, you’re the best man for a bad assignment. Good luck,” she told him seriously. “I keep praying we don’t hear tragic news about Mark.”

3

"Wish I did know something, Coach," Jerry Lett said from his chair across the table in the conference room. "Coach" was what a lot of the kids still called Nick Cotton. He said, "We're not holding anything back from Dr. Voight. Hell, Mark's our best friend. When he wouldn't come with us, I kind'a expected him to maybe beat us back home—you know, maybe fly back. Playing a joke on us. Rob and me took a day and a half to drive it."

"You had no hint he was planning to dump you guys?" Cotton asked.

"No way. We checked out of the motel on schedule. Me and Rob had our bags tossed in Rob's car. Mark wouldn't get in. He goes, 'You guys go on ahead. I'll catch up with you later.' It surprised the hell out of us, Coach. We started talking to him—you know, asking questions—but he just shook his head and goes, 'No, I'm staying. Don't worry 'bout it.' We couldn't change his mind. We still thought it was a joke. That was last Saturday, 'bout noon. We even drove around a bit and went back to get him. He wasn't there, outside or inside."

"What kind of luggage did Mark have?" asked Nick.

"Just the one bag. Leather suitcase that belongs to his dad. Had his dad's nametag on it, with his address."

"And you guys stuck together the whole week?"

"No, Coach, we didn't. That wasn't the plan. I mean, we just let things happen as they happened. We hit the beaches together for the most part, but got separated. It rained two of the six days. Me and Rob stayed in the room, but Mark wasn't there. We don't know where he was. We met other kids, got invited to parties. Mark only stayed those two nights away from the motel though."

"Where?"

"He wouldn't tell us," Jerry said. "We figured he must've scored. He acted like it was some big secret."

"Scored with a girl?"

"What else?"

"Some guys score with drugs."

"Not Mark." Jerry shook his head firmly. "Not the hard stuff anyway. He might'a done a little grass, that I don't know. But Mark's a pretty straight dude. You know he's been accepted to Northwestern."

"Kelly Moore, too."

"Yeah, they're like this." Jerry crossed his middle finger over his index finger. "In love."

"Yet, you think it's possible he scored with a girl. Was he chasing girls?"

"Hell, no," Jerry said. "Me and Rob did. Not Mark."

"Then what made you think so, Jerry?"

Jerry furrowed his brows in concentration. "I see what you mean. I guess I was thinking of the one that kind'a hung around Mark, bumping into him at the beach and, a couple of times, in front of the motel. It looked like she was chasing him."

Nick Cotton smiled a little. Hopefully, Hal Ryerson's theory was taking on a little more plausibility. He asked Jerry, "Did you meet the girl?"

"He wouldn't introduce us." Jerry shrugged. "But I think he did to Rob. Her name's Donnie Ann something-or-other, but neither of us knows anything about her. On the way home, Rob and me talked about it. Wondered if that's what Mark was doing, staying there to get a little. I tell you,

Coach, it was a lousy trip. Me and Rob almost turned around to go back, but what the hell, we wouldn't know where to find him. But, hey, we never mentioned that Donnie Ann to Dr. Voight or to Kelly. We didn't want to hurt Kelly's feelings."

"Describe this girl."

Thoughtfully, Jerry Lett wet his lips with his tongue. "Well, she's a redhead with lots of freckles. Hair cut kind'a short, in bangs. Not filled out like Kelly. Not much up here." He cupped his hands in front of his chest. "Nice looking legs, I remember that, but freckles there, too. I got the feeling she's a little older than us guys. I don't think she could take much of the sun. She had these peeling spots on her shoulders and nose, like maybe she burns instead of tans. She wore the damndest skimpiest bikini, I mean right up the crack of her ass."

"Sounds like you had a good look at her," Nick said. "Will you do me a favor?"

"Sure, Coach, if I can."

"Do you know Mrs. Kyle in the art department?"

"Yeah, but I never had her for a teacher."

"I'll speak with Rob, then I'll give the two of you a pass to go see Mrs. Kyle," Nick told him. "She's an excellent sketch artist, Jerry. You guys describe Donnie Ann's face and hair as exact as you can. Work with her to come up with the closest picture possible. Tell Mrs. Kyle I need it by the end of the day. She'll do it for me. You say you can't remember Donnie Ann's last name?"

"I never heard it. I'm sure, Coach."

"What nights were Mark not with you in the motel?"

Jerry had to think for a moment. "Wednesday and Thursday. He stayed with us Friday night. We were pretty bombed out, and about broke, and we had to drive back the next day."

Rob McKay sat in the chair Jerry Lett had vacated. "I'm worried about the guy, Coach," he said. "This ain't like Mark. Not at all like him."

"Jerry said Mark spent a couple of nights out. Did he tell you about it, Rob? What he did? If he met anybody?"

"He refused to." Rob spread his hands. "We even tried to tease it out of him. Said we'd tell Kelly if he wouldn't give us all the details. Of course, he knew we won't. He was different that Friday."

"How different?" asked Nick.

"Strange, I guess. Like he was preoccupied with something, off in his own thoughts. Barely said a thing to either of us. Know what I thought, Coach? I thought he might'a made it with that redhead and then felt guilty."

"What's Donnie Ann's last name?"

"He never told us. She looked older than most of the kids we ran into. I don't mean real old, not like twenty-two or anything, but maybe like nineteen or twenty. When she'd meet him on the beach, they'd go off and talk. They didn't want Jerry and me around. One day she was hanging out by the motel when we got back from breakfast. They went for a walk then, too. Maybe she had a place of her own. I know what we should'a done. We should'a set him down and asked him what the fuck he was thinking. But we didn't." Rob shrugged his shoulders. "We figured Mark's a big boy."

Nick nodded as he eyes probed into the young man's. "Rob, I know you and Jerry well enough to realize that you two guys sniffed out all the pussy you could find, but I thought Mark was too serious about Kelly."

"Me, too," said Rob. "I wouldn't toss Kelly Moore over for no Donnie Ann. But that's me. Maybe he can't get in Kelly's pants. Nobody else can, that's for sure." Rob turned his head to stare out the big window toward the street. The day was sunny and bright for April, temperature about seventy, car traffic moving steadily along the street in both directions. "Mark's a good guy," he said finally. "He won't tell secrets. So Jerry and I guessed that this Donnie Ann's fucking him." He looked at Nick again. "He's a guy, Coach. He can't beat his meat all the time. Donnie Ann looked like the kind who knows how to play the game."

Nick knew that Jerry and Rob were not lying to him. He did not suspect that these young men were embellishing anything, at least not much. And he hadn't the slightest doubt about their concern for Mark Voight. He said, "The other girls you met, Rob? Would they know this Donnie Ann?"

"I doubt it. I don't even remember their last names. We don't pay much attention to last names. Hell, we won't see 'em again."

"I'll give you a minute to think, Rob," Nick told him. He had been using the back of the itinerary sheet on which to scribble his notes. "See if you can think of anything—other people, places—that might help me find Mark if I look for him."

"That what you're gonna do?"

"Dr. Voight wants me to."

After a little while, Rob shook his head. "I tried, Coach. Believe me. I tried all week to think of something to tell his family. Jesus, I'm sorry."

"Me, too," Nick said. "I'll have Mrs. Zellmer give you and Jerry a pass to see the art teacher."

When Kelly Moore came into the conference room, Nick seated her and went around the table to sit facing her. Kelly smiled at him, but it was a forced smile.

"How you doing, Kel?" he asked.

"I'm okay," she said in a listless voice. She adjusted her skirt, then picked at something on her sweater. She placed her books and purse on the table. "No, I'm not. I'm messing up at practice." Kelly was captain of the cheerleaders squad and also the top player on the girls' spring golf team. From her purse she took a tissue and wiped her nose. Her pretty face clouded, and she started to cry. "I feel like shit, Coach."

For a couple of minutes Nick let her cry. Evidently she needed to, and he wasn't about to bully her. Even her tears couldn't make her unattractive. She had natural blond hair, blue eyes, and a terrific figure for her five foot-five inch height. The skirt and sweater she wore fit her snugly. After awhile she stopped crying, found more tissue, wiped her eyes and blew her nose. She tried to give Nick another smile, this one apologetic.

"I'll be all right," she said, stiffly. She got up to deposit the tissues into a waste basket, came back and sat. "If I start crying again, just tell me to shut up and quit acting like a baby. I've been crying a lot lately."

"I understand," Nick said, as kindly as he could. "Mark's dad wants me to look for him."

Now a glimmer of hope flashed in Kelly's shiny eyes. "Good." Then she snapped, "I don't know why he's waited this long. I'd have gone down there for Mark the second day he wasn't home."

"I'm sure Dr. Voight wanted to," Nick said. "But don't forget, he trusts his son. Did they tell you about the phone messages Mark left?"

Kelly nodded. "Mrs. Voight told me. Dammit! Nobody's doing anything."

Nick sat patiently, waiting, watching Kelly swing on that pendulum between anguish and anger. He watched her get her emotions under control by inhaling and exhaling.

Then her tone softened as she blinked back another tear. "It's weird, Coach. Not like Mark at all. But Mrs. Voight was positive it was his voice. You know, I saw a movie once where some people spliced together a voice tape to make it sound like the person said things he really didn't."

"It's possible," Nick said, "but there would have to be a reason for such thing. You didn't hear from Mark at all during spring break?"

"He didn't call. He didn't write. No e-mails. Not even a postcard."

"Did you have a fight before he left?"

Kelly looked hurt at first, then offended by the question. "We're in love," she said with the assurance of youth in love and wiped another tear with her finger. Her light eye-shadow was already smeared.

Nick said, "Mark and Rob and Jerry stayed at the Blue Swan Motel in Clearwater. Did Mark ever mention anyplace else he wanted to visit? Or any person?"

"No. Actually, he almost decided not to make the trip. We talked about a month or so ago. He said he didn't want to be away from me. But they'd made reservations way back, so I told him to go ahead and have fun. I had a term paper to write anyway. I spent most of my time last week in the library, then went to Chicago with my parents for a couple of days. I was sure when I got home I'd at least have a card waiting."

"Kelly, tell me something about Mark I don't know."

She looked blank. "I don't understand."

"I know what kind of student he is," said Nick. "I know he's a good golfer. He comes from a solid family background and is popular with his classmates. He's a good-looking kid. The two of you have been accepted at Northwestern. And Mark wants to be a journalist. Now—what don't I know?"

"Coach, he's just a wonderful person."

A wonderful person who didn't come home, Nick thought. "What are his bad habits?"

Kelly's brow creased as she pursed her lips. "Nothing bad. Oh, he drinks a little beer once in awhile with the guys. I don't think his folks know that. But he doesn't drink a lot. I mean, it's never bothered me. I never saw him drunk. I just know what he tells me. He's not reckless. He can really curse when he gets ticked, but he's never cursed at me."

"Drugs?" asked Nick.

"No. He couldn't hide it from me if he did. Why'd you think so?"

"I don't. I was asking," Nick said. "Think real hard, Kel. Did Mark seem distracted, secretive, upset before his trip?"

"No. You think I'm lying to you, Coach?"

"Not at all. I'm trying to understand him. My thinking was, he might tell or indicate things to you he wouldn't to his folks. How do you suppose he spent his time on spring break with the guys?"

"On the beach," Kelly said. "Swimming, sunning, eating—maybe going to parties. Maybe drinking a little, too.

I mean, that's what I would expect of guys. And Mark's not a saint. Last year, when Mark's parents took them, he took his golf clubs, but not this time. He told me he never had a chance to play before, so he would just hang out and have some fun."

Nick smiled at her. "While you stayed here and worked hard on your term paper."

Kelly returned a little smile through her sadness. "Well, my folks wouldn't've let me go with him if that's what you mean. They're old-fashioned that way. Anyway, Rob McKay told me this spring break is supposed to be a guy sort'a thing. I didn't want to interfere. It's healthier if Mark's got a little time away from me."

"You're a smart lady," said Nick. "Did you tell him about anyplace you might want to visit in Florida?"

"No, I haven't been to Florida yet."

"That puts you in the minority of S.O.B. students."

"My mom's not a person who can take much sun," Kelly said. "It hurts her skin. Her hair's even lighter than mine."

"I know. I've met your mom. May I ask you one more really personal question?"

"Sure," she said.

"Is Mark a virgin?"

Kelly blushed deeply. "No, he's not. We've been having sex for a year now. Not very often, maybe ten—twelve times a month."

Nick had to look away and concentrate on keeping his expression blank before he looked back at her. That was more than he got—a whole lot more.

"But we're not careless," Kelly added, quickly. "He uses rubbers. I'm not ready to get pregnant yet."

"Real smart," Nick said, still biting his lip.

"Rob McKay's been acting kind'a funny to me," Kelly said. "Like he's not telling me everything. I asked him, joking like, if Mark found another girlfriend, and Rob got all nervous and said I'm being silly."

"Understand, Kelly," Nick said, "they both feel bad about leaving him. But it wasn't their fault."

Kelly chewed her lower lip and nodded slowly. "I'm thinking of jumping on a bus and going there."

"Don't," Nick said, emphatically, but trying not to scare her. "Put it out of your mind. Think of your parents. They'd know what you did and call the police immediately.

Besides, Kel, you wouldn't know what to do once you got there. It wouldn't help you or Mark."

"Not doing anything isn't helping either," she said.

4

In his apartment that evening, Nick Cotton made a phone call to one of his ex-wives who now lived, with her second husband, on the Gulf coast of Florida not far from the Tampa-St. Pete megalopolis. She agreed to put Nick up for a couple of days as long as he refrained from making any snide comments about the man she'd married and promised not to engage her husband in arm wrestling. "You broke his arm last time," she reminded Nick.

"I was ticked," Nick said. "But you got even. You blackened my eye."

She said, "You two get into this macho 'a macho shit again and I'll do more than blacken your eyes. I'll cut your balls off. His, too."

At 6:15 A.M., Nick collected his ticket, checked his single bag at the ATA counter through to Tampa International, went through the security check to the concourse, bought a coffee at a stand, and sat in the waiting area near the designated gate to read the morning Star. For the trip he had put on slacks, a slip-over sports-shirt buttoned to the neck, and a light jacket. He was scanning the sports section of the newspaper when he became aware that a woman had sat down in the seat next to him.

He looked at her in surprise and said, "Marilyn?"

Marilyn Voight gave him a little smile. "Nick, I needed to see you before you got off."

Nick folded the paper and nodded. Circumstances aside, it was always a pleasure to see Marilyn Voight. Subtract a few weeks from the beginning of his tenure at S.O.B. High School, and Nick had known her nearly as long as he knew her husband. She, too, was a teacher in the district at one of the elementary schools. She was an extremely attractive, dark-haired woman, beautiful, or as close to beautiful as could be in Nick's perception of beautiful women, had a lovely oval face, a light touch of make-up this morning, and little lines of gray in her hair that she had not attempted to conceal or cover. The way the little gray lines curved, almost as though they had been applied by an artist's brush, only made her more attractive. She wore a pale-blue jumpsuit outfit and white tennis shoes. Three weeks ago she had celebrated her fortieth birthday when Larry Voight and their two kids had treated her to a steak dinner in the most expensive restaurant in north Indy. Voight had told Nick about it at the time.

Every time Nick Cotton had been in the company of Marilyn Voight, he had appreciated her beauty and class. At those educational seminars and meetings, no matter how mundane Nick considered them, he had noted how this lady possessed the quiet quality of drawing attention without saying a word, her presence in a roomful of educators being impressive. He could see why Dr. Larry Voight considered himself fortunate in his choice of a wife. But, right now, Nick noted the worry lines at the corners of Marilyn's brown eyes.

"First, I want to thank you for helping us," she said, placing a hand over one of Nick's. "You're a good friend, Nick."

"Well—" Nick started and stopped, not sure how to respond. He reversed his hand to hold hers and give it a slight squeeze.

"Is there anything you need for us to do at your place?" she asked. "Take care of goldfish, plants, anything?"

"No. I don't keep goldfish, I can't grow plants, and, basically, my place is a mess."

"Larry said you don't know yet where you'll be staying in Clearwater."

"I got it worked out," Nick said. "One of my ex's, Carol, and her new husband's got a condo at Treasure Island. They're there now, through the season. I called, and she said they can put me up on their couch. She said it's underneath a marlin they got mounted on their wall. Maybe she hopes it'll drop off and stab me."

Marilyn continued to hold onto his hand, occasionally returning light pressure. "Doesn't sound like she holds any grudges. Knowing Carol, I don't think she would."

"We get along fine now. When I get there, I'll have to get a map and find Treasure Island."

"South of Clearwater, on the coast," Marilyn said. "Sounds like Carol's found a nice husband, too."

"Real nice," Nick agreed. "Just right for her. He dotes on her and is home at night instead of at football practice or watching game films."

Marilyn smiled warmly. "Give her my regards. Of course, I never did get to know either of your wives really well. You never kept them around long enough."

"A mis-spent youth I'm still mis-spending."

"Are you taking enough money?" she asked. "I can give you some."

"Now you sound like my mother." Nick grinned at her. "You didn't come to see me off and find out if I got enough money."

"No, that's not the real reason."

"You want to tell me, or must I guess?"

Marilyn's momentary hesitancy was his clue, which Nick had already gathered, that this send-off concerned young Mark. Finally, she nodded. She tried a smile, which appeared strained. Nick could understand why.

"There's a person in Tampa I want you to contact first," she said. "An old friend of mine." She withdrew her hand from Nick's to open her purse and withdraw a folded, blue sheet of her initialed stationery that she handed to him. "That's his name and the address he gave me."

Nick opened the sheet and looked. The name was Frank Carr. The address was on Elizabeth Street in Tampa. There was no phone number. "Who is he? Besides an old friend?"

"Someone Larry and I knew years ago, when we were kids. We were part of a small group that hung out together. He's from that area."

"Okay." Nick refolded the sheet and put it into his jacket pocket. "What's this got to do with Mark?"

"Frank might be able to help you."

"How? Does he know Mark?"

"No."

"Then how can he help?"

"Look at it as a possible contact," she said. "Nick, I can't explain everything right now. You'll have to trust me. Just meet him. Then use your own judgment."

Nick looked into her eyes. She was hiding something. But this was not the time to push her.

"Does he know Mark's missing?"

"I don't see how he can," Marilyn said. "I heard from Frank three weeks ago. First time in many years. He sent me a short note." She stopped to bite at a fingernail.

"And—?"

"That's all," she said. "I didn't keep the note. I read it and threw it away. I didn't show it to Larry."

"Why not? An old friend—"

"It was addressed to me personally," Marilyn said. "I didn't know if Larry even remembered him, or would want to." She uttered a brief laugh without humor. "You're giving me a look. The note wasn't <u>that</u> personal. It was really short. Just 'how are you and the family?'–-'I'm fine,' that sort of stuff. I kept the address so I can put him on my Christmas card list next year."

Nick looked at her until she averted her eyes and started picking at the fingernail she had bitten. She put it to her mouth and bit on it again. When she held the finger out to survey it, a small drop of blood welled up at the corner of the nail. She wiped it on her pants and clasped both hands in her lap.

Nick decided that maybe it was the time after all. "What's bothering you?" he asked.

"My son's missing."

"What else?"

"Believe me, Nick, that's plenty."

"Okay. I asked Larry, now I'll ask you. Was Mark having problems at home?"

"No."

"No fights before he left?"

"No, really," she said. "We expected him home Sunday."

Nick nodded. "He left messages on your answering machine."

"Twice," Marilyn said. "They were exactly the same. It's his voice."

"Larry said the messages were directed to you, not to both of you."

"I guess Mark knew I'd be really worried." Then she added quickly, "And I don't mean to imply Larry's not. I've never seen him this troubled, not for a long time. But you know Larry. You know his sense of obligation to duty. It's his duty now to run the schools in place of the superintendent. This is all very unfair of Mark."

"Mark called when both of you were away from home. He knows your schedules. Why do you think he hasn't called back in the evenings—when you'd be home?"

"I don't know," she said. "It sounds like he doesn't want to talk to us, doesn't it?"

That was exactly what it sounded like. Then Nick caught the end of a PA announcement and saw other passengers lining up at the gate to board. "Did Larry tell you

I'm doing this under protest? I don't want to give either of you false hopes."

"I understand perfectly," Marilyn said.

"You're not sore at him for something, are you?"

"Larry?" she said. "No, not at all. This is not his fault."

"He's afraid he's letting you down."

"He would be." She smiled again, softly this time, with feeling. "Larry worries too much about me. I'm tougher than he thinks."

Listening to her, looking at her, Nick believed it. He said, "Marilyn, I promised Larry a couple of days on this. Unless I'm surprised, I'll wind up hiring some private detective to keep looking. I'll pick somebody I think will do you a job. It might be the best I can offer."

"Yes, he said that's what you told him. Promise me you'll contact Frank Carr first."

"I will."

"Please call me after you do," she said. "I'm staying home. Call as often as you can. I need to know what's happening. Call collect, of course."

She stood up suddenly, smiled at Nick again, then leaned toward him. With her finger she tilted up Nick's chin and planted a kiss on his lips. The kiss was warm and moist. It was a kiss of gratitude, friendship, and maybe even of confidence. But Nick wondered if he was putting too much into it.

"Nick," she said, "don't try to be a hero."

"Me? Trust me. That's the last thing I'd do."

He watched Marilyn Voight walk away, watched the strong, straight carriage and firmness of her legs and rear. Yeah, she was tough all right.

Dr. Voight was a lucky man.

5

At Tampa International, Nick Cotton claimed his bag, picked up a City Metro Map, dodged and shouldered his way through a mass of garishly dressed, milling humanity to find a public phone on the baggage-claim level. An operator informed him that there was no listing for a Frank Carr at the Elizabeth Street address.

Outside the airport, in the bright heat, Nick caught the crowded shuttle bus to the Alamo rental center, which was some distance from the main terminal. Having to stand, wedged upright in the aisle, sweating, crushed between an obese woman from Minnesota, according to her ceaseless chatter to another traveler, the woman in pink pants stretched to their tormented limit, her huge bosom mashed into Nick's chest, and the short, bearded man behind him in a flowered shirt who smelled of cologne and tobacco, he remembered why he had always avoided Florida during the season. The woman pressed to him never stopped talking, except to suck air and flash her toothy smile into Nick's face. The aroma of her breath mixed with that of her perfume assailed his nostrils. Nick would have moved had it been possible, but then that would have left the poor little man behind him at eye-level with the fat woman's breasts, probably his face pressed between them, and, likely, disappearing forever from sight. So Nick tilted his chin upward to stare at the roof of the bus during the lurching ride. The Hispanic driver was the coolest person in the conveyance, adjusting his earphones, driving one-handed, his other hand finger-snapping to the musical beat while his head bobbed rhythmically with half-lidded eyes.

Nick managed to wrest free his map. He had no fear of stumbling or falling as the bus swayed, being as wedged in as he was. Working his arms upward, the map close to his face and between his and the face of the smiling woman, he tried to search the marginal index to locate Elizabeth Street. Finally he found it, in the smallest print possible, and studied it. He was still looking for Treasure Island on the map when the bus jolted to a stop. As the up-front passengers started unloading, the fat woman continued to smile at him.

"We're practically intimate," she said. "I'm from Minnesota. They grow everything big in Minnesota." For emphasis, she cupped one arm beneath her breasts.

Craning past her shoulder, Nick said, "Line's moving."

"Are you staying in Tampa?" the woman asked. "Because if you are—"

"No, I'm going to Treasure Island. I'm meeting a lady."

The woman's hopeful expression drooped. "I see," she said.

"Line's moving."

At the rental counter, Nick stood in line for another thirty minutes to acquire his transportation. The Alamo agent punched buttons on his computer, then looked at Nick. He told Nick that because it was a busy time of year and short notice, the only available vehicle was a tiny, sub-sub compact, miniscule-powered, convertible, evidently something that none of the other customers wanted. If he desired anything larger, even compact-size, he was told he would have to go on a waiting list.

Nick said he would take the sub-sub compact. The Alamo agent snickered. He said the additional insurance was mandatory and was being added to Nick's charge.

When he retrieved his credit card, Nick went outside to locate his waiting chariot.

When he saw it, Nick could understand why no one else wanted it. Was he supposed to drive it?—or carry it? He did not consider himself a huge man at five-eleven and a hundred and eighty-five pounds, but this bordered on the ridiculous. Wedging inside the sub-sub-compact turned into a challenge. Nick had to take off his jacket and lean in to fold it onto the passenger's seat. Then, shrinking his chest, bowing his shoulders, banging his knees and shins, he squeezed his body in behind the wheel. He hoped he wouldn't have to sneeze or fart, fearing he might blow the little car to pieces. The only upside was that the little bugger fired right up and seemed eager to roll.

Driving extra carefully, like a typical snowbird tourist, Nick motored onto I-275 North, nestled into the right lane as everyone else rocketed around him, and started looking for the proper exit. He cut off onto Sligh Avenue, circled under the overpass, and found Elizabeth Street. The address he sought was in an older, peaceful-looking, residential area, a bungalow-sized, frame house with a rose-colored shingled roof. A full-sized Ford, not new, sat in the driveway. Nick parked behind it.

The man who answered the door was in cut-offs, undershirt, barefooted, and had at least two days' growth of beard on his face and a cigarette in the corner of his mouth. He was a good three inches, or more, taller than Nick. Had his face been clean-shaven, he might've looked what people call "ruggedly handsome." He tilted his head, eyes slitted, and waited.

"I'm looking for Frank Carr," Nick told him.

The man peered past his shoulder at the rented car. "Well, you ain't a cop. Not driving that dinky piece of shit. What are you? Process server? Salesman? Collector? You ain't the garbage man. He don't come till Tuesday."

"Are you Frank Carr?"

"Maybe, maybe not. I asked you first."

"My name's Nick Cotton, and—"

"Like that means something?"

"And," Nick finished, "I'm a friend of Marilyn and Larry Voight."

Momentarily, the man's eyes opened wider, then narrowed as he studied Nick, sizing him up. "Hell you are. Well, fuck me. I should know those names."

Nick said, "Marilyn asked me to look up Frank Carr. She gave me this address."

The man leaned his shoulder against the doorframe, the size of him blocking the doorway, blocking any possible view of anything behind him, but he was grinning now. He took the cigarette from his mouth and flipped it onto the lawn. He said in a drawling voice, "Why you think she asked that?"

"Mister, I don't have a clue." As far as Nick was concerned, this was bullshit and he'd had enough. He turned his back on the man and started toward his car.

"Hey, wait a minute! I'm Frank Carr."

Nick stopped and turned.

"You're touchy," Frank Carr said. "What's your stake in this, Nick?"

Nick hesitated. His immediate inclination was to say "screw you" and leave. Frank Carr had not endeared himself to him. It was difficult imagining this red-necked, shit-kicker to be a friend of Marilyn Voight's. But Nick was hot and sweaty and doing this for Marilyn. Finally, he said, "I work with Larry Voight. I'm doing them a favor."

Leaning against the doorjamb, Frank Carr crossed one ankle over the other and folded his arms. "Larry ask you to look me up, too?"

"Just Marilyn," Nick said.

The other man nodded slowly, thoughtfully, then straightened abruptly as though having made up his mind. "Hang on. Gimme a minute to straighten up some 'a my shit. Then I'll invite you in."

Nick waited, finding a place to stand close to the house in the shade. It was a lot longer than a minute. He returned to his car and slipped one of the sketches of Donnie Ann and a school picture of Mark Voight from his jacket pocket. He waited some more before Frank Carr opened the door and motioned to him.

"Sorry 'bout that, Nick. I don't entertain much, and my place is kinda cluttered."

"It's okay, Mr. Carr."

"Fuck that. Call me Frank."

Nick shook hands with him and followed him into a rather smallish living room. The window air-conditioner buzzed noisily. The room was furnished with a sofa and chair with matching slip-covers, a reclining chair and footstool, coffee table, lamp table, and a TV on a roller stand. The carpet was well worn but not ragged or threadbare. On one wall was a glass-enclosed cabinet of nick-nacks, on the opposite wall a large painting of a sunset over still water. A wall shelf and the windowsills held small, colored candles in decorative glass holders. The windows had lace curtains. But Nick didn't see much clutter to speak of. An ashtray on the coffee table held cigarette butts, some of them with lipstick. The air-conditioner could not dissipate the odor of stale cigarette smoke.

Nick's first impression of the man didn't fit with the furnishings in the room. He suspected that a wife might appear at any moment.

"Ugly dump, this place, ain't it," Frank said. "Belonged to a little ol' woman before I took over. I ain't changed a thing yet. Make yourself comfortable, Nick. You look like a man who can handle a cold beer." He waited for Nick's nod. "I'll get 'em."

Nick flexed his shoulders and pinched his damp shirt away from his chest and ribs. He sat in the armchair, stretched his legs and rolled his head side to side. Then he allowed himself a second, longer look around at the living room with its colors, decorative candles and nick-nacks, when Frank returned with two cans of beer.

"All this shit come with the house," Frank said, placing a beer into Nick's hand. He sat in the recliner and took a long drink. "I ain't got a woman here. Not saying I don't have women here when I can, but none here now." He winked and grinned broadly. "So, Nick, Marilyn and Larry Voight sent you. Boy, there's some names from the past. What's your angle? What you getting out of it?"

Drinking from the can, Nick looked at the other man's smile, a smile somewhat incompatible with the glint in Frank's eyes. He shook his head.

"You fucking Marilyn on the side?"

Nick set the beer can aside and started to ease up from the chair.

"Take it easy," Frank Carr said. He laughed and waved Nick off. "I was jerking you, but I couldn't help wondering, so I had to ask."

Nick stared at him, wondering how this pig-fucker could have been a friend of Marilyn Voight's. "No, you didn't. Not if you know Marilyn."

"I know 'er better'n you," Frank said. He took a drink of beer. "Forget it, okay?" After a second, Nick nodded and sat down. He picked up his beer.

Frank took a cigarette from a pack on the coffee table and fired it with his lighter, then leaned back comfortably, resting the beer can on the arm of the chair. As an afterthought, he waggled the pack at Nick, until Nick shook his head.

"What's your job, Nick?"

"I work in the same school district as Marilyn and Larry in Indianapolis."

"Indianapolis," Frank repeated, his voice sounding distant as though his mind were on something else.

Nick said, "That's a city in a state called Indiana in case you're wondering."

"I heard of it," Frank said. "Never heard nothing good about it. Every May they got a race in a cornfield there. I never had the pleasure of visiting."

"You're missing a lot," Nick said.

Frank uttered a short, humorous grunt. "You think I'm full 'a shit, but I'm just kidding. It's 'a way I am. I figure you kid with a guy, you get to know him faster."

"I see," said Nick. "Philosophy of the unwashed." He waited and got what he wanted. Frank's big grin subsided and turned into a look of wary curiosity. The man wasn't sure if he had been insulted. Nick went on, "Larry asked me to do a favor. Their son didn't come home last weekend when he was supposed to. The boy had spent a week with friends at a motel in Clearwater. Nobody knows why he refused to come home." Nick leaned over to hand Frank the photograph of Mark Voight, then the sketch of Donnie Ann. "His friends said he was seeing this girl. All they know about her is the name 'Donnie Ann.'"

Frank studied the faces and drew on the beer, followed by the cigarette. "And Marilyn said you should talk to me?"

Nick shrugged and took another drink.

Frank laid the pictures on the coffee table before sitting back again. "What else she say?"

"Nothing."

Now it was Frank's turn to shrug. "You're thinkin' the kid's found himself a piece 'a tail."

"Maybe, but I'm not sure," Nick said. "You'd have to know Mark to see how this dropping out, if that's what he's doing, is not like him."

"Why? He supposed to be something special?"

"He's been a good kid. Straight 'A' student, prettiest girlfriend in the school, captain of the golf team—"

"All that yuppie shit," Frank interrupted.

Nick nodded. "And a scholarship to Northwestern University. That ain't easy to get. I can't see him tossing everything over for a piece of ass. Not even for an emotional attachment to a new girlfriend."

Frank laughed. "My God, you talk like a school teacher. Here's a lesson in real life, Nick. Pussy's pussy. Now maybe Larry Voight don't realize that, but his wife sure does."

Frank Carr was again on the verge of getting Nick really pissed. He said, "I thought you were a friend of theirs."

Frank made a shrugging motion with one shoulder. "Was. Still am. I knew Marilyn a lot better'n Larry. Him, he was kind 'a wimpish. 'Course, you understand all that was twenty years ago. A man can change, I guess."

"He's not a wimp," Nick said, evenly. "He's the assistant superintendent of a pretty big school system, and he's worried sick about his son. I couldn't explain to him the hopelessness of coming here to look for Mark. The man's a friend of mine."

"Okay," Frank chuckled. "Larry's a jewel. And you're the school teacher doing him a favor. Kissing up to the boss. I get the picture."

One more piece of shit from you, Nick thought, and I'll throw this beer in your face and walk out. But he controlled the urge and didn't say anything.

"Forget it," Frank laughed. "Just my redneck way. I don't mean nothin' by it, Nick. Honest, I don't. Hell, I shit everybody. I take it Larry was the one who planned out this kid's life for him?"

"No. Mark can make his own decisions."

"What d'you think Marilyn wants from me?"

"That, I don't know," Nick said.

"They think the kid might still be in Clearwater?"

Nick shrugged for a reply.

Frank finished his beer and squeezed the can, denting it, before he sat back to mull it over. "Why you, Nick? I mean why didn't Marilyn come herself?"

"She wants to. Larry talked her into giving me a chance first. He's trying to protect her."

"From what?"

Nick hesitated. "Twice this week they received voice messages from Mark. Mark didn't give them much information. If something bad is happening to the boy, Larry wouldn't want Marilyn finding out first and being alone with the knowledge."

Frank shook his head. "The Marilyn I knew wouldn't be sending somebody in her place. Aw, fuck it. My guess is she figures I know the area and you don't. Right? I'm prob'ly the only one she could think of to help you."

"That must be it," Nick said. "I'm not even an educated tourist. I don't know my way around."

"You got a plan, ain't'cha? Something in mind? Or you just gonna settle in for however long it takes to find this kid? Might be the rest of you life, Nick."

"I'm leaving Sunday night."

"Either way? With or without him?"

Nick nodded.

"How much Larry paying you for this job, Nick?"

"Just expenses."

"What? You don't need money?"

"I told you, Larry's a friend. I can get him to cover your expenses, too."

"Yeah, he's prob'ly got money, ain't he?" Frank said. "Superintendent—" he drew the word out with sarcasm, "...title and ever'thing. What's a superintendent make in Indiana?"

None of your fucking business, Nick thought. He said, "More than either of us do."

"Marilyn? She got money of her own?"

"Marilyn is also a teacher," Nick said. "If you're thinking of gouging them for money, forget it. Marilyn said I should contact you, so I've contacted you. Thanks for the beer." He rose and took out his wallet, extracted a five-dollar bill and pitched it at Frank Carr. "That should cover it."

Frank laughed and said, "Hey, take it easy." He kicked the wadded bill aside. "Expenses, huh? You mean, like, gas and meals?"

"Sure."

Frank mashed the butt in the ashtray and lit another cigarette. "Why the hell not?" he said, grinning. "I'll play along. Be your chauffeur. It'll give me something to do. Pick up your money, Nick."

Nick did and returned it to his wallet. "What about your regular job?"

"You caught me at a good time. I'm between jobs. Ain't lookin' for one too hard, either. Guy's like you and Larry couldn't understand. I ain't never been one for all that job security crap. I work when I feel like it, make a little money, move on to something else. Way I like it, Nick. Nobody owns me. Now how 'bout you? Got a place to stay?"

"I've got an ex-wife in Treasure Island. I can bunk with her and her husband. I should call her if I can use your phone."

"Ain't got a phone," Frank said. "I don't get important calls anyway. I got a better idea. Why don't you stay here? Place ain't big, but I got an extra bedroom. I'd appreciate the company. And you don't wanna be finding your way around by yourself from Treasure Island."

"It's arranged," Nick said.

"Fuck that. Unless you're pokin' your ex-wife, why you wanna do that? We can find pussy for you."

"Let's get something clear, Frank." Nick leaned forward to make his point. "My ex is a nice lady. I won't have anybody calling her a 'pussy.'"

Frank looked surprised. "Okay. Hey, I didn't mean to piss you off again."

"You've been working at it."

"Nick—buddy—calm down. I apologize. Really, I do. You ain't got used to me yet, that's all. It's my way, Nick. I needle all my friends. Let's start over, okay? Give 'er a call on your cell phone."

"Don't have one," Nick said.

"Then we'll go someplace where you can call the lady." Frank stood up. "Go get your bags, Nick. I'll fix the spare bedroom for you."

6

Nick carried his bag into the house and found Frank Carr changing the sheets in one of the small bedrooms. The sheets were beige in color and decorated with roses, making Nick wonder if the sheets, like the living room furniture and nick-nacks, had come along with this house from the little old lady. The bedroom had pink curtains and one of the windows with a small air-conditioning unit. Pink window curtains, rose-decorated sheets, and Frank Carr in the same room seemed incongruous.

Nick dropped his bag onto a chair and opened it, watching Frank as he tucked in the corners of the sheet at the foot of the bed, noting how he triangulated them military-style. Maybe they had something in common after all. Years ago, when Nick had been a kid of eighteen, he had started his first of two hitches in the army in order to fund his college education.

"You decide where we wanna start, Nick," Frank said, working with the sheets.

"The Blue Swan Motel at Clearwater Beach was where Mark Voight stayed. It's worth a look. Tell me how you knew Larry and Marilyn."

"Okay. I'm gonna show you something." Frank left the room.

Nick opened the four, empty dresser-drawers. The top two were clean and paper-lined, the bottom two void of the lining and slightly dusty. He took out the few changes of underwear and socks he had brought and tucked them into the top drawer. In the second drawer, he put his shirts. He found hangers in the closet for his pants and extra jacket. He took out his toilet kit and put his empty bag on the closet floor.

Turning around, he found himself face to face with a huge bug.

Nick stared, eye to eye, with the biggest cockroach he had ever seen. The insect apparently had crawled up from the back to the top of the dresser.

Nick examined the insect. "Damn," he said, "a Schwarzenneger bug."

The huge cockroach waggled its antennae at him.

From behind Nick, Frank Carr chuckled. "If you think of him as a palmetto bug, he might not look so disgusting. He can fly, too." In one hand he scooped up the monster and carried it from the room. "Out you go."

Nick heard a door open and shut. From what he'd learned of Frank Carr so far, which wasn't much, he had half expected the man to pop the bug into his mouth and chew on it. Frank returned to the bedroom and handed an old black-and-white photograph to Nick. Nick looked at it.

There were five people in the picture, taken on a beach. Four young men and one young woman in bathing suits all looked to be in their late teens. Probably not much older, if any, than Mark Voight now. The boy on the left was a baby-faced Larry Voight in boxer-type trunks, smiling, just as wiry as a kid as he was now in adulthood. Next to him stood another boy, even thinner, dark-haired, wearing bikini briefs, showing more profile as his face was turned toward Larry, and he appeared to be laughing. In the middle of the group was a young Marilyn Voight in a skimpy, two-piece bathing suit.

Nick couldn't remember what her maiden name was, if indeed he had ever known it. But she was a beauty then, too, in a younger, more arrogant, flashy way. She stood in a hip-cocked, one knee slightly bent, sexy pose, her full dark hair wet and down past her shoulders, smiling mischievously. The tip of her tongue could be seen sticking out ever so slightly between her lips.

To her left side stood a younger, tall, Frank Carr with a full head of dark hair and a tight-lipped grin. He wore a bikini suit also that prominently displayed the bulge of his crotch. His stomach was flatter, harder, than the others, and muscles showed on his chest and thighs. Frank and Marilyn each had an arm around the other's waist.

At the far right in the picture stood the fourth boy, shorter than the others, chunkier but solid looking. He had light-colored hair and a broad, tight smile and hard, little eyes, more round-faced than the others. He wore striped trunks.

"That's our group," Frank Carr said. "The picture's a good twenty—twenty-one—years old. Recognize 'em?"

"Three of them," Nick said. "Including you. How old were you?"

"I don't remember whether we were eighteen or nineteen at the time. That was taken the first or second year we met. After the first time, we met every spring vacation on the beach at Clearwater for three, four years. Larry was the only out-of-stater. Rest of us had been to high school together in Clearwater. Marilyn was the Water Festival Queen our senior year." Frank paused to laugh at a memory. "Man, did we party when the five of us got together. You name it, we done it. We hit it off. Well, sort of, you might say."

"How come you allowed Larry in your group if he was an outsider?"

"Good question," said Frank, his face darkening momentarily. "We met him on the beach the spring of our senior year. Actually, we started teasing him at first. He was all skinny and white, obviously from up north. But he turned out to be a good guy. Instead of getting pissed off, he just grinned and took it, you know, good-natured like. And Marilyn felt sorry for him. Said he looked lonely and lost all by himself. She felt we should adopt him. He told us he'd come down alone and was just goofin' off. Shit, you couldn't help but like the guy. He didn't have an attitude."

"You called him a wimp," Nick reminded him.

"That was compared to the rest of us." Frank stepped around behind Nick to look past his shoulder at the photo. He reached over and put a finger on the face of the boy standing next to Larry Voight. "There was our ringleader. His name was Martin Ruhle. We called 'im 'Ruly,' or Martin, he'd tolerate that. But if anybody called 'im 'Marty,' they'd be in for one helluva fight. He was a cut above anybody I ever met—"

"A what?"

"That's just a phrase I heard. Means somebody who goes after something and don't give up. Martin was a real hellraiser. He thought up most'a the shit we did. Nothing ever scared Martin." Frank crossed a middle finger over his index finger and stuck it in front of Nick's face. "Him and Marilyn was like that. Marilyn and Martin. Martin and Marilyn. A combo, always together. Only guy in school who could fuck Marilyn."

Nick bit down on his lip. He tried to imagine the Larry Voight that he knew fitting in with these other street-wise looking kids in the photograph.

"This other one here—" Frank tapped the face of the kid standing to the far right in the picture, "—is Lenny Wilson.

Suggest something to Lenny, and he'd do it without thinking, no matter how crazy. Lenny and me went to a different school than Ruly and Marilyn. But we hung out together when we could. Then come spring break, and sometimes Christmas break, and Larry'd come down and join in with us. We started lookin' for 'im to come. He always brought money. Said his family wanted him to have a good time. His ol' man taught at some college in Indiana. So Larry was kind'a caught up in that education shit from the start. But he was wilder than you think when we got together."

Nick waggled the picture in front of Frank's face. "If this guy Ruhle and Marilyn were so close, how come you're the one who's got his arm around her?"

"For fun, why you think?" Frank said. "Don't think I wouldn't pat her ass when I got the chance. Hey, she teased with all of us. Ruly didn't care. He knew what he had. 'Course, that was kept in our group. Some outsider make a move on Marilyn, and Ruly'd beat the shit out of him. We seen it happen. If you was smart, you just never wanted to piss Ruly off." He paused to grunt a short laugh. "Who knew then that Marilyn and Larry were falling in love? He was shy with her. If Ruly had knowed, well—there's no tellin' what he'd'a done to Larry."

"And that's the kind of person you guys followed," Nick said.

Frank grinned. "Had to. Martin Ruhle was a natural leader. I tol' you—a cut above." He tapped his forefinger to his temple. "That's 'cause he was smart."

Nick studied the picture for another minute before handing it back. "What kind of things did you do?"

Grinning, Frank appeared to be enjoying the memory. "What you think? We pooled our money and had Larry pitch in all his. He was so fuckin' trusting. We had booze, beer, coke, grass—hell, what didn't we try? We chased pussy when Marilyn wasn't with us. Run out'a money, and we'd steal from the tourists." He laughed. "Lenny Wilson knew how to hotwire cars, only one of us who did, so we'd joyride. Some 'a the things we done scared poor Larry to death, but he went along. Gotta give him that. He showed a little guts from time to time. Ruly said it was just 'cause he wanted to be liked. Maybe that's so. One time—" Frank laughed louder at the memory, "—one time we set him up with the biggest, ugliest whore we could find and got him laid. Few days later he gets the itchy crotch and thinks his dick's gonna fall off. The guy actually cried. Funniest thing I ever seen. We had to show him how to get rid of the crabs." He changed expression as he added, "Then a guy got killed, and Larry stopped comin' down."

"One of your group?" asked Nick.

"No. Snowbird. On the beach. It was late at night, last night of Larry's last spring vacation before he hadda fly back to Indiana. Odd thing, that. Happened on a stretch 'a beach that wasn't wall-to-wall tourists. We'd been partying and were pretty strung out. Here was this beach, the moonlight, no crowd, so we stripped and went skinny-dippin'. We come out'a the water, and Ruly spots this fat guy stretched out on his towel, fast asleep. Only other guy we seen on that piece 'a beach. The fatty was middle-aged, wearing swimming trunks, had his big belly rollin' up in the air as he breathed. When we got dressed and walked closer to him, we seen he had a goddam, thick money-belt 'round his waist. Can you beat it?"

Nick, checking to see if any other palmetto bugs were lying in wait for him, leaned his elbow on the dresser as he listened.

"Tell me, Nick, what do you think 'a that? Guy all alone on a beach wearing his money-belt."

"I'd guess it was a temptation," Nick said.

"Yeah," Frank said. "Ruly gets the idea we oughta take it. Like I said, our heads were screwed. After we got all our clothes on, Lenny an' me jumped the fat guy to hold him down. Larry didn't want nothing to do with it. Ruly went for the belt. The fat guy was stronger than we'd thought. He bucked us off. Me and Lenny start to run, but not Ruly. Ruly takes the guy on. They punch it out. Suddenly, the guy goes down, and that's it. Not just out cold, but no pulse. Don't know if it was a heart attack, or got his neck broken, or what. We were one scared ratpack. Ruly takes the money-belt, and we get out asses out'a there." He shrugged. "That's what happened."

"I see," Nick said. "You killed a man and walked away from it."

"You make it sound like that was our plan. No, there was something wrong with the fat guy. Ruly didn't do it intentionally, more like in self-defense. Anyway, things changed for us at that point. I thought Larry was gonna turn us all in, go to the cops and confess. We talked him out of it.

Made him see how it'd look for him, and even for his ol' man back in Indiana. Larry went home. Never came back to see us, and we never heard no more from him."

"Marilyn did. She and Larry wound up getting married."

Again, Frank's expression clouded. His eyes glinted. "Yeah, I never did figure out how that managed to take place. We all thought she lived for Ruly." He stretched his arms out, interlocked his fingers and cracked his knuckles. "So you see, Nick, there's a side to Larry Voight you didn't know."

"I guess," Nick said.

"Hell, Nick, we all got our secrets."

In the late afternoon they were in Frank Carr's Ford, crossing Old Tampa Bay on Highway 60. Frank had stopped in Tampa for a six-pack and more cigarettes, giving Nick the opportunity to place his phone call to his ex-wife.

He told Carol about his change in arrangements and wondered if she really did sound disappointed or if it was only his hopeful imagination. He said to her, "It's better this way. Your husband won't feel threatened or upset." He heard Carol laugh. She concluded the call by saying, "Maybe next time."

As an afterthought, and with the realization that he'd forgotten to pack anything like it, Nick detoured into a convenience store and purchased an off-the-rack pair of swimming trunks and a beach towel at grossly inflated prices.

As he drove, Frank Carr pointed toward the bay.

"Blue water, blue sky, fleecy clouds, circling birds. Tourist postcard shit, huh, Nick?"

Nick was looking at the different sizes and types of boats on the water, some wind-driven, others motor-powered, all leaving short white wakes behind. Gulls and pelicans floated and swooped. "Looks nice to me," he said.

"Tourist shit," Frank chuckled, rubbing his chin. He had shaved before they left the house. A piece of toilet paper was stuck to a tiny bloody spot on his chin. "Boring. Like this goddam traffic. Three out'a four cars are rentals, or out-of-state licenses."

"Your number one industry," said Nick.

Frank looked at him. "I spent a few years as a fishing guide in the swamps, Nick. Only tourists I had to contend with were rich fuckers who didn't know one end of an air-boat from the other. I hated 'em, but I kept grinning because they paid big bucks to try and impress each other 'bout how much they know how to fish or hunt when they don't know shit. 'Yes, sir,'—'no, sir,' I hadda say and just grin like they were the nicest people I ever seen. I came dammed close to leaving some of those parties in the swamp. See if they could find their own way out, which I knew dammed well they couldn't." He uttered a soft laugh. "So—you'll forgive me if I'm up to here with tourists."

They were on the bridge now, and a police car drew alongside in the lane next to the Ford. Frank grinned and stabbed his middle finger at the officer driving. The cop looked blandly back at him. Nick quickly averted his gaze.

"Fucking cop," Frank said. "Don't trust 'em, Nick. They'll screw you if they can."

"What's he doing now?" Nick asked.

"Who? The cop? Prob'ly wishing he could nail me for something."

Nick lifted his eyes to see the police car speed on ahead of them. For several seconds he rode in silence. Then he asked, "Whatever happened to your friend Ruly? Martin Ruhle."

"Depends on if you believe in heaven or hell, or both," Frank said. "Him and Lenny Wilson got killed some years ago."

Nick peered out the window at two pelicans swooping low and then banking off. "Accident?"

"Naw," Frank said, braking behind a line of traffic. "Murder. Payback, I should call it."

Nick stared at him, waiting.

Frank gave him a quick look. "I don't know the whole story myself. I read about it, what the cops thought, and heard some of it from Lenny on the phone before he was killed. Seems Ruly and Lenny fell in a piece 'a luck, which turned out to be bad for 'em. They were down in Fort Myers doin' some crazy shit, I don't know what, and they fell in on the tag end of a armored car stick-up."

"They were in on it?"

"No. Right place at the wrong time. Happened right in front of 'em. They were in Ruly's car and seen it. A guard was killed, and these four masked guys were shoving money sacks in a duffel bag. They piled in a van and took off. Another guard was knocked cold. Well, Ruly steps on the gas and follows the van. Then the dummies up front run a light and sideswipe a police car. Talk about shit for brains. The cops get turned around and give chase. Ruly falls in behind the police, see? Couple 'a blocks, and the van swings into an alley. Cops right behind 'em. Ruly comes along into the alley and puts on the brakes. Guess what he seen?"

"I give," Nick said.

Frank shook another cigarette out to clamp it between his lips, tossed the pack onto the dash, and punched in the car lighter. Nick was glad the windows were down.

Frank said, "The duffel bag, man. The robbers had pitched it out toward a dumpster. Cops were already long gone after the van. Ruly jumps out and tosses the bag in his car, then eases on out'a the alley, and him and Lenny go in the other direction. They get to their motel and take it inside."

"Was it the money bag?"

"Yup." Frank bore down on his horn to warn off a driver trying to cut in front of him. "Son of a bitch," he muttered, lighting his cigarette. "Goddam tourist. Yeah, it had the money in it, along with three pistols, a sawed-off shotgun, four masks and four pair 'a rubber gloves. Over half million dollars in those sacks. It was like hittin' the fucking state lottery. Five hundred grand. Funny though that the bank and armored car service reported almost a million stolen. They must'a got together to scam the insurance companies, or rake some for themselves. You can't trust nobody, Nick."

I'll keep that in mind, Nick thought. He said, "Then what?"

"That's when Lenny Wilson give me a call. I had a job at a car wash in St. Pete. He told me the story over the phone and asked me to git myself down there and help 'em decide what to do. So I grab a bus. But I got there too late."

Now they were heading west on Gulf to Bay Boulevard. Nick sat quietly for another moment before looking at Frank and raising his brows in question.

"Rest of it I pieced together from the newspaper," Frank said. "Seems when the cops finally stopped that van, it had only three guys in it. Means one must'a got out somewhere in that alley to keep an eye on the money or go back and get it. My guess is, he spotted Ruly's car and license plate. Anyway, the cops couldn't pin the robbery on the guys in the van 'cause they didn't have nothin'. There were no reliable witnesses in front 'a the bank. The guard that was knocked out didn't know what hit him. All kinds 'a conflicting reports. The van boys got tagged with some piddly charges and turned loose when they come up with a high-powered lawyer. I don't know how they did it, but they tracked down Ruly's car. Prob'ly at the motel."

"Ruly and Lenny were killed?" asked Nick.

"That's right." Frank nodded soberly. "Not much left of 'em when they were found in a swamp. No heads, arms, or legs. Just the trunks of the bodies. Ruly's car was found torched in the Glades. The bodies were pulled out'a water, been chewed on by fish, birds, crabs, maybe gators. Cops made the identification from the personal effects in their clothes. Of course, there was no connection of them to the stolen money, and none of the money was found. Cops down there just had two dead guys on their hands. But I figure they got murdered by those van guys and chopped up, you know—sending a message to others, parts of 'em scattered around in different places for gator bait. Some speculation that they weren't chopped up at all, that the critters done it. Either way—" he shrugged, "—they were in little pieces with no heads. Those guys were my best friends."

Nick nodded. "Dammed near impossible to identify a portion of a human body without hands, feet, or a head. Unless the DNA was on record someplace, and then the pathologist would have to know what he was looking for."

"Sounds like you know your shit, Nick."

"I read it somewhere," Nick said. He had no desire to tell Frank Carr that he had been in the military police while in the service. Let Frank think of him as a hick school teacher. Nick added, "Anyway, you said there was I.D. on the bodies, so it sounds like the killers were making a point. They don't like people ripping them off. What happened to the money?"

"Never found," said Frank. "But those robbers got it, I'm sure. Hell, they could'a taken it from Ruly and Lenny without having to kill 'em. God, I hated to hear that."

"Did you talk to the police?" Nick asked.

"Not me. I didn't volunteer nothin'. Cops were at the motel by the time I got there. I hung around a couple extra days, then caught the bus back to St. Pete. I was the one hadda tell Marilyn about Ruly. It hit her hard. Not long after that, she left Clearwater and went to Indiana. To Larry Voight. Last I heard from her."

"You sent her a note recently. What made you decide to get in touch?"

"I'm mellowing with age, Nick. I made some inquiries and found out the Voights are living in Indianapolis. I wrote her a short letter saying as how it's been a long time and I'd appreciate hearing from her. I addressed it to her instead'a Larry 'cause I knew Marilyn a lot better. I bet she's still a gorgeous babe."

"She's still a beautiful woman," Nick said. "She and Larry are good together. She's also highly respected in her field."

"Looks the same as her picture, huh?"

"Better. Older and better."

One corner of Frank's mouth quirked up in a little grin. After a few seconds of silence, he asked, "You married, Nick?"

"Not now. I had a couple tries at it."

"Kids?"

"Lot of good kids, but not my own," Nick said. "I was a football coach."

"Football? You're kidding me. I like football. You said was. What? Had a losing season and got your ass canned?"

"Yeah, I got canned." Nick wasn't about to relate to Frank Carr the incident of losing his temper and pushing a school board member's head into a locker room toilet.

"But you're still a school teacher," Frank said sardonically. "Nice, safe job. Don't have to get your hands dirty." He clucked his tongue. "I never cared much for teachers when I was in school. All pussies and wimps."

More bullshit, Nick thought. He was sorry Marilyn Voight had directed him to Frank Carr. And he was doubly sorry he had accepted Frank's invitation to stay with him at the house. He said, "Sounds like you got a lot out of school, Frank."

"Got myself out, that's what I got. Never did pick up a diploma and dammed proud of it." He grinned over at Nick. "We can be pals, Nick, even if I don't like teachers."

"Sure. Why not?"

"Mark Voight one 'a your ballplayers?"

"No. Golf's his game."

"Bet Larry put him to it," Frank said, "so he wouldn't get hurt. Take care 'a the little boy."

"No, he lets Mark decide for himself."

Again, Frank grinned at him. "Bothers you, don't it?—when I badmouth Larry?"

"It does."

"I just ain't crazy about wimps." Frank changed the subject. "Maybe we'll get lucky, Nick. Maybe we'll find his kid for him."

7

The Blue Swan Motel was not in the community of Clearwater Beach, which had been what Nick had expected, but was in the city of Clearwater itself. Set back off the main street, it consisted of a stucco office building, painted pale blue, separated from a single, long, white-washed building that housed the units. The turn-in from the street served both as entrance and exit. The only swan in view was painted on the sign out front. On each side of the entrance/exit was a metallic flamingo with chipped and fading pink paint.

"Off season you could prob'ly get a room here for fifty, sixty bucks a night," Frank Carr said. "Maybe less. This time 'a year, it cost those kids at least double that, and that's per person." He found a vacant space in front of one of the units and wheeled the Ford into it. "I'll wait out here for you, Nick, where I can smoke."

Nick left his jacket in Frank's car and took the pictures of Mark Voight and Donnie Ann something-or-other into the office. He spoke with a man behind the counter who was wearing white shorts and pink shirt with its tail out. The man sighed as he glanced at the pictures.

"I can't tell one kid from another," he said. "Lots of 'em come and go, and most of 'em don't hang around the office. They grab the first bus to the beach. Unless there's some trouble, I don't notice who's who. These I don't remember, but, hell, I mighta seen 'em yesterday and not remember it."

"He came with two friends," Nick said. "Two other young men. It would've been three in the room." Now he wished he had had the foresight to bring pictures of Rob McKay and Jerry Lett, also, but it probably wouldn't have mattered with this guy. "I don't know if the girl stayed here or not. Would you please take a closer look?"

The man looked and shook his head. "I don't remember 'em." He raised his eyes to Nick. "My brother works the desk nights. You can come back and ask him. But I bet a dollar he'll tell you the same thing."

Frank Carr, smoking his cigarette, was sitting in one of the bamboo chairs under the hot, afternoon sun. He shaded his eyes and tilted his head at Nick. "Disappointed?"

"What I expected," Nick told him. "The man doesn't remember them, but why should he? Said I can come back tonight when there's another one on duty."

"We can check lots 'a different motels," Frank drawled. "Whatever turns you on. But I think you're pissing in the wind, Nick."

Nick nodded in agreement.

Frank said, "Maybe you oughta buy some ad space in the newspaper, run both pictures there. Let somebody contact you. But that's a longshot. What'cha think?"

"How far's the beach from here?"

"Not far."

"I'd like to see it," Nick said. "We can start walking and showing. It's something to do."

Frank pushed himself up from the chair and brushed the seat of his pants. He ground the cigarette underfoot. "Fine. We'll do it," he said without enthusiasm.

In the car, Nick grumbled, "First dammed setback and I'm ready to chuck it all. I'm wasting Larry's time and money."

"Go easy on yourself. All you can do is try. You're goin' home when you say?—Sunday night?"

"Yeah. Sunday night."

"Do what you can an' then leave. Nobody can blame you for that."

It turned into a long, fruitless afternoon.

Nick changed into his new swimming trunks, locked his clothes in Frank's car in a public lot, except for his shoes which he wore to protect his feet from the hot sand, and set off southward on the beach while Frank plodded in the other direction. Both of them carried a photo of Mark and a copy of the Donnie Ann sketch. Nick draped his towel over his shoulders to ward off sunburn. White as his skin was, he felt he must have looked like a Sno-cone. Nobody was going to mistake him for a native Floridian.

After awhile, he lost count of the number of kids he stopped and asked. Their faces and bodies began to look alike. Almost all of them, impatient at having their busy sun and sex schedules interrupted, glanced at the pictures and responded with "huh uh's," "no, sir's," "not me's," and "shit no's." A few asked why he was looking for them, then shrugged and didn't wait for an answer.

As the sun was setting through a thin line of dark clouds, Nick burrowed a place in the sand and deposited his shoes, the pictures, and his towel. He took a running plunge into the surf and swam outward, rising and falling on the waves, the saltiness invading his nostrils and mouth. The formerly light ocean breeze had intensified. Nick swam past the bobbing heads of other swimmers and surfers until he was alone. Then he rested, letting the current pull at him, before swimming back to shore.

He swam abreast of a young, bronzed wavesurfer wearing a bikini-style bathing suit. The surfboard swung toward him, giving him a scare, and the young man tried to veer off. He lost his balance and pitched into the waves, came up scowling and cursing.

"Goddammit!" he shouted at Nick. "Fucking tourist! Why don't you fucking go home!"

Nick tried to shout an apology, got a middle finger in return, and struck out for shore.

Frank Carr, smoking again, was waiting for him beside the Ford. Nick went into one of the public restrooms, splashed water on his chest, arms and legs, then ducked his head under to wash off as much of the salt water as he could. He changed clothes and came out running his hand through his short hair.

"Bet I walked two miles, at least," said Frank Carr. If he had, he wasn't sweating. "Have a good swim?"

"Okay for a workout. When I don't have one every day, I miss it."

"Hungry?"

"A little," Nick said. "What I really need is a hot shower with soap."

"I'm starved," Frank said. "Let's eat first, and you can shower at the house."

Nick looked at Frank's unkempt appearance but said nothing. At least the man had shaved and put on a shirt.

"We can be casual as we want here, Nick," Frank said. "You can pay for the meal." He grinned crookedly. "Use up some of Larry Voight's expense money."

It was nightfall when they got back to Tampa and stopped at a small, bar-grill restaurant on Seventh Avenue in Ybor City, Tampa's Latin Quarter, that Frank selected. They had a pitcher of beer brought to the table, ordered fish steaks from the menu, and then Nick went to the pay phone and placed a collect call to the Voights in Indianapolis.

Marilyn answered the phone.

"It's me," he said. "I'm with Frank Carr now. No way you can get in touch with me. Did you hear from Mark?"

"No," Marilyn said. "Nick? What—what did Frank say about Mark?

"He claims he wants to help. All we can do is show Mark's picture around. You better believe he'll come home on his own, when he's ready. Marilyn, I don't know what else to do."

"I know," she said. "I'm afraid I've put you in the middle of a bad situation."

Nick didn't understand what she meant, but she was a distraught mother wanting her son to come home. He said, "I'm not bitching. I'll keep at it through tomorrow, most of Sunday."

"I think you'd better talk to Kelly Moore," Marilyn told him. "She called here tonight, about Mark, and sounded—different. I'm not sure how, exactly. But she asked me how to reach you, and I told her I didn't know. I've got her number here."

Nick pulled out his map from jacket pocket, found his pen, and wrote the number in a margin.

Larry Voight's voice broke in: "Nick! I'm on the extension. How's it going?"

"No news to report, Larry. I'm sorry. I was telling Marilyn I'll be staying at Frank Carr's house, and he doesn't have a phone."

Larry's voice changed abruptly. "Who?"

Shit, Nick thought. Marilyn hadn't told Larry about hearing from Frank. He had forgotten that.

"Did you say Frank Carr?" Voight asked.

Marilyn's voice interrupted and said, "Honey, I gave Nick Frank's address. I forgot to tell you. We got a Christmas card from him. It just slipped my mind."

There was a silence before Voight said, "No shit? Is Frank there, Nick?"

"Not right here, Larry."

"I can't believe it. Frank Carr."

Marilyn interrupted again. "Larry, Nick's told us all he can to this point." It sounded to Nick that she was telling her husband to leave the subject of Frank Carr alone.

Voight said, "Is there anything we can do from this end?"

"No," Nick told him. "It's a lot of legwork, Larry, and no leads. I'm sticking with it another day and a half. I'll check back with you guys a couple of times tomorrow. I hope by then you've heard from Mark."

"Thanks, Nick," Marilyn said.

"We appreciate it," Voight said. "We'll talk to you later. Be careful with Frank. Don't let him cop your joint."

The Voights hung up almost simultaneously. Nick stared at the phone for a moment, puzzled by Voight's comment, then made his second collect call.

A man answered, and when the operator cut in to ask if he'd accept a collect call from Nick Cotton, the man's voice faded from the phone to ask someone else: "Do we know a Nick Cotton?" It must have been his wife he had asked because, a second later, his voice came back strongly. "Sure, we'll take it."

"Hello?" he said. "Hello? Mr. Cotton? This is Ralph Moore."

"Sorry to bother you like this," Nick said. "Can I speak to Kelly please?"

The wife's voice could be heard faintly in the background, most of her words indistinct. "Where you calling from?" Ralph Moore asked. "Suzanne says Kelly told her you're gonna look for Mark."

"I'm in Tampa. Is Kelly there?"

"No, she's not. She called a girlfriend and they went out together." His voice faded again. "Honey, when's Kelly coming home?" Then it was back to normal. "She should be back no later than ten-thirty. Is it urgent? Did you find Mark?"

"No. No, I haven't. Do you mind if I call Kelly in the morning? I'll try and get some change by then."

"Of course. Don't worry about it," Ralph Moore told him. "Just call collect. What time can we tell her to expect your call?"

"I plan to get an early start."

"That's okay. If we're still in bed, you can wake us up. Is it possible for Kelly to call you when she comes in?"

"No. Where I'm staying there's no phone."

"Well, we'll tell her to expect your call," Ralph Moore said. "Good luck, Mr. Cotton."

Nick returned to the table. Frank eyed him as he refilled his glass with beer from the pitcher. Their salads had been delivered, and Frank was almost finished with his.

"Talk to Marilyn?" Frank asked.

"Both of 'em. They haven't heard from Mark."

"How'd she sound?"

"What you'd expect. She's worried and holding on."

"What's your game plan tomorrow, Nick? More 'a the same?"

"Unless you come up with a better idea." Nick punched into his salad. After the first bite, he realized how good it tasted and how hungry he had become. He hadn't eaten since the peanuts served that morning on the airplane. "There's a cop I need to talk to tomorrow if I can. I want to show him the sketch of Donnie Ann."

"A particular cop?" asked Frank.

"Larry's been in touch with a man in missing persons. You know any cops, Frank?"

"I told you, I stay away from cops. Ever since that shit went down with Lenny and Ruly in Fort Myers, I don't want nothin' to do with 'em." He refilled his own glass and drank. "What time you figure to start in the morning?"

Nick chewed, swallowed, and said, "Might as well be early. Okay by you?"

"Only reason I'm asking is I gotta see somebody tonight," Frank said. "You won't mind if I drop you at the house. You'll have plenty of beer and the TV."

"I don't mind tagging along, Frank."

"I mind," Frank said. "It's a woman."

"Gotcha. When will the kids be on the beach again?"

"All night," Frank said. "Some of 'em. I'd say when the sun comes up. Depends on the day. I heard it might rain tomorrow. Squall can blow in here anytime."

Nick nodded. "Then we'll do the stores near the motel."

"Fine," Frank said, again without enthusiasm.

The waitress brought their baked fish, and Nick dug in.

8

Back in Frank's house, Nick stood under the steaming shower wondering what else he could do about finding Mark Voight, anything he hadn't thought of yet. Frank Carr's off-hand suggestion, advertising in the newspaper, might not be too far-fetched. He wondered if he might buy space in the classified section and speak directly to Mark: Mark Voight—Please talk to your parents. But that would work only if Mark bothered reading the classifieds.

Nick assumed he was in the house alone. Frank had let him out on the driveway, saying, "Make yourself at home. Take these beers in with you." Then Frank had backed out into the street and was gone.

Nick had found the lights, put the beers in the fridge along with the two cold cans already there, and noted that Frank obviously did not eat his meals at home. Other than the beer and a plastic-wrapped chunk of Colby Cheese, there was nothing else in the refrigerator. Then Nick had spread his towel and wet trunks in the bathroom and undressed.

He finished his shower and started toweling himself when he thought he heard someone in the kitchen, heard the fridge door being opened and shut. His initial assumption was that Frank had come back sooner than expected. Maybe his woman had kicked him out. Nick wouldn't blame her if she had. He draped the bath-towel around his neck and padded into the living room.

A stranger, a man, was bending forward toward the TV to turn it on. He didn't see Nick, and Nick stopped in surprise. The stranger was a bulky man, about five-eight, with gray fringes of hair at the sides of his head that stuck straight out, the top of his head shiny and bald. The clothes he wore were mismatched in colors and wrinkled, as was the sports jacket, which looked like it had been slept in. He wore loafers on his feet but no socks.

"Hey!" Nick said.

The man straightened up, his eyes opening wide, and said, "What the hell?"

The man's jacket flipped open, revealing a holstered gun on his belt. His left hand placed the beer can on top of the TV, and his right hand reached for the butt of the gun.

"No!" Nick shouted, but the man wasn't stopping. He was trying to tug out the gun but was in too much of a hurry.

Nick did the only thing he could think of and tackled the stranger, wrapping his arms around his body, pinning his arms, head-butting him in the chest to drive him to the floor. It was a pretty good tackle. It knocked the man's breath from him, and gave Nick the chance to roll him over. He straddled the stranger from behind, seizing the right arm, hoisting the elbow and locking it, at the same time forcing the man's face down, none too gently, on the carpet. Nick pinned him with a knee to the spine, his other hand griping and squeezing the stranger at the back of his neck. When Nick had his full attention, he released his hand from the neck, reached under and dragged the revolver free of the clip-on holster.

Nick tossed the gun onto the chair. He worked with his free hand, hauling out a hip-pocket wallet and flipping it open. The old boy had a badge and an I.D. card in a deteriorated plastic holder. The card said Department of Corrections. The card said the man's name was Clarence T. Bettis. A probation officer.

Nick got up and retrieved his towel. He kept himself positioned between the man and the gun on the chair.

Bettis, prone on the floor, rolled over and looked at Nick. "Jesus Christ," he moaned.

Nick wound the towel around his waist and tucked in the corners.

"Jesus Christ," Bettis said again, sitting up, scowling. "I got attacked by fuckin' Tarzan."

"You shouldn't've reached for your gun," Nick said.

"Well, fuck you, too." Bettis got to his feet, flexing his neck, facing Nick and watching him warily. "I wasn't gonna shoot you."

"I didn't know that," Nick said. A fucking probation officer?—with a gun?

Bettis adjusted his wrinkled jacket and continued to roll his head from side to side to flex the neck muscles. He bent down to retrieve his walled, folded it and put it in his hip pocket. "That hurt, you mother-fucker. You a cop? I seen cops take guns from people like that."

"You scared me," Nick told him. "I didn't hurt you."

"Yeah? You a doctor now? Who the fuck are you an' what'cha doin' here?"

"Waiting for Frank to come back."

"What?"

"Frank Carr. You're in his living room."

Bettis stared at Nick for a long moment. Then his expression changed. A little smile quirked the corner of his mouth. "Don't shit me. I know Frank's friends. I ain't never seen you before. Who are you?"

"What's a probation officer doing in Frank Carr's house?" Nick asked him.

"You one 'a Kenny's buddies?"

"I don't know a Kenny. Not any Kenny around here."

"Then who the fuck are you, Tarzan? Let's start with that."

"You got it backwards, pal," Nick said. "I'm here by invitation. What are <u>you</u> doing here?"

"Something funny goin' on," Bettis said. "You got business with Frank?"

"Personal business."

"Yeah? What kind?"

"You ain't part of it, far as I know," Nick said. "Talk to Frank when he comes home."

"And when's that gonna be? I ain't heard from him all day. What you cooking up with Frank?" Bettis looked at his gun. "So far, I ain't seen nothin' about you I like."

"That worries the shit out of me," Nick said.

"Fuck you," Bettis said. "I can make you tell me."

Nick laughed out loud.

Bettis's face reddened. So did the shiny top of his head. "You don't know me," he said. "My name is Clarence T. Bettis. Guys've thought they could fuck with ol' Clarence T. before and found out they're wrong. Don't get a big head, Tarzan, 'cause you jumped me. You caught me by surprise, that's all. Means nothin'."

"Means I took your gun away from you," Nick said.

Bettis looked him over. "You been inside? Naw, I don't think so. You ain't got the right look. And you ain't local. You're a Snow White. Who you workin' for?"

"Myself."

Bettis made a step toward the chair, but Nick stepped in front of him and waggled a finger in his face. Bettis scowled.

"Bullshit," Bettis said. "Okay. Tell me you an' Frank's old buddies gittin' together, and maybe I'll believe it."

"It's none of your business," said Nick. "And maybe Frank don't want you to know our business. Think of that?"

The other man's expression indicated that he might've been churning the possibility in his mind. "Maybe I better wait for Frank. Hear what he's gotta say."

"You can take your beer and wait outside," Nick told him. "I'll keep your gun. Come back in uninvited, and I'll shoot you."

"Fuck you mean you'll keep my gun?"

"Did I stammer?"

"So that's it, huh? You got a lot to learn. Nobody takes advantage of Clarence T. Bettis."

"I just did," Nick said.

"That's round one, Tarzan. If you an' Frank think you can fuck me out of this deal, you're both crazy." He stopped and licked his lips. "I'm leavin'. You gonna try and stop me?"

Nick pretended to give it some thought before he laughed. "No, I won't chase after you. I might lose my towel."

"Wise-ass," Bettis said. "Lemme have the gun. You can unload it."

"No. That's the penalty for losing round one."

"You sonuvabitch," Bettis said. "It belongs to me."

Nick shrugged.

Bettis looked around, possibly for another weapon of some kind, but apparently realized that wasn't a viable option and let his shoulders sag. Nodding his head, he backed toward the front door. "I'll see you again, asshole."

"Counting on it," Nick said. "Clarence T.?"

Bettis stopped after opening the door.

"I meant what I said. If you've got another weapon outside, leave it. I will shoot you if you come back through that door."

Nick watched him step outside and shut the door. He went to the window and watched Bettis climb into an older model car, he couldn't tell what make on the darkened driveway, back out and leave.

Nick carried the pistol into the bedroom and put on his clothes, minus his jacket. He sat on the bed and inspected the revolver. It was a Colt .38, the cylinder holding five rounds, the slot directly under the hammer empty. The hammer action was a bit stiff. The gun had not been oiled recently. Specks of ingrained rust showed on the frame above the stock and in the curve of the trigger guard.

Clarence T. Bettis did not spend a lot of time caring for his weapon.

What, Nick wondered again, was a probation officer doing in Frank's house? Walking in, getting a beer, making himself at home. Armed, too. Nick wondered if probation officers were allowed to carry firearms in Florida.

He adjusted the cylinder so that the empty chamber was beneath the hammer again and laid the gun aside. He decided it was time to search Frank Carr's house.

Nick went into the other bedroom, Frank's room, and opened drawers. Frank was not a man of many possessions, not even a hell of a lot of clothing. There were no family pictures in the bedroom, no material objects of any consequence. This bedroom, in fact, was almost as Spartan as the one assigned to Nick. He did find the beach photograph Frank had showed him earlier and stuck it into his shirt pocket.

There were a few shirts and pants, nothing dressy, on hangers in the closet. All the pockets were empty. A pair of boots and a pair of shoes were on the floor. Behind them, a cardboard box. Nick hauled it out.

It contained more clothing, older, more worn, that hadn't been washed in a long time. The smell of sweat was strong. Nick pawed through the clothes, most of which were discarded shirts with frayed collars, buttons missing, snags or tears. One long-sleeved shirt, blue-gray, had the name tag Carr over the left breast pocket and another I.D. patch on the upper left arm. The patch said: Dugger Security. The color-matched pants were wadded under the shirt.

So Frank either was, or had been, a security cop for somebody named Dugger. Interesting, Nick thought. And Frank's buddy was Clarence T. Bettis, a probation officer for the D.O.C.

Nick stuffed everything back into the box and returned it to the corner of the closet.

In the living room, he switched on the TV, took Bettis's untouched beer and seated himself in the chair facing the screen. His first day in Florida had gained him nothing but a redneck house companion, currently chasing after some woman, and a gun he had lifted from a probation officer, another redneck. He thought about getting into his rented car and driving back to Clearwater to check the Blue

Swan Motel, but after reconsideration dismissed it. It would be too long a trip with too little hope for anything positive.

So Nick sat and drank the beer, watched mindless television, waited, and wondered how the Voights were feeling that night.

9

Nick Cotton awoke to rain rattling the windows.

For a few seconds, coming out of a sound sleep, he felt disoriented. Momentarily, he thought he was back inside his own apartment. Then he remembered Frank Carr and Clarence T. Bettis and knew he wasn't that fortunate.

He had no idea when the rain had started, but the bedroom was still dark. He fumbled his watch from a small bedside table and discovered, to his surprise, that the time was past 7:00 A.M. The cracking and rumbling outside told him the darkness was due to the thunderstorm. Nick felt for and confirmed that Clarence T. Bettis's gun was on the bedside table.

A look in the other bedroom further confirmed that Frank Carr had not come home last night.

Nick shaved, dressed, and turned on the TV in the living room to find a weather channel. He looked out front, and Frank's Ford wasn't there, the only car on the driveway being his own little, sub-sub-compact rental. At least he had had the foresight last night to put the top up. He went into the kitchen to look through the cupboards. All he found to eat was a box of dry cereal. There was nothing to moisten it except water or beer. Nick munched it dry, by the handful, as he went back to check on the weather on the TV.

The local weatherman said all of central Florida would be in for thundershowers and a decrease in temperature. Today's high was predicted to reach the low sixties. So much for going back to the beach, Nick thought. But he would have to stir himself from the house. He had a couple of long distance calls to Indiana to make that he considered a priority. He thought about leaving a note for Frank but decided to hell with it.

In Frank's closet, Nick found a light raincoat and put it on over his jacket. As an afterthought, he took Clarence T.'s gun with him, turned off the lights and went outside into the rain.

At a house angled across the street, an older man in flannel shirt and jeans stood on his narrow porch, hands in hip pockets, staring at the pelting rain. When he saw Nick, he began watching him. Nick saw that the man was still watching as he unlocked the door of his rental car. He put the revolver in the glove box, then leaned back out to raise his hand in greeting to the older man. Tentatively, the man lifted a palm out in return.

Nick ducked his head and hurried across the street toward the other house, then realized that he must have scared the old guy. The man backed up toward his door, watching Nick warily. Nick waved again and called, "Hi!" and stopped short of the porch so as not to alarm the man further.

"Do you know Frank?" Nick asked him.

The older man peered back at him. "Frank?"

"Frank Carr." Nick motioned over his shoulder. "The man who owns that house over there."

"You mean the big guy? Drives the Ford?"

"That's him."

"He don't own the house. Mrs. McNally does." Lifting a brow at Nick's mild surprise, the man continued, "You didn't know that? He say he owns it?"

Come to think of it, Frank hadn't said that it was his house. Nick had just come to assume it was. That could explain some of the more delicate furnishings. "I guess not," Nick said. "My mistake. Where's Mrs. McNally?"

"Out 'a town. You a friend of that guy's?—Frank's?"

"Sort of. He's letting me stay there temporarily."

The older man continued to look Nick over. He said, "Son, you don't look like a criminal, so I'm gonna take a chance. Come up on the porch out 'a the rain."

"Thanks." Nick stepped up, took his hand from the raincoat pocket and extended it. "My name's Nick Cotton."

"Where you from?"

"Indiana."

"You're kidding."

"Nope."

"Really?" The older man's face brightened as he smiled. He took Nick's hand and pumped it. "Where in Indiana?"

"Indianapolis."

"Hell, I grew up in Fort Wayne. Worked there a long time. Twenty-five years. I been here twenty-three years now. My name's Christopherson. You can call me Chris. You a tourist?"

"Business trip," Nick said. "I met Frank yesterday, and he invited me to stay with him. I made the wrong assumption. I thought the house belonged to him."

"No. I've known Mrs. McNally since before her husband died, and that was nine, ten years ago. She's in Palm Springs, California, for the time being. Her daughter lives there and took sick. Missus Mac went out a couple months ago to help 'er. Don't know how long she'll be away. I offered to look after her place for her, but she said she'd arranged for a housesitter. Day after she left, your friend moved in. Brought some stuff in his car and that's all. I watched him. He never locks the house. Sometimes stays away days at a time."

Nick studied Christopherson, nodding to him, seeing in the old man a curious and watchful neighbor. Nosy, but possibly useful. "He claims he's got a girlfriend," Nick said.

Chris nodded. "That explains it."

Nick brushed water from his short hair and wiped his forehead. "Except for a TV, there's not much in there worth stealing."

"Even so," Chris said, "you'd think he'd wanna be more careful. You just invite trouble if you don't lock your doors."

"Mrs. McNally doesn't have a phone in her house," Nick said.

"Did have. Had it took out before she went away. Said she didn't want somebody goin' in and running up big phone bills on her. Maybe she don't trust the housesitter all that much."

"Did you meet him, Chris?"

"Hell, I tried to," Chris said. "Not friendly at all. Acted like I was intruding on his privacy. I was gonna ask him if he needed anything, but when he acted like that, I thought 'fuck him.'"

"Any idea how Mrs. McNally met him?" asked Nick.

"Huh uh." Chris stuck both hands into his hip pockets again. "I tried to talk to him only that one time. I don't force myself on people, but I don't want to see Mrs. Mac get taken advantage of."

Nick looked back toward the house, then back to Chris. "Chris, did you ever see a stocky man, bald on top, go in or out?"

"More'n once. He don't bother knocking either. Drives an old beat-up car. Sometimes they go out together. You asking questions like this, should I start worrying about something?"

"Right now I'm only curious," Nick said.

"Mind if I ask what kind'a business you're in?"

Nick reached inside the raincoat to his jacket pocket and brought out Mark Voight's photograph and the sketch of Donnie Ann. "I'm looking for these kids. I'm a friend of the boy's parents."

Christopherson studied the faces, frowning slightly. "The boy—he a runaway?" He waited for Nick to give him a shrug. "I can't be sure," he said, handing the pictures back. Nick folded the sketch around the photograph and put them away. "There was a couple of kids in there last week. At least, they looked young enough to be kids. It was dark, and I was sitting here on the porch and didn't get a good look at 'em. Saw 'em briefly in the light when they went in the door. They came with the bald guy."

"When did they leave?"

"They didn't, not that I saw. The bald guy left by himself. He come back two or three times over the next couple days. The girl took your friend's car once in awhile to go somewhere. I know she was there yesterday morning, but I don't know when she left 'cause I wasn't paying close enough attention. Then I noticed your little car over there yesterday afternoon."

Nick asked him to take another look at the Donnie Ann sketch. Christopherson did and shrugged before handing it back.

"I got pretty good eyesight," he said, "but I couldn't tell you it's the same girl. I'd be lyin' if I said so."

"Thank you, Chris." Nick smiled at him. "Now I got to find a phone and call the boy's folks."

"Hell, both of us being from Indiana, I'll take a chance on you," Chris said. "Come on in and use mine."

"Thanks. I'll call collect."

"What the hey." Chris motioned Nick inside, and followed him into a carpeted foyer. "Take off your raincoat, Indy. You can hang it there by the door."

"I don't want to disturb anybody."

"I'm alone," Chris said. "My wife, God bless 'er, died almost ten years ago. Kids long gone. You won't disturb me." He pointed. "Phone's around the corner on the wall."

He went into another part of the house while Nick found the phone and placed his first collect call. It was to the Moore residence.

Ralph Moore, Kelly's father, answered again. Nick asked for Kelly.

"We got a problem, Mr. Cotton. Kelly's on her way to Florida right now." The man's words spilled out. "Nancy, her best friend, confessed this morning when Kelly didn't come home. She dropped her at the bus station last night. Her mom and I found out Kelly took a small bag and some money from Suzanne's bedroom."

"Hell," Nick said. "I'm sorry, Mr. Moore."

"Not your fault. I called the station, and there was a southbound bus that left at ten-thirty. We think she got on that one. If so, she's scheduled to arrive in Tampa at two A.M., tomorrow morning. I need your help."

"I'll meet the bus," Nick assured him.

"Thanks." The man's grateful sigh was long. "Thanks a lot. We haven't called the police, and we don't want to. But we don't want her down there by herself looking for Mark Voight. You can give her a spanking for me and put her right back on the next bus home."

"Except," Nick said, "if she's determined, and I know Kelly, she'll get off at the first stop. I'll look after her."

"Jesus, that's asking a lot of you," Ralph Moore said.

"I don't want anything bad happening to her," Nick told him.

"Mr. Cotton, I just don't know what the hell got into her."

"She's in love," Nick said. "She didn't do it to hurt you."

"Yeah, well, we do believe that. Listen, we can't thank you enough. Anything we can do—?"

"I'll have her call you when she gets in. If she's not on that bus, I'll call you. We'll take it from there."

"Any luck finding Mark yet?" asked Ralph Moore.

"Not a bit."

The man said, "Listen, Kelly might know something, or thought of something, we don't know. It might be why she wanted you to call her yesterday."

"I'll take care of her, Mr. Moore."

Nick broke the connection and heaved a long sigh. This responsibly he didn't need. But what else could he do? He put the phone to his ear and placed another collect call to the Voights.

Larry Voight, sounding out of breath, answered the phone.

The first thing he said was, "Nick, we've got problems."

Two for two, Nick thought. Great.

"Marilyn's on her way down," Voight said.

Nick groaned inwardly.

"She left this morning before I woke up," Voight continued. "Took one bag and the van. She left me a note. Told me not to try to stop her."

"What in God's name made her do it?"

"I think she got a phone call. Maybe from Mark."

"You <u>think</u>?"

"The phone rang early, before daylight. She answered it before I could get myself up. It was really brief, then she hung up. She told me it was a wrong number. I don't believe it."

"Wonderful," Nick muttered, sarcastically. "Did she give you an address? Her destination?"

"Just to Florida," Voight said miserably. "What should I do, Nick?"

"Hell, what can you do? You gotta take care of Monica. If Marilyn comes here, to Tampa, how long do you think it'll take her to drive it?"

"Eighteen to twenty-four hours, unless she stops overnight. I don't think she will. Jesus, I am flat losing my mind."

"Well, hang in there," Nick said, more grumpily than he had intended. "I don't know what the hell to say. She gave me Frank Carr's address, so I might be seeing her."

"Take care of her, won't you?" Voight said. "Of course, you will."

"Larry, I got a bad feeling I won't be making that return flight tomorrow night."

"I don't give a shit about that," Voight said.

"Did you ever meet a man down here named Clarence Bettis?"

"No. He say I did?"

"No. Tell me more about your friend, Frank Carr."

"I wouldn't call him a friend," Voight said. "Maybe, one time, I thought he was. A group of us hung out together when we were kids, and he was one of us. I felt he'd do just about anything another guy told him to. I mean anything. What's he doing now?"

"Apparently not much," Nick said. "Last night, you cracked about him making a pass at me. I took it as an implication that he's gay. Were you joking?"

"By God, he did, didn't he? I was serious, Nick. Frank's as homo as they come. He used to make passes at me until Martin Ruhle told him to lay off. A guy named Martin Ruhle sort of led our group. Frank always wanted to please Martin. I suspected Martin was fucking him sometimes."

"Frank told me about this Ruhle."

"I understand he's dead," said Voight. "Him and another boy named Lenny. That's what Marilyn told me."

"When did she tell you?" Nick asked.

"Oh, that was a long time ago. Just before we got married. I can't remember exactly. You see, something bad happened, and I stopped hanging out with those guys."

"Something like a man with a money-belt getting killed on a beach?"

Voight was silent for a moment. "Frank did tell you a lot. Yeah, I've never forgot that. I'll carry that shame with me as long as I live. I didn't do anything to stop it, Nick. Then I was too much of a coward to report it. I think Martin Ruhle counted on my being a coward."

"It's done, so don't torture yourself," Nick said. "Larry, I might be racking up some expenses. I want you to know."

"I don't care. You got a blank check, Nick. Just bring my wife and my son home with you."

"You keep an eye on Monica," Nick said. "Don't let her catch the next bus or plane down here. I'll talk to you later."

Nick hung up and stood shaking his head. Now he had two women coming in his direction, neither one of whom he wanted there. A seventeen-year-old senior he would have to play daddy to, or at least be a Dutch uncle. And a grown woman with some insane notion that she could find her son. Both of them would be descending on him within twenty-four hours.

Christopherson, holding two cups of steaming black coffee, came back into the living room as Nick turned around. He said, "You gotta go to the kitchen if you want milk or sugar, Indy. It's through that way." He grinned as Nick accepted a cup. "You got a troubled look on your face."

"Bad news and more bad news." Nick sipped the coffee and nodded another thanks. "Chris, can I ask a big favor of you?"

"You can ask. We're both Hoosiers."

"Do you have a phone number where I can reach Mrs. McNally?" He sipped more coffee as Chris nodded. "I want to ask her just exactly what her arrangement is with Frank Carr."

Chris carried his coffee and saucer into the living room and placed them on a small table-stand. "Let me do it," he said. "I prob'ly should call her anyway. You got specific questions?"

"How they met. What instructions she's given him."

"I get it," Chris said. "Anything she can tell me about him. I don't know what time it is in California. Early, I think. Missus Mac's not much an early riser."

"Doesn't have to be this minute," Nick told him. "I can check back with you later. I got some things to do anyway." He took time to finish his coffee and then placed his cup next to the other man's. "I appreciate this, Chris. Okay if I write your phone number?"

"No problem." The older man watched as Nick put on his raincoat. "I'll sort'a keep an eye on things across the street. See who comes and goes."

10

The Sheriff's office of Pinellas County looked and smelled, with its slight leathery and oil scent, like all the other police stations Nick Cotton had ever had occasion to visit, even the post provost building he had worked out of when he was in the military police, except the furnishings of this one were newer, the lighting considerably better.

And, too, like the army, it turned into a hurry-up-and-wait situation. After leaving his name and stating the purpose of his visit with a receptionist, Nick had to sit for a long, boring time until the receptionist, speaking on the phone, caught his eye, nodded to him, and gave him directions to Sergeant Melton's cubicle.

The sergeant greeted Nick with a handshake, told him to hang up his raincoat, and invited him to sit. Melton was about Nick's height, five-eleven, but heavier with wider shoulders, wearing a khaki uniform of dark pants and lighter-colored shirt with three gold chevrons on his sleeve.

After listening, Sergeant Melton rocked back in his chair and said, "I got the information Mr. Voight sent, but I don't have anything for him. Sir, I'm afraid you made a wasted trip." He pointed to one of the file cabinets. "Those drawers are full of reports of missing kids and F.B.I. cross references. And those in that cabinet are just the thirteen to eighteen-year-olds. That other cabinet, kids not yet in their teens. Unless something happens to those kids that bring 'em to our attention, or to the feds—" he let the statement drop and shrugged his shoulders. "I get lots of parents asking 'is there a chance you'll find my son or daughter?' and 'should I come there and help?' I tell 'em no. Hard maybe, but I gotta tell them the truth."

"I understand," Nick said, "but perhaps you can help me another way. I need a recommendation from you. I'd like to hire a local man, a private detective. It's the best way to put Mr. Voight's money to use. I could check ads in the yellow pages, but I'll have more confidence in your choice."

Melton rocked as he considered. "You gonna want this private eye to pound the pavement? Up and down the streets to show those pictures to anybody who'll look?"

Nick thought it was an odd question. He said, "It will be up to him. Nobody will tell him how to do his job. I'll want him to check up on one or two other people as well."

"Leads to the boy?" asked Melton.

"I don't know yet," Nick said, truthfully. "Might turn out to be nothing."

Melton nodded. "I do know someone. A real good person, but maybe a little strange. Former cop."

Nick nodded. "I imagine most private eyes are."

"What? Strange, or former cops?"

"Former cops," Nick said. <u>Strange</u>?

The sergeant scribbled on a notepad, got out his phone directory, looked in it and wrote some more. He tore off the sheet and passed it across to Nick. Then he turned the sketch of Donnie Ann around and pushed it toward him. "Want this back, or should I keep it?"

"Keep it. I've got more." Nick looked at the name on the slip of paper. "Gus Dick?"

"That's the name," Melton said, grinning a little. "Gus needs the work."

Nick raised his brows. "What's wrong with him?"

Melton's expression underwent a sudden change. He appeared to bristle momentarily as though Nick had struck a nerve. "Not a dammed thing," he said. "Gus was a good cop and a personal friend of mine. Still is."

Nick changed the subject. "Ever hear of a man named Frank Carr?"

Melton thought and shook his head.

"How about a probation officer name of Clarence T. Bettis?"

"Never heard of him either," Melton said. "Good luck with Gus."

Gus Dick? Sounded like another redneck, Nick thought as he ducked through the rain to the parking lot where he had left his teacup of a car. Squeezed inside, painfully, Nick looked at the slip of paper again. Gus Dick, with an address in Clearwater and a phone number. It took him another half hour, fighting traffic and asking directions, to locate the proper building and find another parking space.

The private detective's office was on the first floor of an aged and slightly run-down building that housed other offices entitled: Argosy Travel, Festival Commission, Shear Delights, Sun Incorporated, plus names of two dentists, a podiatrist, and six lawyers, the names all on a display board in the foyer. The P.I.'s office had a single word stenciled on the door: Dick. Nothing else. Nick wondered how many people with different expectations might have gone into that office and come out disillusioned.

He opened the door and went in.

There was no outer office, only one large room with short, filing cabinets, two chairs on this side of a desk, a bare table holding a coffee maker and a carafe of black coffee, and a woman behind the desk. A desk lamp was turned on because there was but little light coming through the window behind the woman. Nick paused to let his eyes adjust.

The woman was leaning slightly forward, her elbows planted on the desk. In each hand she held a barbell, looked to be about a ten-pounder, that she was alternately flexing up and down. A stack of magazines lay on one side of the desk.

"Don't smoke in here," she said sharply, concentrating on her exercise.

"I don't," Nick said. "I'm looking for Gus Dick."

"I'm Augusta Dick."

Nick stood and stared with his mouth slightly open.

"Come on in," she said, still working at her muscle-toning. "You can hang your coat by the door."

Nick saw the coat-tree at one side. On a low peg hung a woman's raincoat. He shrugged out of his, rather Frank Carr's, and hooked it on the top peg.

"Are you Mr. Cotton?" Augusta Dick asked.

"Yes."

"Good. Dave called me, said you'd be coming over. Sergeant Melton. He and I worked together when I was with the locals. Come closer, Mr. Cotton, and have a seat."

Nick approached the desk and got another surprise. The woman was in a wheelchair.

She must have noted something in his face because her hopeful expression changed as she laid the barbells on the desk, worked the joy-stick and backed the chair up to wheel it around to the side of the desk. Her hands folded themselves on her lap, fingers interlocking.

Up close, she was an attractive woman. Nice face with clear skin, brown hair cut short, dark eyes, probably brown Nick guessed, a smallish nose that was pointed, and full lips tinged with a light gloss. She had slim shoulders and uplifted breasts under her pale-colored, lightweight blouse. Her lower body was clothed in dark pants, hose that could be seen covering slim ankles, and black shoes. Both feet were braced against the tilted footrest of the wheelchair.

Nick realized he was staring and felt suddenly embarrassed.

"You're disappointed," Augusta Dick said evenly. "You can turn around and leave, and I'll understand. You won't be the first."

"No," Nick said. He felt for the back of the nearest chair.

"I'll even give you the names of a couple other good p.i.'s," she said.

"I'm sorry." Nick sat down. "You took me by surprise is all. When Sergeant Melton said—well, I assumed—I thought you'd be a man."

"Are you one of those Neanderthals who think a woman can't do a man's job?"

"I know better than that," Nick said.

"But you figure what the hell good's a cripple."

"Stop," Nick said, sharply. "I've offended you somehow, and I apologize. I won't play games or tuck my tail. Unload your baggage someplace else. I'll tell you what I need, and you can tell me if you want the job."

Augusta Dick laughed and nodded. "Good for you. I like you already, Mr. Cotton. What's your first name?"

"Nick."

"Where you from, Nick?"

"Indianapolis, Indiana."

"What do you do there?"

"School teacher."

She smiled and said, "Probably makes you an honest man. Okay, Nick, you better call me Gus. Everybody else does." She placed her elbows on the chair's armrests and steepled her fingers. She wore no rings at all. The only jewelry that Nick could see were tiny earrings at her lobes. "What do you think of my name on the door?"

"Could imply a lot of things," Nick said.

"Yeah. I didn't want something ordinary like 'investigations' or 'private detective' or 'detective agency.' I wanted a slight air of mystery."

"You got it."

"More than I need," she said. "Last week a condom salesman came to see me."

"How long have you been detecting?" Nick asked.

"I opened this office four months ago," Gus said. "You're my second client. I hope you're going to be my second. My first was a seventy-three-year-old lady who wanted to know where her husband had gone. The 'old fart' was what she called him. He was eighty-one and constantly badgering her for sex. She said you'd think he'd grow out 'a that nonsense. I got all the particulars and found him in a single day. He was shacked up in Daytona Beach with a professional stripper. All smiles, but claimed he'd had a bout of memory loss of who he was or where he belonged. Only he hadn't forgot how to use his credit card."

Nick wondered if Augusta Dick always talked so fast. "You took him home to his wife?"

"Talked him into it," she said. "She shot him that same night. Aimed for his pecker, but her aim wasn't that steady, and she hit him in the thigh. I felt bad for him, bringing him back to get shot. So I visited him in the hospital and found him trying to make out with a nurse. He wasn't even mad at me, he had such high hopes of getting that nurse to climb into bed with him. That, Nick, is the history of my first and only fee. So far."

Now Nick wondered if she always talked so <u>much</u>. She probably was lonely sitting here by herself in this office.

"I do know how to get things done," Gus said. "I've got good contacts. Now I've got to make a go of this business strictly for myself. It's not just the money, though that's part of it. I'm on full disability pension for the rest of my life. Only I don't want the rest of my life to be a rest, if you get my meaning. I believe I can do anything I put my mind to. I mastered this chair. You should see me do spins, wheelies, figure-eights. Want to know how I got hurt?"

Nick opened his mouth, but before he could speak, she went on, "Drug bust that turned heavy. Guns going off all over. I took a bullet in the spine, broke my back. That was over two years ago. Ask me if I miss it. Police work." She paused for a breath and a change of expression that made the semi-question rhetorical and the answer obvious. "So Dave's trying to help me out by sending you to me. Well, I'm ready and—almost able—"

Nick broke in: "Can we get to my problem?"

"Yeah, sure. I talk too much. I don't see a lot 'a people. Want some coffee?"

"Thanks," Nick said. Maybe if she was busy drinking coffee, she might stop talking long enough to listen. But he did like her already. He figured that she had about as healthy a view of her condition as possible, under the circumstances.

Gus wheeled around, took two paper cups from a desk drawer, swung over to the coffee carafe and poured. Nick got up to take one from her so she would be free to maneuver her chair. He sat down and sampled the coffee as she rolled to her desk and set her cup on it.

Gus opened another drawer and took out packets of sugar and powdered cream and a stack of stir sticks rubber-banded together. She looked a question at Nick, and he shook his head, before she went to work opening and dumping three sugars and two creams into her cup. She stirred the concoction and said, "Okay, Nick, you were about to tell me."

Nick told her about the missing young man, everything that he knew, and gave her pictures of Mark Voight and Donnie Ann. Gus looked at the pictures as Nick talked.

Finally, Gus said, "Without a starting point, other than the Blue Swan Motel, which runs hundreds of guests through its door weekly, we don't have much to work with. But you already know that. I can take Mr. Voight's money and give this my full attention. We could get lucky. As you can guess, I'm not overburdened with a caseload. What I suggest is a couple of weeks. Maybe the boy will go home before then. If not, and I can't come up with any other leads by that time, I'll tell Mr. Voight the truth. Leave it up to him if he wants me to keep on it. But I would also have to tell him that he's wasting his money. Will he go for it?"

"I'm sure he will," Nick said. "And I'll tell him that you're the p.i. that Sergeant Melton recommended."

"There's more. Right, Nick?"

She was perceptive, too. Nick nodded. "Yes. Can you check out a couple of men for me? They might or might not be involved. Both are local—well, Tampa anyway. One's name is Frank Carr. He was connected to the boy's family over twenty years ago. According to Dr. Voight, he's homosexual, but I would never have figured that out for myself. A couple of months ago, he contacted the boy's mother, the first time in all those years. He's house-sitting for a Mrs. McNally on Elizabeth Street in Tampa. I'll give you the address. He invited me to stay with him."

Gus was writing on a legal pad. She had put on small-framed glasses to write. She jotted the address Nick gave her. "Why?" she asked.

"Why do I want to check on him?"

"No. Why did he invite you to stay with him?"

"Concern for the son of his old friends, he said. And for my convenience. He offered to help me look for Mark. But I haven't seen him since last night. He didn't return to the house this morning. There's no telephone."

"And you don't trust him."

"He might have a record."

Gus looked up from the notepad.

"The way he corners his sheets on a bed," said Nick. "That, or military service."

Gus grinned. "You sound like a cop."

"I served some time in the military police."

"See?" Gus said. "My instincts are pretty good. Describe Frank Carr."

Nick did, giving her time to write as he spoke. "Six-one, or two. Lean, hard body type. Full head of hair with some gray in it now." He took out the old beach photo and showed it to Gus. "Here he is when he was a teenager. Same face. He looks composed, tough, in this picture. You can see the muscle definition. Same now. I had him pegged as a redneck shitkicker when we first met."

Gus peered at the old photograph. "The woman. This the mother?"

"Yes. And here's Mark's father." Nick leaned forward the tap the face of the young Larry Voight in the picture. He traced his finger to the others. "Martin Ruhle. Lenny Wilson. They're dead." He related the story as Frank had told him, even the part of the killing of the tourist on the beach for the money-belt. He saw Gus's brows shoot up at that part. He sat back in the chair and took his coffee from the corner of the desk. "That's the gang."

"You're right," Gus said. "I can see where your friend Mr. Voight looks out of place with this bunch. They were taking advantage of him, and he didn't know it."

"Or if he knew it," Nick said, "he chose to overlook that fact because he wanted to be liked. Whatever Marilyn Voight was at the time, she's changed. I've known the Voights a few years, and they're both good people."

"With a big problem," Gus said. "Do you think she's concealing something from you?"

"I do. Maybe the story Frank told. Maybe more. I know she wants her son back. And she's on her way here now, driving. I talked with Larry this morning. She left before he got up, so I'm guesstimating twenty hours."

"This could complicate things. Where will she be staying?"

"Since she provided me with the address," Nick said, "my guess is that she'll head straight to Frank Carr's house."

"Mrs. McNally's," Gus corrected with a smile. "Does this Frank Carr have a job?"

"He says not. He might've worked for a place called Dugger Security. I went through his things and found a patch on a shirt."

Gus folded a page back on the pad to get a fresh sheet in front of her. "I can check Frank Carr's police and employment records without any trouble. You said a couple of guys. Who's the other one?"

"Probation officer name of Clarence T. Bettis. Probably out of Tampa. He's fortyish, five-seven or eight, chunky soft, ratty-looking dresser, round face, bald on top with sideburns that stick straight out when I saw him. He looks like a boozer to me. Last night he let himself into Frank's house, uninvited, and made himself at home. We surprised each other. I had to take a gun away from him."

"Nick, you fascinate me," Gus said, her head down, writing. "Did he tell you he's a probation officer?"

"I saw his shield and I.D. But I didn't check to see if it's up to date. I'd like to know his connection with Frank. A neighbor reported seeing Bettis escort a couple of kids into the house. Boy and girl."

"The ones you're looking for?"

"Neighbor couldn't see 'em that well."

Gus finished writing, put down her pen, and sat back in her wheelchair. "Be nice to know why Clarence T. Bettis is packing, wouldn't it? I can reach you at Mrs. McNally's house?"

"I told you, no phone. The neighbor's name is Christopherson. I have his number here. Leave a message with him, and I'll get back to you."

"May we discuss my rates?" Gus said as she wrote the number. "They're high."

"I can understand that since you have so many potential customers beating down your door."

"I think we'll get along, Nick," Gus said.

11

The rain continued. It was middle of the afternoon when Nick parked in the driveway outside the McNally house on Elizabeth Street. Frank Carr's Ford was not there. Nick did notice that the front door was ajar, and he hadn't left it that way.

He studied the situation for a moment, not willing to go waltzing inside in case Clarence T. Bettis was lurking there with another gun. Nick scanned each corner of the house to see if any heads poked out toward him, though he doubted anybody would be waiting outside in the rain. Still, someone could have seen him drive in, slipped out the back of the house and come around the side. He took Bettis's gun from the glove box.

Nick wormed his way out of the little car, cocked the revolver, held it in his right hand alongside his leg, and, warily, approached the half-open front door, making sure he stayed out of line of a clear view from anyone who might be peering from a window.

For another few seconds he stood still in the rain, feeling the drops running down his face, dripping from nose and chin, then kicked the door full open and ducked back away from it, flattening his back against the house.

"Man with a gun!" he called, the entry cry he remembered from his M.P. days.

Nothing happened.

Nick hesitated to stick his head inside. He edged over to one of the windows and tried to see in. The rivulets of water and darkness inside the house made it impossible. If this was a standoff, he wondered who could be patient the longest. Most likely the person waiting inside the house, if there was one, because that sucker wasn't getting his ass wet. But Clarence T. Bettis had not impressed Nick as a patient man.

Nick eased his way back to the front door and, using his left hand, his right being occupied holding the gun, pushed it in wider. From here, peering around the corner, what he could see of the living room looked vacant. His M.P. training taking over, Nick cupped his left hand beneath his right fist around the butt of the pistol, stepped into the house and moved quickly to one side. Dropping into a shooting stance, he pivoted left and right.

Still nothing happened.

Nick took each room in turn, slowly and cautiously, using the same entry method, before he relaxed with the satisfaction that he was the only person inside the house. He took off the raincoat and dropped it on the hallway floor.

In the bedroom, the one bag he'd brought was open and upside down on the bed. There hadn't been anything left inside it to dump. From the scruff marks on it, it looked like the bag had been drop-kicked a time or two. The two dresser drawers containing his clothing were open, his underwear, shirts, and socks tossed randomly on the floor. In the bathroom, his toilet articles had been raked off the shelf.

Clarence T. Bettis would be a good guess. Still pissed at Nick and letting him know it. Frank Carr might have looked through his things, but Frank wouldn't have had a reason to toss them like that. It could have been that Bettis was merely looking for his gun.

Nick found a note taped to the refrigerator door. It said: Nick—call me at 235-1617—F.

Nick popped a beer and stood looking at the note. He wondered if Bettis and Frank had come to the house separately, or together. That would be a good question to ask Frank when he talked with him.

He took his beer into the bathroom, used a towel to wipe his head and neck, and picked up his toilet articles. Next, in the bedroom, he repacked his bag, in case he had to move out quickly, and set the bag in the living room near the front door. After a few swallows, he set the beer aside, put on the raincoat, and walked across the street to Christopherson's house. The old man answered the knock and nodded him inside.

"You're all wet again, Indy," he said.

In the hallway, Nick shrugged out of the raincoat and hung it up. "Somebody has been in Mrs. McNally's house since I left."

"I know," Chris said, eying the gun in Nick's belt. "Your friend in the Ford came back couple of hours afterward. The heavy bald one was with him. They went in but didn't stay long."

"They left me a note. Can I use your phone again?"

"Help yourself," the old man said and slipped out of sight.

Nick dialed the number, let it ring several times, and finally Frank Carr's voice answered.

"Hey, Nick," Frank said cheerfully, "I missed you, pal. How's it goin'?"

"Not good, Frank. Somebody got in your house. Went through my things."

"You don't say," Frank said. "He went through my things, too. Took my raincoat. That's not all. That picture I showed you's missing. Kind'a dumb of me just to leave it there like that. Since it's got nostalgic value, I'd sure like to have it back."

"I bet it's gone for good, Frank."

"Too bad. Nick, we could putz around and waste another day or two, but I don't really see no point in it. Suppose we get right to what I want."

"I'm all ears, pal." Nick put a similar, slightly sardonic tone on "pal" just as Frank had done.

"Where you calling from?" asked Frank.

"Neighbor's house," Nick said.

"Lemme guess," Frank said. "That old fart catty-cornered across the street. You know, I don't think he likes me. Is he listening now?"

"Nope. Just the two of us, Frank."

"Good boy, Nick. What'cha hear from the Voights?"

"They're waiting patiently. It's all they can do."

"Really?" Frank made a thoughtful humming noise into Nick's ear. "Nick, why do I think you're holding out on me? Don't you trust me? We're buddies."

"Asshole buddies," Nick said.

"Now I believe you when you said Larry's waiting patiently. He don't have the balls for nothin' else. But Marilyn? Huh uh, not that lady. I'll make a prediction, Nick. I predict she's on her way here, right now, as we speak. When do you think she'll get here?"

Nick swore inwardly. He hoped to hell that Marilyn hadn't already informed Frank that she was on the road. He decided to play it as though she hadn't. He said, "She won't. She's smart enough to know that if I can't get to Mark, she can't either. She'll wait for him to contact her."

Frank's voice turned testier. "You are bullshitting me, my friend. Did you actually talk to her?"

"Sure," Nick said, and took a shot. "I spoke with her after you did."

"So she told you I called her this morning?"

"How else would I know?"

"Goddamn," Frank said. "I don't know whether to believe you or not. You just might'a talked her out 'a coming, like you said. Or you could be bullshitting me some more. Looks like I should be asking you face to face."

"Hey, that's fine with me," Nick told him. "Marilyn ain't coming, Frank. I convinced her to wait. Don't bother phoning her again, she won't talk to you anymore. You have to deal with me."

Frank Carr laughed. "Hell, Nick, it's been fun playing with you, but we can stop now. My pal Clarence is foaming at the mouth to get at you. He fucked up last night, says you got lucky and took his gun. He don't like that one little bit. It's all I can do to keep him from coming after you right now."

"Hell, Frank, let him," Nick said. "I believe in giving a guy more'n one chance."

"You don't know Clarence when he's mad. Clarence has got guys who owe him favors. They don't pay much attention to bein' nice. Know what I'm saying?"

"Tell Clarence he's scary as hell."

"Nick, you're out'a your league," Frank said. "Lemme tell you what's a good idea. You pack up and go home. Nobody needs you. Marilyn don't. I still think she's on her way."

"Suppose she's not? Then who's your contact? Larry Voight? I'm here and ready."

There was a silence at the other end of the line. Nick smiled to himself. He had Frank Carr thinking.

Nick gave him another moment and said, "I didn't peg you for a kidnapper, Frank. Redneck pigfucker maybe, but not a kidnapper."

"Fuck that," Frank snapped. "Ain't nobody kidnapped nobody."

"I have to see Mark," Nick said. "Marilyn's waiting for me to tell her I've seen him and that he's okay. You know she's not a fool."

"She didn't say that to me."

"How much chance did you give her to say anything?" Nick was taking another long shot, but he was relying on what Larry Voight had told him. The call Marilyn answered had been short enough that she claimed it to be a wrong number. He said, "Call her home again. She won't answer. Larry will. You can tell him you want to talk to his wife."

Again, Frank was quiet for several seconds. Finally, he said, "We'll do it the other way around. You make the call for me, Nick. Tell Marilyn I want her <u>here</u>. Her alone. She's to come to the house. I'll meet her there."

"No, I won't do that."

"What? Think I'm gonna hurt that woman? That ain't what I want."

"What do you want, Frank? You kidnapped their son. I think they should contact the police and the F.B.I."

"It ain't a kidnapping," Frank said. "I keep telling you that. Mark told 'em he's okay."

"Maybe you held a gun to his head. I have to see him first."

"You don't make the rules here," Frank said.

"I might contact the F.B.I. myself. I can turn Clarence's gun over to them. Maybe you won't mind the feds chasing your asses, but you better ask Clarence if he'll mind."

"Nick, this don't hafta go like that."

"You think it over," Nick said. "I'll call you later, Frank, and we can discuss it further. In the meantime, don't count on seeing Marilyn until you deal with me."

He hung up the phone as Frank was starting to say something. "Piss on you, Frank," he said aloud. One thing for sure, he waned a chance at Marilyn Voight before she got together with Frank Carr. Staring at the phone, Nick sighed.

Christopherson, grinning, appeared beside him. "Well, Indy?" he asked. "I overheard some of it. Sounded like you're trying to piss the guy off. I wasn't eavesdropping. Come in the living room and sit with me. Can I get you coffee or a beer?"

Nick told him a beer, followed Chris into his living room and lowered himself into one of the soft chairs. Chris came back a minute later with two bottles, handed one to Nick, and took another chair. He stretched out and crossed his ankles.

"I talked to Mrs. Mac," he said. "Her daughter's doing better, but she's gonna stay a couple more weeks. It took some prodding, and I didn't wanna scare the lady, make her think there's something wrong at her house. Way it happened, she advertised for a house-sitter in the paper.

That's how she met the big guy—Frank Carr. He told her he was looking for a place to stay until he found something permanent. Promised he'd take good care of the house and convinced her he's an honest man. My guess is he turned on the charm."

Charm? Nick smiled at that.

Chris continued, "And she probably was flattered by male attention. But she was wise enough to take some precautions. Had her clothes and valuables put in storage. The guy said it was fine with him, that it was smart for her to do so. Said you don't know who you can trust."

"A favorite line of his," Nick said. "Is she paying him?"

"Nominal fee is what she said. He didn't ask for much money. Mostly wanted a place to stay temporarily. She wanted to know why I was asking."

"What'd you tell her?"

"Just that I was curious," Chris said. "I think it satisfied her." He worked on his beer, scratched his head and looked at Nick. "Now you tell me, Indy. Is he a kidnapper?"

"No, I don't think so. I'm not sure what he is."

"But you don't trust him."

"Not one little bit," Nick said.

"If it ain't safe for you there, you're welcome to stay with me. I got room. I'd try not to talk your ear off, and you can always tell me to butt out if I get too nosy."

Nick smiled his appreciation at the offer, set the beer on the floor beside the chair, and stood up. "I need to call the boy's father."

"Help yourself."

Nick told the operator he wanted to place a collect call to Larry Voight and gave her the number. The phone rang several times at the other end but was not answered. Then he tried the administrative offices of the school district and got a receptionist who was pulling Saturday duty. No, Dr. Voight was not in the building so far this weekend. She could leave a message if he checks in that Nick was trying to reach him.

Nick hung up, not liking the sound of what he had heard or what he was thinking. How long would Larry Voight wait, with both his wife and son in Florida God-knows-where, and not set out to find them? He hoped that Larry Voight hadn't turned into the third foolish person within the past few hours.

"Hey, Indy!" Chris said. He was standing in his living room now, at the front window, looking out toward the street. From that vantage point, he could see the McNally house. "You got company over there."

For a brief second, Nick felt a surge of hopefulness. Marilyn, already? He went to stand beside Christopherson and look through the parted curtains.

Across the street, a Ford Broncho had stopped at the mouth of the driveway, blocking it. Two men wearing ponchos with hoods had gotten out, standing now one on each side of the vehicle and looking toward the house. Nick peered through the droplets on the window. He couldn't see the men clearly, but from this distance they looked Hispanic or black. Each man carried an automatic weapon. Nick could see the banana-shaped magazines on the guns.

"They got what I think they got?" Chris asked in an awed whisper.

The gunmen took positions at either side of the McNally front door. The one nearest the doorknob reached over, turned it, and pushed the door open. They went into the house fast.

"Want me to call the cops?" Chris asked, still whispering.

"How fast can they get here?"

"Depends on how far they are into their doughnuts," Chris said.

"Let's wait a minute."

The two men were inside no more than three minutes. They came out, chucked their guns into the Broncho and stood in the rain talking. One opened the back of the vehicle and took out a gas-can. The other went to the door on the driver's side of Nick's rental, tried it, and opened it. The first one joined him and began slopping the contents of the can into the little car, spreading it around. He leaned in and backed out without the can.

"Jesus," Chris said softly, "you gonna let 'em do that, Indy?"

"What do you suggest?"

"You've got a gun."

"They've got bigger ones," Nick said.

"That is a point," Chris admitted.

The second man was searching his pockets beneath the poncho. He shook his head at his partner. The partner began patting himself down. Nick wondered what would happen if he strolled across the street and offered them a match.

One man had to go back to the Broncho and climb inside. A few seconds later, he got out and approached his partner, who was gesturing and saying something to him. The first one showed him something, and they hunched close together to cup their hands around it. Then they stepped apart, and the first one was holding fire. The second one was flipping one hand in the air like he had been burned.

The first guy stepped forward and tossed the flaming matchbook through the open door of the small car.

Both of them raced to the Broncho, climbed in, backed the vehicle out into the street and stopped. Nick couldn't see them inside the Broncho, but he guessed that they were watching the same thing he was, the glow of the fire growing inside the rental.

They must have been satisfied because, a few seconds later, they gunned off down the street.

Nick had the front door open and was stepping onto the porch just as the gas-can inside the rental exploded. Flames engulfed the little car, sending a corkscrewed cloud upward into the afternoon rain.

"Holy shit!" Chris said.

"Now you can call the cops," Nick said. "The fire department, too."

12

"You didn't see or hear anybody messing around out there?" asked the uniformed cop in the rain slicker.

"I was across the street in Mr. Christopherson's house," Nick explained for the second time. "We didn't see anything till we heard the explosion."

The cop had his ballpoint pen poised over his clipboard. The plastic cover of his cap and the slicker's shoulders were peppered with raindrops, the rest of the slicker simply wet where streaks of water had run down the sides and front. He didn't seem to mind that he was dripping on Mrs. McNally's rug. He touched the tip of his ballpoint pen to his tongue. Apparently he had been in the habit of writing with a pencil. The pen tip left a blue smudge on his tongue and lower lip. He said, "So you're telling me it must'a been vandals."

"Had to be," Nick said. "Or somebody who don't like tourists."

"Made a mess out of that car," the cop said in understatement.

They were standing in the living room of the McNally house. This was the fourth time Nick had answered the same questions from three different officers. Most of the curious on-lookers outside, hunched against the rain that had lightened, had by this time strolled away. Just a car fire, nothing exciting. The two fire trucks were out on the street, and the firemen in their slickers and helmets milled around the charred remnants of the rental and assisted in the roll-up of the hoses. One of them burst out in laughter that could be heard inside the house.

"It happens," the cop said, licked the tip of his pen once more and wrote something on the sheet on his clipboard. "Did you take out insurance when you rented it?"

"Yes," Nick replied. "The papers, or what's left of 'em, are in the glove box."

The cop halfway grinned. "You didn't torch it yourself, did you?"

"Why would I do that?"

"I might've," the cop said. "Some rental company stick me with a peanut like that."

A glum-looking young man, wearing a blue jacket, with the blue and gold Alamo logo on the breast pocket, stood in the doorway, hands stuffed in his raincoat pockets, shaking his head and staring out at what was left of his car. He sniffed like he had a cold, or was about to cry. Nick hoped he wouldn't cry. He couldn't see that particular rental as anything to cry over.

The cop, squeezing past the Alamo rep, said with a straight face, "I don't think it's drivable."

"Drivable? Shit, it's a cinder," the young man said. He looked at Nick and sighed. "I imagine you'll want another car, Mr. Cotton."

"I imagine so," Nick told him.

"I'll see what we can do. Might take a little while."

"Not too long, I hope."

"It was a pretty little thing," the rep said.

Was he serious, Nick wondered. He said, to cheer up the rep, "Prettiest thing I ever saw."

The rep gave him a business card. It was the second card he'd given Nick. The rep appeared slightly catatonic after viewing the specter of his car in the driveway. "If you don't hear from us by morning, give us a call. It's Sunday tomorrow, but somebody will be available."

The fire trucks and three police cars left. A tow-truck waited patiently on the street. It started forward with headlights on, eased around the Alamo rep's parked car, and, digging furrows in the yard, entered the driveway. The driver got out and went to work.

"Would you like a beer?" Nick asked the Alamo rep, feeling sorry for him. The young man looked like he needed something.

"No, thanks." The rep patted his breast pocket. "I guess my report's done. We'll have our insurance adjuster look at it, but I know what he'll say. Can I use your phone?"

"None in the house," Nick told him. "The owner had it removed when she left on her trip."

"Look, I'll see if we can possibly get you another car tonight," the rep told him, almost apologetically. "I'll really try."

"Do what you can."

"It's the busy time of year, you know."

"I know. Everybody tells me that."

"I never had anything like this happen before," the rep said.

"Hey, shit happens," Nick said.

But there was just no cheering up the young man. Trance-like, the rep went outside to talk with the tow-truck driver. Nick left a living room light on and, still wearing Frank Carr's raincoat, walked past them to cross the street to Christopherson's house. It was full dark now, and the rain had slackened some more. Chris was waiting on his porch.

"One 'a the cops asked me," Chris said. "I did like you said. I told 'em we don't know what happened."

Nick nodded. "No need to bother them with a couple guys we can't identify."

"Indy, you sure as hell can't stay over there any longer. They might come back. I got my car in the back. Why don't we go someplace for dinner? I know a good place for fettucini and clam sauce, and we can crack a bottle of red."

"Okay, we both have to eat," Nick said. "I need to use your phone first."

"You know where it is."

Nick dialed the number Frank Carr had left for him. Frank answered immediately.

"Had a couple visitors," Nick told him. "Hispanic types, I think. My rented car's history."

"That's no loss," Frank said. "You met Paulo and Hector Garcia. They do jobs for Clarence. They're nasty boys, Nick. What'd they tell you?"

"Nothing. I wasn't home to greet them."

"Then how'd you know they're spics?"

"I saw 'em leave."

"You can stop sweating, Nick," Frank said. "They wasn't supposed to kill you. Not yet, anyhow. I made Clarence promise. So look at it as a message. Now, back to what we were discussing before you rudely hung up on me. You were bullshitting about going to the F.B.I."

"Not unless I talk to Mark," Nick said. "I only have your word it's not a kidnapping."

"I think you're bullshitting about Marilyn not coming, too," Frank went on. "But—point is, I just don't know for sure, do I? I did what you said and tried calling 'em, and nobody answered. You got me puzzled a little bit. I ain't exactly sure what you are in all this."

"I have a way to reach Marilyn that you don't," Nick said. "How 'bout it, Frank? Do I get to talk with Mark?"

"You say she'll listen to you?"

"Right."

After a moment's silence, Frank said, "You win. Hang on and I'll let you talk to the boy."

"Not this way," Nick said. "Face to face, that's how. I don't trust you."

"You don't trust <u>me</u>? Boy, that's good. You're the outsider with the big nose. We don't need you in this mix at all."

"What's it gonna be, Frank? F.B.I., or do you want to see Marilyn?"

There was more silence at the other end. Nick let him think it over.

Frank said, "If I agree, you'll contact Marilyn and tell her to get started, right? I'll take your word on it. Clarence says I'm a fool to do it your way, but it might be cleaner."

"I'll deliver any message you want to Marilyn, but I won't persuade her to come here."

"Then you're out altogether, my man. Leave town, Nick. Fast as you can. Or I'll unleash Clarence and his boys."

"I told you what I'll do."

Frank grunted. "For a fucking school teacher, you got balls. I'll give you that. This must be my day for bein' stupid. Got something to write on?"

Nick grabbed his pen and a sketch of Donnie Ann to write on the back of it. He folded it over and said, "Go ahead."

"First, understand this. You bring any cops, or suits that look like they might be feds, anybody but yourself for that matter, and the kid will be killed. No matter what happens to me. I'm saying I'm in for the whole ride, Nick. It's all or nothing. Are we clear on this?"

"I hear you," Nick said.

"I'll give you directions. It's a Denny's. Be there in forty minutes." Frank rattled off the street address and directions as Nick wrote. "Think you can find it?"

"I taught geography," Nick said. "I can find it."

"Wise-ass," Frank said and hung up.

Chris called to Nick from the living room. He was at the window. "You got another visitor."

Nick peered out, frowning when he saw a dark-colored van stopped just past the driveway in front of the McNally house. He couldn't see who was inside because of the tinted windows and the darkness. Nick did see the tow-man, checking his harness attached to the wreck, pause and speak with the van's driver on the opposite side of the vehicle from himself and Christopherson. The two-truck driver nodded to something and motioned across the street.

"I wouldn't go out there," Chris warned.

The sliding door on the near side of the van opened, and a ramp eased out. Seated in her wheelchair on the ramp was Augusta Dick, private eye. The ramp lowered to the street, and Augusta rode free of it. She wheeled around, pressed a control under a flap near the front of the van, and the ramp retracted, the sliding door closing after it.

"This one's okay," Nick said to Chris. "We'll make that clam sauce dinner another time, Chris."

He crossed the street and greeted Gus. She had her light coat pulled around her shoulders with a hood up over her hair.

"You must be psychic," he told her. "I was thinking of calling you."

She nodded at the ruin behind the tow-truck. "Was that your car?"

"What's left of it belongs to Alamo." Nick smiled at her. "Want to do a taxi service for me?"

"I'm on the payroll," she said. "What happened?"

"Two Garcia's, pals of Clarence Bettis, paid a visit. Their names are Hector and Paulo. I think they meant to tell me I'm in over my head."

"Are you?"

"I wasn't here to get their message."

"And you're okay with this?" Gus tilted her head at him with a quizzical look. "Aren't you scared?"

"I'd be more scared if I'd been here when they came. They had automatic weapons."

"You told the police," Gus said.

"I forgot."

Gus chuckled and shook her head. "You forgot? I wouldn't fool with automatic weapons, Nick."

The tow-truck honked and came out of the driveway pulling the ruined rental. The driver waved, and Nick waved back to him.

"How about," Nick said to Gus, "I treat you to dinner after you take me to a meeting?"

"I accept," she said. "What kind of meeting?"

"I'll tell you on the way."

Nick stood beside the van as Gus worked the lift, maneuvered herself backwards onto it, and set it in motion to deposit her inside. She thanked him for the offer but told him there wasn't anything he needed to do to help. He watched her leverage herself out of the wheelchair and into the driver's seat, then turn the seat around to face forward. She pushed another button, and the sliding door closed.

Nick opened the smaller forward door with the handle and climbed in on the passenger's side. Under the dome light, he read aloud the directions Frank had given him.

As they rode, he told Gus about his phone conversations with Frank Carr.

"So you found the kid without me," Gus said. "Am I out of a job?"

"Not yet. I'm going to need a babysitter. Mark's girlfriend is coming in on a bus after midnight. Her folks couldn't stop her."

"That's not good," Gus said.

"In capitals. This little girl can be stubborn. I was thinking of asking you to put her up at your place. Keep an eye on her."

"Who's gonna keep an eye on you?"

"I'm thinking of her safety, Gus. This wasn't supposed to be part of the deal."

"I can try, sure," Gus said. "But my apartment's in Clearwater. Am I supposed to detain her by any means? Reason I'm asking, I doubt if it's possible unless I handcuff her to something. You don't think she'll make a fuss?"

"Oh, she'll make a fuss," Nick said. "Let's think about this. Damn! I got two women descending on me who shouldn't be here. What's your suggestion?"

"Let 'em in on what's happening. I'll help you."

"I'm worried Frank might go screwy and send those guys with the guns back."

"Look. We can try to persuade Mrs. Voight and this girl to stay at my place," Gus said. "I'm just saying I don't think it'll work. What're you gonna do when you see the boy?"

"Ask him what the hell's going on. If he's not with Frank under duress, then how did Frank Carr suck him in?

What's his mother got to do with it? When I first met Frank, he was upset that Marilyn hadn't come herself. I believe he was expecting her. But she never told me that. I showed up, and it confused him. Hell, I was just as confused. Neither one of us knew what the other was up to."

"Ready for some info? Your instincts are on target," Gus said. "I made a number of calls about Frank Carr and Clarence Bettis. Bettis was a probation officer until he was suspended under suspicion of some shady dealings. Nothing solid, but one of my sources said he suspects Bettis and some of his clients rip off houses and deal in stolen goods. Incidentally, Bettis drew Frank Carr."

"So Frank did serve time."

Gus nodded, her eyes on the road. "Frank has matriculated at Raiford and Lake Butler. First time, nine years for second-degree murder. Second time, eight years for armed robbery. He's got arrest sheets all along the Gulf Coast. Your boy's got quite a record. He and Bettis make a dangerous pair."

"According to Frank, they didn't kidnap Mark."

"If we catch Frank Carr with a gun in his possession," Gus said, "he can go back to prison for violation of parole."

"He'll be smart enough not to have a gun in sight."

"Don' bet your life on it." They rode in silence before Gus asked, "Garcia, you say? How'd you find out their last names?"

"Frank told me."

"I've got a cell in that side pocket." Gus indicated the pocket of the door on Nick's side. "While you talk to the boy, I'll make a call regarding Hector and Paulo Garcia." She smiled, looking ahead at the traffic. "Bettis probably was their probation officer as well. What'll you do if they come back?"

"They won't right away," Nick said. "Frank won't let it happen. He's counting on me to convince Marilyn to come here. I'm buying a little time."

"And you need me for transportation. Why is it not a kidnapping, Nick?"

"Larry and Marilyn Voight make a good living, but they don't have the kind of money that attracts kidnappers. At least, I don't think so. And had it been, they would've been contacted about a ransom. No, this is something between Frank and Marilyn."

Gus said, "I also checked on the other names you gave me. I called the Fort Myers police. Their research specialist confirmed the deaths of Martin Ruhle and Lenny Wilson. Both had had a string of minor arrests, but nothing big. Of course, that was eighteen years ago. By this time, had they lived, they'd probably be as hard as Frank Carr. Their remains, what were found, were shipped home to their respective parents. Ruhle's folks are gone—somewhere. Lenny Wilson's father's dead, but his mother's still living. She moved to Dade City. I located her through a sister of Lenny's who happens to be a hooker in this fair town. Mrs. Wilson told me about the double funeral service they had for Lenny and Martin Ruhle. She has no idea where Ruhle's parents are now. Her main memory of the graveside service was that a couple of former high school classmates of Lenny's played taps on their clarinets, off-key she said. She called it 'very moving.' Lenny's the only one of the group who had siblings."

Then Gus motioned ahead, through the glare of headlights, and slowed to turn into the driveway of the restaurant. She parked the van in a handicapped space and started to activate her seat to swing around toward the wheelchair.

Nick stopped her with a hand on her arm. "Gus, I'd appreciate it if you wait here for me. I don't know how Frank will take it if we go in together."

"Don't I get dinner?"

"Please," Nick said. "If I want to eat at Denny's, I can do that in Indianapolis. You think of a good restaurant for us."

A clouded expression touched Gus's features. "I'm not a helpless cripple, Nick. I won't be a burden. What if Frank gets tough?"

"He won't, not here." Nick smiled to reassure her and make her think that he knew what he was doing. "If I'm wrong, you can send <u>my</u> remains home. Who's your boss on this case?"

Gus relented. "Mr. Voight is. Wanna take a gun?"

"Lord, no," Nick said. "I might be tempted to use it."

He passed the cell-phone over to Gus, left his raincoat in the van, went inside and stopped to look around. The checkout kiosk stood directly in front of him with a <u>please wait to be seated</u> sign in front of it. To his left was the brightly lighted dining room, to his right the counter area in a smaller room. He spotted Frank Carr sitting alone at the counter.

Frank saw him, got up, and approached. "How you doin', pal?"

"I'm here," Nick said. "Where's Mark?"

"Always in a hurry, Nick. You gotta learn to slow down. And don't look so grim. You don't wanna scare the kid. I had a hard time convincing Mark to talk to you. Did you give Marilyn my message?"

"Not yet. Mark first."

Frank's smile was still in place, but his eyes were steely. "Warn you, Nick. Guys don't get far playing hardball with me."

"I'll put that in my memory bank," Nick said.

They fell silent and edged to one side as a family came in to be greeted by the hostess.

"Okay," Frank said. He pointed toward the dining room. "Booth at the end, on your right. You got ten minutes. Say what you gotta say, and that's it. After that, you call Marilyn for me. Ten minutes, Nick, then I'm breaking it up."

"Fine," Nick said and walked away from him.

13

They were sitting close together, their backs to Nick Cotton as he approached, Mark Voight and the thin, redhaired girl with all the freckles. When Nick stopped beside the booth table, Mark didn't look up. The redhead did.

She was smoking a cigarette. Donnie Ann's face had been almost perfectly captured in the sketch. She blinked large, green eyes at Nick and mashed the cigarette in an ashtray. She wore jeans and a transparent, sleeveless blouse, with a tight little bra adorned with tiny bows visible under it. Her lipstick was bright red.

Nick slipped into the seat opposite them. Both of the kids had tall glasses of iced cola with straws. The tip of Donnie Ann's straw was coated with the red lipstick. Mark's fingers moved nervously on his glass, and his mouth formed a hard, straight line. He was a handsome kid, but not particularly so when attempting a grim or "go to hell" expression. He still hadn't looked straight at Nick. Donnie Ann got busy striking a match to another cigarette.

After a few seconds, Mark did look up, saw Nick staring at him, and averted his eyes.

Nick said pleasantly, “How you doing, Mark?”

“Fine.” Just that one word—short and clipped.

Nick waited another couple of seconds. “Just fine?”

“Yeah.” Same delivery. An attitude, no eye-contact.

Nick looked at the girl and gave her what he hoped was his charming smile. She smoked in short, quick puffs, her heart not into it. “Hello, Donnie Ann,” he said. “It doesn’t look like Mark’s going to introduce us. My name’s Nick Cotton. I don’t know your last name.”

She turned her head and threw a quick, bright-eyed, inquisitive look at Mark. The corner of Mark’s mouth twitched. Trying for that “go to hell” attitude, and carrying it off, was difficult work for him. He said out of the corner of his mouth to Donnie Ann, “Jerry and Rob must’a told him. It’s okay.” To Nick, without meeting his eyes, Mark said, “She’s with me.”

Nick leaned back comfortably, resting an arm along the back of the booth. Smiling, he stared at Mark until the young man raised, then lowered, his eyes, grabbed his glass and sucked on the straw.

"Mark, are you in trouble?"

"No!" Quick and snappy.

"Look at me, little boy."

It surprised Mark, and he did look at Nick.

"What's going on?"

"None of your business," Mark said. "Leave me alone."

"I can't. Your mom and dad asked me to do the favor of looking for you. Tell me why you neglected to go home."

"Home," Mark said, sarcastically.

"That's what they call it, you know, the place where you live," Nick said, keeping his voice mild and even. "Like the song says, 'Back Home in Indiana.'"

"Bullshit," Mark said. "You should'a stayed there if it's so fucking great."

Nick glanced at Donnie Ann and gave her his 'who me?' expression. "Did I say it's great? I said it's home." Then to Mark: "What's going on between you and your folks?"

Mark looked down, his lips working together in some kind of expression between pursing and pouting.

"He don't wanna talk to you," Donnie Ann said.

Nick let his eyes shift to her, then back to Mark. "Okay. I'm no great shakes to talk to. At least, call home. Tell your dad what's happening. He's worried about you."

Mark's eyes darted up and then down again. Emphatically, he shook his head.

"Are you afraid of something? Or somebody?"

Mark looked at Nick, a little longer this time. Nick hoped they were starting to get somewhere. Mark said, "Frank said if I showed you I'm okay, you'd leave us alone. Well, I'm okay. So there."

By this time Nick was forcing his smile to hide his loss of patience. He leaned forward, planting his elbows on the table. "You're not making this easy."

"Then go away."

"Yeah," Donnie Ann piped up. She furiously stabbed her cigarette into the glass ashtray.

"I will when you provide some information," Nick said. "Do you like Frank Carr?"

Mark's eyes went up and down again. He was getting good at that meaningless gesture. He said, "Sure."

"He's your buddy, huh? Well, Mark, I'm going to cause your buddy some grief."

"Hah!" said Mark.

"Yes. Kidnapping's a federal offense."

"Who's been kidnapped?" Mark snapped. "Not me. That's a dammed lie."

"Then tell me the dammed truth."

Mark looked at Donnie Ann. She looked back at him.

"Kid," Nick said to Mark, "you know me well enough to know I don't like attitudes. Yours stinks. I told Frank I'll report you as kidnapped. There's already a missing persons cop on your trail." Which wasn't exactly the truth.

"Can't you just leave us alone?" Donnie Ann cried. "Why you gotta keep pickin' at him?"

"Because Mark is acting like an asshole."

"Mr. Cotton is a big man at S.O.B.," Mark said to the girl. "He's chief of security because they fired him from coaching football. But they had to give him a job." His words dripped with sarcasm. "But he's forgot that's at S.O.B. and not here." He gave Nick a corner of the mouth quirk. "Or maybe he's gonna hit me now."

"It's a temptation," Nick said. "I'll tell the cop you're with Frank Carr, and I'll tell the F.B.I. you're being held against your will—"

"That's not true," Mark blurted.

"I don't give a shit," Nick said. "Frank won't like it. He didn't put us together so you can sit here with your mouth flapping. Give me something to take back to your folks, and I'm out of here."

"You don't unnerstand," Donnie Ann said, plaintively. "Mark's sensitive. It's a sensitive subject."

"Oh, that explains it." It was Nick's turn to be sarcastic. "Where do you fit in?"

"Don't talk to him," Mark told her.

Nick sighed and shook his head. "Kid, you must have a reason for not going home."

"I got a reason."

"And that is?"

"Just because," Mark said.

"Beautiful," Nick grunted. "It's like this, Mark. See if you can follow my reasoning. I have to tell them something, or they'll be here asking you themselves."

Mark flinched. "Tell 'em not to do that." He looked up and saw that Nick was waiting. "They're fucking liars, both of 'em."

"Why are they liars?"

"They just are."

"Just because, huh? That sounds like all the wisdom of seventeen years. I had you pegged smarter than that."

"Go back there," Mark said. "Tell them you seen me, I'm okay, and I'm staying here awhile."

Donnie Ann laid her head against Mark's shoulder.

Several more seconds passed before Mark said, "This was not a good idea, Mr. Cotton. I didn't want to talk to you."

"What're you afraid of?" asked Nick.

Mark raised himself up in the booth and looked back over his shoulder as though scanning for somebody to help him. Maybe Frank Carr. But Frank wasn't in sight. From Nick's vantage point, he could see Frank at the counter. Frank wasn't looking in their direction. Mark sat back down and said, "Nothing."

"So you're afraid of Frank."

Mark laughed. "No. Not at all."

"Then what's your problem?"

Donnie Ann put her head back onto Mark's shoulder. "Don't bully him," she said to Nick.

"It was a simple question," Nick said. "An 'A' student with a scholarship to Northwestern should be able to handle it."

"He don't wanna tell you."

"That makes it okay, huh? He's got a mom and dad waiting to hear from him. They're worried. That gives him a responsibility."

"What 'bout their responsibility to him?" Donnie Ann asked.

"They've been lying to me all my life," Mark said. "Well, I got to figure things out for myself now. You tell them that, Mr. Cotton. I'm doing all right. I can stay here with Frank."

"For how long?" Nick asked.

"I don't know yet."

"How the hell did you get yourself connected to Frank Carr?" Nick nodded toward Donnie Ann. "Her?"

Mark looked quickly at him and away again. He was getting that nervous habit down pat.

Donnie Ann straightened up. "What's that supposed to mean? You insulting me? Mark, you don't hafta say nothing."

Mark tightened his lips and followed her advice, saying nothing. The girl took one of his hands and held it, squeezing it. Mark leaned closer to her until their shoulders touched. He appeared to need that closeness.

"Call your dad, Mark," Nick said.

Mark laughed shortly, harshly, his eyes lowered again.

"He deserves to hear from you."

Mark uttered another short laugh.

"Okay," Nick said, "what about school? Your plans to graduate and go to college? What about Kelly?"

Mark's mouth twitched again, but his eyes blinked, as he shook his head.

"Who's Kelly?" Donnie Ann wanted to know.

Mark looked at her, looking guilty now. "A girl I knew. That's all. Just a high school kid."

"That's pathetic," Nick said. "What about your scholarship?"

"I don't know," Mark muttered, looking down.

"You don't seem to know much of anything."

"It's all phony," Mark said, not looking at Nick.

Donnie Ann sniffed in sympathy and put her head back onto Mark's shoulder. "You should leave us alone," she whined.

"Who the fuck are you anyway?" Nick snapped at her.

"Don't talk to her like that," Mark flared.

"Why not?" Nick said. "Whatever this self-pity thing is you got, it ain't working. Maybe Donnie Ann can give me a clue. How about it, Donnie Ann? What suddenly has become phony with Mark's life?"

"They lied to him," she said.

"His parents?"

"Yes."

"Don't," Mark said, more to her than to Nick. "They don't think I'm entitled to know the truth."

"What is this great truth you've suddenly discovered?" asked Nick.

"Go ahead," Mark sneered. "Be sarcastic all you want."

Nick leaned forward to make his point. He didn't smile at Mark now. He glared at him. "Your mother and father need to hear from you."

"Dr. Lawrence Voight is not my father," Mark said bitterly. "It's all been a lie."

Nick laughed.

Mark's face turned red. "He's not, goddammit! Frank is. Frank Carr's my father."

"Yeah, right," said Nick.

"He is. He told me all about it. Mr. Bettis told me, too."

"Great," Nick said. "Couple of fucking crooks."

Now Donnie Ann sat up straight and said, "Don't call my daddy a crook."

Nick raised his brows at her. "And which one is your daddy? Did they pick you up off the street and tell you a story, too?"

"My daddy is Clarence Bettis," Donnie Ann said.

Nick folded his arms because he had the temptation to slap both of them. "You don't even get it, do you, Mark?

They spin you a fairy tale, and you go in like a fish to a lure. They got you hooked. Now you sit here, role-playing the mistreated child. Next, you'll talk yourself into believing you were abused. Your mommy and daddy are the people who raised you and love you. But forget that. What's this new 'Big Daddy' of yours want from you?"

"His rights," Mark said softly.

"What makes you think it's not a lie?"

Donnie Ann spoke up. "Because Frank knows things about his mother. She got pregnant and ran away from him because he didn't have a good future like Lawrence Voight. All he wants is to claim what's really his."

"Which is?"

"Me—as his son," Mark said. "He just wants recognition of that."

Nick said, "Shit."

"I knew you wouldn't believe me. I've been lied to for eighteen years. They could'a told me."

"They gave you a pretty goddamn good eighteen years," Nick reminded him.

"They could'a told me the truth," Mark insisted. "Don't they think I'm smart enough to handle the truth? They were scared I'd want to know my real father. And I do. They think they're so much better than he is."

"Which they are," Nick said. "Did Frank Carr tell you he's an ex-con? That's he's been to prison twice at least?"

"Yes, he did," Mark said, with a note of triumph in his voice. "Now he's trying to get his life in order, and he wants to know me. I don't see anything wrong with that. It's admirable. The mistakes he made are all in the past."

"Am I hearing this?" Nick had to shake his head. "You've gone past dumb. Something happens to shake your secure little world, and all of a sudden you're ready to kiss it off. You got your feelings hurt. You're not a survivor, Mark."

"You're one to talk," Mark said. "You been married and divorced two times. You can't keep a wife."

"Kid, I'll be the first to tell you I can screw up. But I don't like to stay screwed up. I hate to see you toss everything over, your graduation, your scholarship, your girlfriend—"

"I'm his girlfriend," Donnie Ann said.

"A real step up," Nick said with dripping sarcasm.

Mark said, "What would you do if you found out everything's not like you thought? I don't want lies anymore.

I told you I'll figure out what to do, and I will. You tell my mother and her husband that. I'll be in touch with them, you can tell them that, too. Until then—" he shrugged.

Frank Carr, grinning at Nick, appeared beside the table. "Time's up, Nick."

Mark looked up at Frank with a nervous, expectant look on his face. So did Donnie Ann.

"You kids go to the car and wait for me," Frank said gently. "I'll be right there."

Mark and Donnie Ann scooted out of the booth. Mark started to pick up the check for their drinks, but Frank took it from him. He smiled at them as they brushed past him and headed out. Mark didn't look around at Nick.

Frank slid into the vacated seat. "See? He's doing fine."

"What kind of bullshit are you giving him, Frank?"

"No shit, Nick. I'm his daddy. Didn't he tell you? Marilyn and me had it goin' good after Martin Ruhle died. Even before. Hot pants, she was. It's some memory. Yeah, that was a long time ago. Then she left me."

"Frank, you're about as paternal as a rattlesnake."

Frank laughed and spread his hands. "Don't you think I can get all teary-eyed about bein' a daddy?"

"What is it you really want?"

"I want Marilyn here." Frank stabbed his forefinger onto the table for emphasis. "I want her to see how good me and Mark get along. So we can all be friends."

"You're a fucking liar, Frank."

Frank puckered his lips and blew out a breath. "That old man across the street—what's his name?"

"What's that got to do with anything?"

Frank grinned. "Let's say it ain't my plan to hurt him. I don't wanna have to do that. He's got a telephone. You give me his name, I can get his phone number. You don't have a cell phone, so we need a way to keep in closer contact, Nick."

"Screw you," said Nick.

"You don't want me to go ask him myself."

"Leave him alone, Frank."

"Leave him alone, Frank," Frank mimicked. "Think that little plea means shit to me? Or the old man himself? Lemme tell you something, school teacher. You deliver my message and call me at the same number by morning. At that time, you will tell me exactly when Marilyn will get here. You will convince her that she must come. You know why?"

"I'm sure you'll tell me."

"Because if you don't, Nick, something very bad will happen to you. To that old man as well. Long time ago, I killed lots 'a dogs. Not that those dogs did nothing to me, just that I could. I can describe all the nasty things I done to those dogs before they got smart and died. Understand, buddy? If you don't get my message to Marilyn, and make her understand it, you better be running like hell for home. All the way back to Indiana. You don't wanna be my next dead dog. I will get Mrs. Voight here sooner or later, with or without your help. It's faster and safer for you, and anybody you might'a took a liking to, if you do what I tell you." He paused for effect and added, "I think we understand each other." He leaned back and grinned broadly. "Nine o'clock in the morning, Nick. Call me by then with the good news. If I don't hear from you—well, I'll just let Clarence send his boys for you again. Only this time they won't be trying to scare you."

He stood up, hooked his thumbs in his belt, and looked down at Nick.

"Can't say it's been a pleasure. I never liked school teachers. Never met one I couldn't hate. But you're in my classroom now, Nick. My territory." Frank interlocked his fingers and popped his knuckles. "Just 'tween us, I've been known to kill people that bother me. Do you bother me? I don't consider you even a pimple on my ass. Be smart and keep it that way. Give Marilyn the message."

"Every single word," Nick said.

Frank wadded the check for the kids' drinks and threw it in Nick's face. He turned and strode away.

14

Nick Cotton and Augusta Dick, private eye, ate dinner in the dining room of the Westshore Marriott since it was conveniently close and handicapped-accessible. They shared a bottle of white wine and talked.

The first thing Gus wanted to know was Nick's impression of Mark Voight after talking to the lad. He told her the kid had no concept of what he was doing to his folks, and, apparently, no sense of responsibility that had kicked in yet.

Nick said, "Frank Carr's playing him. Frank's sole objective is to get Marilyn here. Being a daddy couldn't be further from Frank's mind, so he's got another agenda. Plus, I don't believe anything Frank tells me."

Gus changed the subject over to Nick himself, peering into his eyes in a straight-forward manner, probing for more information on his background. Nick told her a bit of his own youth, his participation in sports, army service, college, his former coaching job, and his current meaningless, in his words, position. Gus kept mixing her bright-eyed looks with her crinkled, little smiles. She was one of those women who listen with their whole bodies, not only their ears. She laughed in a few places, and Nick felt like he was rattling on like an idiot.

"Your school really is called S.O.B.?" Gus asked.

Nick nodded. "Named for Sylvester Overton Barton, a lovable politician and crook. He was the township trustee who ran the school in the days before consolidation. It was small then, kindergarten through twelfth grade. Sylvester was trustee, school principal, teacher of science and math, and athletic coach for football and basketball. His teams always lost, except for one year."

"You mean he won a game?" asked Gus.

"He won the county championship in football. With a lot of luck and a lot of rain that fall. I mean a <u>lot</u> of rain. Oldtimers say all the local football fields were mudholes every week. The team he assembled must have been mudders. They won five games in the slop and two more by forfeiture." He paused as Gus giggled. "The two forfeitures involved accidents with the buses bringing in the opposing teams. They never made it to the ballpark. Coincidentally, both buses were rammed by a gravel truck driven by

Sylvester's younger brother. It turned out to be the only perfect football season in the school's history. The following year, sixty-year-old Sylvester Overton Barton ran off with a thirteen-year-old cheerleader and the school funds. Rumor was that he and the child fled the country. But when a new stadium was built, and the new school, patrons never forgot that championship. They named both after Sylvester Overton Barton, an indication that they had their priorities straight. Now the students can truly say they graduate from the S.O.B."

Gus laughed, drank wine, and said, "You miss the coaching, don't you?"

"That," Nick said, "is an understatement."

"Pushing the board member's head into a toilet was not smart."

"That," Nick said, "is a fact."

"You keep yourself in shape," she said. "How much do you weigh, Nick?"

"One eighty-five. Rarely varies."

"You're lucky," Gus said. "I have to work to keep my weight down. Right after I got hurt, I thought to hell with everything. I was really wishing I'd died instead of being a cripple. I'm glad you didn't know me then."

"Augusta, you're a very attractive woman."

"Not then," she said. "I was a self-pitying bitch. In the hospital, and I never told anybody else this, I begged Dave Melton to bring me a gun. He wouldn't, of course. My first night home, home being a new apartment for me, one that's wheelchair accessible—the guys in the department all pitched in to build the ramps, put the bars in the bathroom and bedroom, moved all my stuff from my old place—anyway, that first night I searched for my second gun, a nine-millimeter Baretta. I couldn't find it. Figured one of my cop buddies lifted it in the moving. I cried all that night. Funny thing is, I never even considered cutting my wrists or poisoning myself. I wanted to end it by eating a bullet. Lots 'a cops do it that way."

"You don't have to talk about this," Nick told her.

"It's therapy now." Gus smiled again. "When I got pretty handy with my new surroundings and started gaining too much weight, Melton dropped in on me one night. He had my gun, my Baretta. He handed it to me and said he guessed I was over my foolishness. Then he took me to bed and fucked me. It wasn't the first time we'd fucked, but I like to think it was the best. He wanted to show me I was still a woman. Afterwards, he said, 'Goddammit, Gus, don't get fat. You don't need it. It's time for you to go to work."

It struck Nick that he suddenly had new respect, and a small touch of envy, for Sergeant Melton. "Smart man," he said.

Gus nodded. "He guided me into getting my p.i.'s license through some contacts who owed him favors. Helped me pick out my office when I insisted I wanted one. And today—" She toasted Nick with her glass, "—he sends me a client. With money, yet. I'm in hog heaven."

"So," Nick said, "are you and Sergeant Melton still—?" He waggled his fingers.

"Sergeant Melton is a married man," Gus said. "He's a good friend." Looking at he wine glass, she shook her head. "I know, I talk too much. Trying to impress you, I guess, the way you impress me."

Nick laughed.

"You do," Gus said. "The way you took Bettis's gun, the way you watched two guys torch your car but didn't risk your life, and the way you handled Mark Voight and Frank Carr tonight."

"I didn't handle them yet."

"Mark's a victim of the climate," Gus said, and Nick couldn't tell if she was kidding him. "The beach party mentality. Grabs up these young snowbirds."

"Believe it or not, Augusta, I know some sharp people back home. We don't all chew hayseeds."

She giggled again into her glass. "Besides my parents, you're the only one who calls me Augusta."

"You better eat more than a salad," Nick said.

"Watching my weight. Why don't you have dessert?"

"I missed my workout today," Nick said.

Gus tilted her head at him. "Day's not over yet."

Nick had to let that thought hang between them.

Gus changed the subject again. "Nick, don't get too down on Mark Voight. The kid's confused now. He might go dumb for a little while, but he won't change what he is."

"I believe that."

"Okay. Now, what do we do until your little girl gets here on the bus? Want to come to my place?"

"I better stay at the house," Nick said. "I need to be there when Mrs. Voight arrives."

"What if the nasty boys come back again?"

"I'll have you to protect me."

Gus looked momentarily pleased by his comment. "Can I get in with this wheelchair?"

"I'll have to tilt you, maybe even carry you, but I'll get you in," Nick told her. "Better count on all night, maybe longer. Do we need to go to your place for anything?"

Gus shook her head. "I keep a duffel in the van with changes for just such emergencies." She smiled again. "Or opportunities," she added with a wink.

Later, as Gus inched the van along with some heavy nighttime traffic on Kennedy Boulevard, she said, "I checked with Dugger Security. They had a Frank Carr working for them until a month ago. He quit and left no forwarding address. The man I spoke with was surprised when I told him Frank was a parolee."

"Don't security agencies have to check on that?" asked Nick.

"Apparently he owed Mr. Bettis a favor. Also, they have a hard enough time finding able-bodied men to work, or stick with it very long. Minimum wage. Frank's got more ambition than that. The guy told me Frank could've been a helluva security cop. Said he took no shit off anybody."

"If Frank had a badge and could throw his weight around, that would appeal to him."

"Bettis, his probation officer until his suspension, continued to report Frank as employed to satisfy the court. So far, I couldn't find out if Bettis is married, let alone has a daughter. He's not listed in the phone book. But I've got friends in the sheriff's department and the court, and I left word I want an address. I probably can't get it until after the weekend."

"It'll be good to know where Bettis lives," Nick agreed. "He and Frank, and those two kids, have a home base somewhere. I believe it was Mrs. McNally's house until I showed up. In fact, I think those kids were there when I first went to the door. He ran them out the back way and told them to wait somewhere. The old gent across the street saw the girl that same morning."

Gus said, "I also know someone who might be able to track down that phone number you called. Trouble is, I won't be able to reach her until Monday. How do you want to handle it after the mother gets here?"

"I want her to talk to me. One thing's sure. I can't let her get together with Frank by herself. What I'll try to do is stall Frank until you get that number traced. First, I'll have to find a place to stash Marilyn. Bettis will have his boys checking on that house."

"We can put her in my apartment," Gus said. "They won't look for her there. If you explain things to her, she'll probably stay. Maybe she can persuade the little girl to stay with her." After another moment, she added, "Nick, sooner or later we'll have to deal with Frank Carr."

"I know."

"Why is he so hot to get the mother here?" Gus queried. "Can't be he just wants to fuck her again."

Nick braced himself as Gus braked the van at a changing light. "It shoots to hell the theory that he's queer."

"Mr. Voight was wrong, that's all. So Frank's got some other reason. Revenge? Carrying a torch after all these years? Or just a nut case? You've talked to him, and I haven't. You don't believe he's insane."

"No."

"So, whatever Frank's reason, it bodes ill for Mrs. Voight."

Nick laughed. "Jesus, do you really talk like that? Bodes ill?"

"I'm trying to show you I'm educated, also."

"Augusta, I'm afraid he wants to hurt her. Frank Carr is capable of inflicting hurt on people."

Gus looked sideways at him. "The question is, are you? You were in the M.P.'s. I assume you can shoot. I hope so if it's necessary. Does Frank know you were in the military police?"

"I neglected to tell him," Nick said.

"You want him to keep thinking he's got you scared."

"I want whatever it takes to get Mark and his mother away from the son of a bitch."

"So if Frank thinks you're scared of him, he might make a mistake," said Gus. "You have to let me in on what we're doing. If we're setting a trap, that's fine. Just tell me." She swung the van into the parking lot of a convenience store and stopped. "You're right, I'm still hungry. I've got a yearning for dessert, strawberries and whipped cream. Would you mind?"

"I'll pick up some other things too. There's no food in the house unless you like dry cereal, or cereal with beer on it."

Nick went inside and shopped. He also bought two lottery tickets for the next weekend's state jackpot. He carried the grocery bags to the van and set them behind the seat. He gave the tickets to Gus and told her that if they won they could split it.

When they got to the McNally house, it looked quiet enough, the lights that Nick had left on inside still on. The Broncho wasn't to be seen, nor were Bettis's car or Frank's Ford. Across the street the Christopherson house was well-lighted, and Nick could see the man's silhouette peering from a window with the curtains parted.

"Park the van across the street a ways," Nick told Gus. "Just in case." He saw Gus look at him in the dark. "If anybody shows up, which I don't think they will, in fact—I don't think Frank will let anything happen to me before I talk with him tomorrow—I don't want your van getting damaged."

Gus maneuvered back out of the driveway, angled across the street and parked a space beyond Christopherson's house. Nick got out and waved to the old man. Chris saw him because he waved back from his window.

Nick lifted the grocery bags and waited until Gus, in her chair, had lowered herself on the lift to the pavement. She retracted the lift but didn't close the side door. Her large handbag was tucked beside her hip in the chair.

She said, "Put those sacks on my lap, Nick, and reach inside for my duffel. It's at the rear."

Nick had to get on his knees inside and crawl back to find it. He said over his shoulder, "There are two back here."

"Bring both," Gus told him.

"You got your weights in this one? It's heavy."

"Be careful with it," she said. "Try not to bang it around."

Nick crawled out backwards with a duffel in each hand. Gus, at the front of the vehicle, activated the door to close and used her key to lock the front door on the passenger side. "All tightened up," she said. "I'll handle the groceries if you'll bring those."

Using her battery control, she wheeled around in front of the van, crossed the street and rolled up the driveway to the McNally house. Nick stepped around her, lowered the duffels and, with Bettis's gun in his hand, eased open the front door. Taking his time, he used the same basic entry technique he had employed earlier, calling out first, then going in quickly to sweep right and left, then taking each room and the kitchen in turn before going back for Gus. He carried the bags inside, put them on the couch, went back and brought in the groceries and the handbag. Then he stood looking at Gus Dick.

"This stoop's too high," she said. "You won't be able to tilt me in the chair to get me up there."

Nick slipped one arm under her back and the other beneath her knees and lifted her out. He carried her inside, deposited her on the couch and went back to bring in the chair. He shut the door and rolled the chair to the middle of the living room.

"Get me mobile again," Gus said.

"Shut up, Augusta. I'm getting to it."

He picked her up and put her back into the wheelchair.

She looked up at him. "You're not even out of breath."

"Sergeant Melton was wrong. You're not fat."

"Thanks, I guess," she said.

Nick took the grocery bags into the kitchen, turned on the light, and started putting their purchases away. Gus followed him, stopping at the doorway. It was wide enough for her to get through, but she waited there. She had wiggled out of her light coat and apparently left it in the living room. Nick showed her a bottle of white wine and asked her if she wanted more to drink. She nodded.

Nick found two water glasses in a cabinet, washed them in the sink, dried them and poured each about half full of the wine. Gus backed her chair up to let him pass as he carried the glasses to the living room.

Nick handed her a glass and took the other to the couch, setting it on the coffee table. He picked up the lighter duffel bag. "I take it your clothes are in this one. We got two bedrooms. I'll put it in mine and take the other bedroom for myself. I don't know if Frank changed his sheets."

"We could sleep in the same bed," offered Gus.

Nick carried the light duffel to the bedroom he had used and laid it at the foot of the bed. He returned to the living room and hefted the heavy duffel. "What's in here?"

"Open it," Gus said.

He did.

Packed in carefully with towels were two guns. One was the 9mm. Baretta, the pistol. The other was a Remington shotgun. The shotgun had been outfitted with a pistol grip behind the trigger guard and a folding metal-stock on top. The stock could be unfolded and the butt plate snapped down in position for conventional firing from the shoulder. A strip of rubber padding had been super-glued to the butt plate to reduce discomfort. Nick balanced the shotgun in both hands and looked at Gus.

"The chamber's empty," Gus said. "Seven round capacity. I'm pretty good with it on the skeet range. You familiar with shotguns, Nick?"

"Not this particular Remington," Nick said. "I had a car in the M.P.'s with a rig between the seats for a 69-R Savage. I had to qualify with it."

"Handguns?"

"In the army my standard issue was the .38 Police Special. I also had to qualify with the .45 automatic."

"Good," Gus said. "Then we can take care of ourselves, can't we."

The last thing Nick wanted was a shootout with Frank Carr, or Clarence T. Bettis and his boys with the automatic weapons. He dug further into the duffel and found a box of shells and a box of cartridges. He ejected the clip from the Baretta. It was full. There was no round in the gun's chamber. He checked that the safety was on before inserting the clip.

Gus seemed to approve. "You're doing everything by the numbers. Let's keep them out and handy. We're in a lighted room. If your guess about our security is wrong, we won't have time to reach back in the bag for the guns or ammo. Humor me, Nick."

Nick folded one of the towels, laid the Baretta on it, and handed it to her. Gus flipped one more fold over the handgun and squeezed it down beside her right hip with the butt within easy reach. Nick laid the shotgun on top of the duffel on the couch. Then he gave her a look that asked if she was satisfied.

"Thank you," she said and sipped her wine.

Nick settled back with his. He looked at his watch.

Only thing to do now was wait for the arrival of Kelly Moore. Nick turned on the TV.

15

Augusta Dick parked the van in a convenient handicapped-space outside the bus depot. Nick Cotton suggested that she wait for him while he went inside to check on Kelly Moore's arrival.

"Can't," Gus said. "I gotta potty."

"Why didn't you do that before we left the house?"

"You would've had to help me on and off the toilet, and I didn't want to embarrass you," she said. "I took a look in the bathroom. It's too confined to get my chair in."

"Yeah, I got a lot to learn," Nick said. "I don't know how to take care of the handicapped unless you tell me."

"Quit talking, and let's go. I'm in a hurry."

There wasn't anything Nick could do to help her from the van, so he stood outside and let her get herself into the chair and lower it to ground level. "Don't get in my way, buster," Gus said. "I'm putting this sucker in overdrive."

Nick bought a coffee and carried it to a seat in the waiting area. The terminal was active for this hour of the morning. Lots of kids with duffels, suitcases, and backpacks waited in lines at the doors leading to the loading ramps for the buses that would take them to points north, home, and back to school. He saw red faces, tanned faces, smiles, scowls, and weary expressions. He people-watched until Gus wheeled alongside him.

"This kid we got to babysit," Gus asked, "what's she like?"

"Real nice girl. Brains plus beauty."

"Not too smart to be doing this." Gus took Nick's cup and sipped coffee, made a face and handed it back. "That's awful." She looked at the waiting lines. "All these youngsters going home." She pointed at a girl not far from them who was easing off her backpack to set it on the tiled floor by her feet. "That one must be miserable. Look at her face peeling."

"That's what they come for. Spend hours in the sun and go home burnt."

"Some come to get laid," Gus said. "I used to get a good tan. Living here, it wasn't hard to keep it. Now I'm as white as you snowbirds. Simply not convenient for me to get to a beach."

"Maybe when this is over, we'll go to a beach. I'll carry you."

Gus laughed. "And put a bathing suit on me, too?"

"Sure. Whatever."

She gave him a look. "You said you've been married twice. Did you like your wives, Nick?"

Nick nodded. "Very much. I was the problem, the fanatic football coach. Funny how you don't know what's going on around you when you get over-involved in something. I let my classes suffer because I concentrated on football more than their education. Since I lost the coaching job, I've had to do some re-evaluation."

"We always get smart too late, don't we?" Gus patted his arm like a matronly aunt. "I hope you haven't given up women."

"Lord, no."

It was ten minutes past two when another bus unloaded, and Kelly Moore came inside with a large, leather bag in one hand and her purse by its strap on her shoulder. She stopped and looked around as if not quite certain what to do now.

Nick got up and went to her.

Kelly's expression showed sudden relief. She dropped the large bag and put her arms around Nick. Her eyes were puffy and red. He wondered if she had been crying all the way from Indiana.

"I hoped you'd be here," Kelly said. "I thought my parents might get in touch with you."

Nick kissed her lightly on the forehead. Then, taking her by the shoulders, he shook her gently. "I ought'a spank you, Kel. This is the dumbest thing you've ever done."

"I had to. Do you know where Mark is?"

"No." He saw the tears well up in her eyes. "Do you have a cell phone?"

"At home," she said. "I didn't think to bring it. I borrowed this suitcase and some clothes from my friend, Nancy. I didn't bring much money either."

Nick dug a handful of change from his pants pocket. "First thing you're gonna do, young lady, is go over to that public phone and call your folks. Tell them you're here, and I'm with you."

"They'll chew me out," Kelly said.

"You deserve it. I'm not asking you, Kelly, I'm telling you. Long as you're here, I'm going to be worse than a parent."

"Then I can stay," she said, hopefully.

"If I say no?"

"I won't leave until I see Mark. I mean it."

"Make your call, Kelly. Right now. They're waiting to hear from you."

She left her bags at his feet and headed to the bank of phones. Nick carried Kelly's bags to where Gus Dick was waiting and sat in the plastic chair next to her.

Gus said, "I've been thinking, Nick. I can call Dave Melton and ask if his family would mind putting Kelly up for awhile. He'd do me the favor."

"Augusta, she'd see right through it," Nick said. "She wouldn't stay there. The only way we can stop her from going off on her own is to keep her with us. She's determined to find Mark Voight. I'm stuck with her."

Gus smiled a little. "Maybe we can get her arrested. Might be safer for her in jail."

"With the other jailbirds? I can't do that to her." Nick looked over at Kelly, her back to them, gesturing with one hand as she held the phone in the other. "Wait till she finds out about Mark's new girlfriend?"

"Don't tell her," Gus cautioned. "It wouldn't send her home. She'd be more determined than ever to confront him."

Kelly hung up and came toward them, looking curiously at Gus but trying not to stare. Nick introduced them and informed Kelly that Augusta Dick was a private eye.

Kelly said, "My parent units are royally pissed at me. But I expected that. I told them I'll be safe with you, Coach."

Nick groaned.

"You're as pretty as a model," Gus told Kelly. "Tight buns, nice tits. But you're really screwing up your face with all that crying. A man's not worth it."

Kelly's face flushed.

"Of course, you don't believe me." Gus smiled. "So I guess we'll have to find your wayward boyfriend and bring him back to you."

"That's all I want," Kelly said.

"Well, we can't do it tonight, girlie, so you might as well relax. Everybody ready to go?"

In the van, Kelly sat on a fold-down jumpseat in the back. Nick rode up front beside Gus. When they were moving, Kelly answered his question.

"Mark called me night before last," she said. "That's when I called his mother to ask how I could talk to you. Mark said he wasn't gonna see me anymore, that I should forget him. He said he's got another girl, and that it's goodbye."

Glancing through the rearview mirror, Gus said, "You're not gonna cry again, are you?"

Sitting sideways to look back at Kelly, Nick watched her cry. He caught Gus's expression as Gus rolled her eyes.

"How can he do that?" wept Kelly.

"Honey, men are beasts," Gus said.

"That's not true," Kelly sniffed. "Not Mark. Mark's not like that. Something's happened to him, and he's not telling me. Coach? What's going on with him?"

"He's even dumber than you," Nick said. "What else did he say?"

"That's all," Kelly said. "He said not to worry about him and to forget him. He wouldn't say if he was coming back or not. He hung up on me. I couldn't stay there after that. Nobody understands."

"Sure, we do," Gus said. "Love is hell, babe."

Kelly sniffed again. "You're so cynical." She dug a handkerchief from her purse. "My parent units are good people, but sometimes they treat me like I'm a little child. I mean, they kind'a laugh at the idea I can really be in love. My dad was pissed when I talked to him. He said to do everything you tell me, Coach."

"You should meet my folks," Gus said, keeping her eyes on the street. "They never forgave me for wanting to be a cop. Now that I'm crippled, they're embarrassed and over-indulgent every time we get together. It's why I don't see them often, because it turns awkward. We just have to put up with parents."

It must have been the right thing to say to Kelly because Nick saw her smile a little, wipe her eyes, and put away the handkerchief.

Lights were off in Christopherson's house when Gus parked her van in front of it. A light inside the front door of the house came on when Nick climbed out. Chris stepped onto the porch and called to him.

Nick let Gus and Kelly take care of themselves exiting the van and took Kelly's bags to the front door. He returned to the van and collected his raincoat, took Bettis's revolver that he had placed beneath the front seat, tucked the gun into his belt and walked up to Chris's front porch. "You're up late," he said.

"Standing guard," Chris said. "I ain't much good at it. I've been dozing off in my chair. What'cha got, Indy? Two women with you now?"

"And one's just a kid," Nick said. As he came closer, he saw that the old man held a rifle pointed downward at his side. "What's that for?"

"Guard duty. Hell, it's just a little .22," Chris said. "Only gun I got. First time I took it out in over ten years."

"Don't shoot anybody," Nick said.

"Those guys we seen today got guns. Tell me you ain't thinking of staying in that house with those women."

Nick told him that it was indeed his thinking. "The lady in the wheelchair's a private detective, Chris, a former cop. I signed her up to work for my boss. The girl wants her boyfriend back."

"And you gotta look after 'em? Indy, I gotta tell you it just ain't a good idea."

"I appreciate what you're doing for me, Chris. But what's not a good idea is for you to get involved. You'll be living here after we're gone. Put that gun away and go to bed."

"And don't worry till I hear the shooting, right?" In the dark, Chris grunted a soft laugh. "I ain't doing it just for you, Indy. I'm looking after Mrs. Mac's property, too. Maybe I'm an old fart, but I ain't helpless yet. Since you came, it's got exciting around here. I might be able to help."

"I don't want you getting hurt," Nick said.

"Now won't that be my call, Indy?"

Okay. So now Nick had two women, one in a wheelchair and the other a teenager, a third female on the way, and a stubborn old man. Exactly what he needed as he tried, somehow, to plot out what to do about Frank Carr, Clarence T. Bettis, and the two Hispanic flame-throwers. On top of that, Frank had issued a not-so-subtle threat against Christopherson. But the old man would be better off not knowing that.

"Can I use your phone?" Nick asked.

"Anytime."

Nick went into the house and asked to place a collect call to Dr. Larry Voight. He let the phone ring several times and got no answer. In Gus Dick's phraseology, this did not bode well.

"What's wrong?" asked Chris. In the lighted foyer, Nick could see that the old guy was wearing a robe belted over pajamas and floppy house-slippers.

"Can't reach the boy's father," Nick said. "He should be home, and he's not. His wife's on her way here now. I have the God-awful feeling that the father is coming, too. It's gotten way out of hand."

Nick stood there and thought about calling the cops. But what would he tell them? Please sit patiently outside the house until I can sort out all these arriving outsiders? Because I think there are four guys with guns who are dangerous? No, I can't tell you exactly who and where they are, but I'd certainly appreciate your looking out for us. Yeah, right.

As though reading his mind, Chris said, "Cops won't have a reason to get involved until after you're dead."

"You're determined to get mixed up in this, aren't you?"

"Am already," Chris said. "That's Mrs. Mac's house I'm watching."

"There's a way you might help," Nick told him. "You said you've got a spare room. When the boy's mother gets here, if I can convince her, I'd like to put her in with you. I have to talk with her. The baddies might not be expecting her to arrive as soon as she will. So they might not be watching the house yet. I want to intercept her before they know she's here."

Chris nodded. "Good idea, Indy. I'll protect her. It'll give us a chance to figure out our plan of attack."

Plan of attack? Nick shook his head and left Christopherson's house.

He found Gus Dick and Kelly Moore waiting for him at the mouth of the McNally driveway. Gus was smart enough not to approach the house first even though she had the Baretta out of her purse and in her hand. For the third time that day, gun in hand, Nick utilized the same entry method after he had walked around out back and spotted no one in the vicinity. He carried Gus Dick in through the front door before he allowed Kelly to bing in her bags. In another minute he had Gus seated in her wheelchair.

Kelly said, "Most people just lock their doors, Coach."

"I don't have a key," Nick said.

"I'm hungry," she announced. "I haven't eaten since we stopped in Tennesee."

"There's stuff in the fridge," Nick told her. "Kitchen's that way. Fix whatever you want. Hey, make sure that sliding lock on the back door's fastened."

"Cheer up, Nick," Gus Dick told him. She wrapped the Baretta inside the towel again and tucked it in at her side. "We're okay so far."

Nick told her of his unsuccessful attempt to reach Larry Voight.

"You know what he's doing," Gus said. "He's following his wife."

Nick sat in the chair and shook his head. "Both of them—goddam fools. Jesus Christ! How many people we gonna have to protect? I can't be responsible for all this."

"You're not," Gus said. "We've been playing Frank Carr's game, but we can't let him make all the rules. You know we can't stop Mrs. Voight from seeing him if that's what she decides to do. We have to make sure she doesn't see him alone. Now if he's half smart, and he finds out I'm with you, he'll realize violence can get messy. The man's an ex-con. A step out of line and he goes back to Raiford for keeps."

"He's not concerned about consequences," Nick said. "Something, the way he said it, made me believe him when he said if it got down to a tight spot he'd kill Mark. His own son."

"That's why we keep the guns handy." Gus looked up at Kelly, eating a ham sandwich, coming into the living room. "How much do we want to tell this child?"

"Child?" Kelly said, indignantly. She flopped down on the couch, yelped and scooted sideways. Gingerly, she lifted a corner of Gus's duffel she had sat on and realized she had been goosed by the barrel of the shotgun beneath it. "Holy shit!" she said.

Nick got up and took the gun. He propped it in a corner of the room and saw Gus give him a critical look. "Don't worry. It's fine there."

Kelly was still wide-eyed. "We're not gonna <u>shoot</u> Mark?"

Nick sat down and said, "Kel, I think you ought to know about two people Mark's got himself involved with."

16

"Why does he trust people like that?" Kelly Moore wanted to know.

"I imagine it was a shock to him." Nick shrugged. "Mark's sheltered life doesn't make sense now, or makes a different kind of sense. He's struggling with it."

Gus Dick had wheeled close to a living room window facing the street where she could edge aside the curtain and look out.

"But why's he dumping me?" Kelly was on the verge of real tears again.

Gus turned her head toward Kelly. "You're part of a pretty picture he had, and the picture got distorted. How you deal with it is part of maturing."

"Can we kidnap him back?" Kelly asked, seriously.

Gus turned her face away to conceal a laugh. It wasn't all that insane a suggestion, Nick thought. If he ever got close enough to get his hands on Mark again, he just might physically manhandle him away from Frank Carr.

Nick said, “We'll know more when his mother gets here.” He looked at his watch. “Guys, it's past three in the morning, and we need to get some sleep. We've got two bedrooms. I'll sack it out here on the couch.” He looked at Kelly. “You and Augusta take the beds.”

“I think I should stay mobile,” Gus said to Nick. “I can nap in my chair.”

“Doesn't your ass get sore in that thing?”

“I feel it higher in my back,” Gus said. “Main thing I gotta watch out for are boils.”

“Here's your chance to stretch out on a bed. You got night clothes?”

“I sleep naked,” Gus grinned. “In case I get callers in the middle of the night.”

“Am I hearing what I think I'm hearing?” Kelly asked.

“Forget it, kid,” Gus told her. “Your friend Mr. Cotton is a gentleman. He won't sleep with either one of us. I gotta pee. How about you?”

“Uh, yes,” Kelly said.

Gus grabbed Kelly's handbag from the end of the couch, wheeled around toward the bathroom, and Kelly, after another wide-eyed glance at Nick Cotton, picked up her other bag and followed.

Nick slumped down on the couch. He took Clarence Bettis's revolver in his hand for a moment, trying to decide whether he wanted it under one of the couch cushions or on the end-table. He selected the end-table, within easy reach, and started to rearrange the cushions. He was debating having the living room light on or off when a heavy hand pounded on the front door.

Nick tucked the revolver into his belt at the small of his back and opened the door a few inches.

Clarence T. Bettis stood there, grinning at him.

"Tarzan," he said, "you got clothes on. I was gonna show these guys the size 'a your dick."

"These guys" were three men lounging at the front of Bettis's car in the driveway. Two were Hispanics in colored shirts and light jackets, and the third was a thin, long-faced, white man wearing a wrinkled, brown suit. Nick could see them clearly in the light from the living room. All of them had their hands free, in the posture of showing them to Nick. None of them had guns in sight.

"We ain't gonna hurt you," Bettis said. "But I still owe you one. See these boys? That's Hector and Paulo, left to right, way you're facing. This is the first time they seen you, but they seen that little car you had and didn't much care for it. You know that already. Gotta be careful around Hector and Paulo. Know what turn's 'em on? Guns 'at go rat-a-tat-tat. They like that sound. But you don't wanna be in the way of that rat-a-tat-tat." He chuckled, his grin still in place. "That skinny guy there's Kenny Neeves. Killed three people, he tells me. Kenny's like me, likes handguns. Speakin' of which—"

"Forget it, Clarence," Nick said.

Bettis shrugged. "We'll settle that point later. Here to get some information from you and to give you a message."

"Which is?"

"Information first. Who's the two broads? The crip and the young 'un? What's their stake in this?"

Nick suddenly felt inclined to kick Bettis's ass again. "Watch your mouth, Clarence."

"You ain't smart, Tarzan. You think anybody can go in or out without us knowin'? We got you covered."

Nick was not surprised. It answered one question in his mind. He said, "The lady in the wheelchair is an ex-cop. The other is Mark Voight's girlfriend."

"Both of 'em from Indiana? Come to protect you?" Bettis laughed and looked around to get his pals to join in his humor. "You'll need it, Tarzan. Frank's not happy that he's gotta wait for you to call him. Thinks you might try to fuck him. So he wants a nice clear line 'a communication between you. Your buddy across the street—" Bettis thumbed over his shoulder, "—is going to cooperate."

Nick leaned out and looked at the Christopherson house. A downstairs light was on behind curtained windows.

Bettis said, "When Frank wants to talk to you, he's gonna send a message through the old guy. We went over and got his name and phone number. See what I mean about covered?"

Nick clenched his fists. "What did you do to him?"

"Oh, he thought he was a tough ol' bird," Bettis said. "Pointed a little rifle at us when we went in on him. Hector jus' walked over, put his hand around the barrel, and took it away from him. No problem. Then—can you beat it?—he wasn't gonna tell us his name and phone number. We asked him real nice. I finally hadda ask him myself."

Nick stared at Clarence Bettis.

"He sent you a present," Bettis said. His right hand came from his jacket pocket, and he held his closed fist toward Nick. "Here."

An ivory-looking object dropped into the palm of Nick's left hand.

It was a tooth. A molar. Specks of blood showed encrusted at the base of the root.

"Guy hates to lose those big 'un's," Bettis said and clucked his tongue. "How 'bout it, Tarzan? The woman Frank wants, you got a message I can take back to him?"

"Yeah, I got a message," Nick said.

"Well, give it to me."

Nick's right fist exploded upward, smashing squarely into Bettis's nose. The man collapsed quickly and soundlessly.

Hector and Paulo both straightened at once. They froze when they saw the revolver in Nick's right hand pointed in their direction. Then both men looked at Bettis, who was stirring and moaning, and started laughing. Kenny Neeves joined in the laughter.

Paulo Garcia looked at his brother. "Why don' you walk up an' take the gun out of his hand?"

"I don't theenk so," Hector said.

"Keep your hands where I can see 'em," Nick said.

"You got it, mon," Paulo Garcia giggled.

Kenny Neeves stopped laughing long enough to rub a tear from the corner of his eye with a knuckle. "What you want us to do with ol' Clarence?"

"Get him out of here," Nick said. "Take him back to Frank. Tell Frank I'll call him in the morning. Move carefully."

"Yeah, we see your back-up," Neeves said.

Nick threw a quick glance behind him to see Gus Dick in her wheelchair in the doorway. She had the shotgun, pointed outwards, resting on her lap, a finger on the trigger. Nick moved a bit to one side to give her a clear shot if she needed it.

The two brothers and Neeves leaned over the squirming probation officer. When he was lifted on rubber legs, Bettis had one hand cupped over his nose and mouth, his eyes unfocused. He made a sound that was muffled behind his hand. Blood dribbled below the hand, down his neck and onto his shirt. He couldn't walk.

The other men maneuvered him into the backseat of the car. One Garcia got in back with him, the other in the passenger seat up front. Neeves hesitated before getting behind the wheel.

"You know he's gonna wanna kill you," Neeves said.

"I guess," said Nick.

"No guess about it."

"What's your stake in this?" Nick asked.

"Money, what else?" Neeves said as he got into the car.

When they were gone, Nick crossed the street at a run to the Christopherson house. He knocked on the door, tried it, and went inside. The old man sat in his living room recliner, leaning back, holding a bundled towel filled with ice cubes to his mouth and side of his face.

Chris gave Nick a dejected look through moist eyes. "Sorry, Indy. I ain't as tough as I thought. I'm no help to you."

Nick patted the man's shoulder, then examined the discoloration along his jaw. "You're plenty tough. I'm the one who's sorry. I didn't think they'd bother you."

"Hell, all they wanted was my name and phone number," Chris grunted. "They walked right in. I recognized the bald one. Figured two of the other three for the guys that burned your car. I should've started shooting, but I hesitated."

"It ain't easy to shoot at a man," Nick told him gently.

"They took my rifle easy as candy from a baby. I was a coward. Guess a man's never too old to learn 'bout himself."

"Who's your doctor, Chris?"

"Fuck that," Chris shot back. "Sorry. Didn't mean to snap at you. I don't want a doctor."

"You might have a broken bone. I can't tell."

"Well, I don't."

Carefully, Nick placed the molar on the table beside the man. "If the tooth's not damaged, a good orthodontist might put it back in and anchor it."

"I'll keep it as a trophy. Remind me what I am. Hell, it don't hurt that much now," Chris said. He couldn't look straight at Nick. "My teeth ain't all that solid as is. I'll tell my dentist it fell out. Know where I hurt? It ain't here." He pointed to his jaw. "It's here." He poked himself in the chest. "Not literally. Don't worry, Indy. I'm not having a heart attack."

"Sure you don't want a doctor? Jesus, I don't know what to do for you."

"Nothing to do. Take care 'a those women you got. About that other one you're expecting. Won't be a good idea now for her to stay here. I won't be nothing but an errand boy, run to you when the phone rings. They had me pegged."

"Cut it out, Chris," Nick said. "We know their names. We can call the police and charge 'em with assault and battery. It might be a good idea to do that, give 'em something to think about."

"Let's don't." Chris looked at Nick with a new gleam in his eye. "Maybe I'll get another chance." He looked at his rifle on the floor. "Next time might be different."

"I don't like the way you're thinking. I might take your gun."

"You won't do that," Chris said. "You won't leave me here with nothing. You sure as hell can't stay here to guard me. Do what you gotta do for that kid you're after. I'm serious, Indy. I'll be okay."

Nick went to Chris's phone and again tried to call Larry Voight's number in Indianapolis. Again, there was no answer at the Voight house.

Chris was out of his chair and had picked up his rifle. With thumb and forefinger of one hand he worked his jaw around. "What'cha think?"

"I'm pretty sure the boy's father is on his way," Nick said.

"Kid's got something to tell you," Gus Dick said to Nick in the living room of the McNally house.

Kelly Moore in her underwear stood by the end of the couch. She had undressed down to pink bikini panties and tight little bra. It didn't seem to bother her any, but it bothered the hell out of Nick Cotton. Had he been Mark Voight and had a choice between Kelly Moore and Donnie

Ann Bettis, he would have made a fucking bee-line back to Indianapolis and Kelly.

"I saw those men leaving," Kelly said. "Augusta described the one named Bettis. I'd seen him before. At S.O.B., last winter. December, I think. Mark and I were leaving school, and he met us outside. I don't think he ever told us his name. He asked Mark if he's Marilyn Lesser's son."

"Lesser? Mrs. Voight's maiden name?"

"Yes," Kelly said. "He kept asking questions. Wanted to know if Mark had ever been to Florida, then asked if he was planning another trip. Mark told him about spring break coming up, that he and Rob and Jerry were going down. The man wanted to know where they'd be staying."

"And Mark answered all his questions?" Nick asked.

"The man seemed kind enough. He said he was an old friend of Marilyn Lesser's and he'd get in touch with her sometime, that he was happy to meet Marilyn's son. He wanted to know how old Mark is, and who his father is, their address—everything. Mark finally got tired of all the questions and got us away from there, but he was nice about it. The bald-headed man seemed satisfied, too."

Nick looked over at Gus. "That answers one of my questions for Marilyn. How those guys knew when and where to locate Mark Voight. Thanks, Kel." He was working hard to keep his eyes off of her full-bodied, nearly naked figure. "Either get some clothes on, or go to bed."

After Kelly left the room, Gus said, "They had this whole thing planned before Mark left Indiana."

"You get some sleep, too," Nick told her. "I don't think those guys will return tonight. I'll be here on the couch."

"I can use your help getting undressed," Gus said. "Kelly has a hard time lifting me."

Nick followed as Gus wheeled her way into the hallway to the first bedroom. He looked past her into the kitchen to Kelly Moore, her back to them, leaning forward with her cute butt stuck out, positioning a chair at an angle with its back braced under the rear door knob.

"Tear your eyes away, Nick," Gus told him. "She's too young for you."

"Way too young," Nick agreed.

Smiling, Kelly turned off the kitchen light and came into the hallway. "I saw that in a movie," she said. "If somebody tries to come in, it'll make some noise."

"Way to go, kiddo," Gus said to her. "I'm a light sleeper, but yell out if you hear anything."

Nick accompanied Gus to her bedroom and hoisted her from her chair to undress her. He held Gus up, sat her down, lifted her and leaned her against him, but got the job done. Gus insisted that panties and bra go off, too. Finally, Nick lifted her onto the bed.

Keeping her arms around his neck, Gus said, "You're a difficult man to entice. I'll bet you've never had a meaningful sexual relationship with a cripple."

"Handicapped person," Nick said, "and the answer is neither meaningful nor otherwise. We've got a date for the beach after this is over."

Gus pulled his head down and kissed him on the mouth. "I'll take that as a promise, Nick." Then she released him.

"Oh, brother," Kelly Moore said from the doorway, then stepped out of sight.

"Put my gun next to me," Gus said.

Nick did, turned out the light and retreated to the living room. Kelly followed him to the entryway. He saw her and said, "Go to bed, young lady."

"Can't I sit up with you?" she asked. "I don't mind the dark."

"You cannot," Nick told her. "I don't intend to spend all night listening to how wonderful Mark Voight is, or how misunderstood, or how you're crazy about him. I'd like to get at least a couple of hours rest. You should, too. We might need it."

"I'm nervous about being alone," Kelly said.

"Out!"

She left the living room. Nick stripped to his underwear, turned off the lights, and tried to find a comfortable position in which to lie on the couch. He couldn't stretch out fully without hanging his feet and ankles off the other end. He had to draw his knees up and turn on his side.

The shotgun was across the chair close to the couch, and Bettis's pistol was within easy reach on the end-table.

17

Nick, his face toward the back of the couch, awakened to daylight feeling a warm pressure behind him, full body-length, knees hooked into the backs of his own. He blinked in surprise. Slowly he lifted his left arm, crooked it as much as possible, and tried to feel behind himself. His fingers brushed soft, smooth skin. The person pressed into him on the couch stirred and murmured something. Nick made little stabbing motions with his groping fingers, found a naked hip, an arm, a rounded butt—nothing covered. He contorted himself to reach below his left arm with his right, and the fingertips of his right hand alighted on a female nipple. Suddenly, Nick was wide-awake!

Nick twisted his body around to get a look.

The sudden movement of his turning dislodged his companion from the confined space of the couch. She rolled off, landing on her bare butt on the floor and said, "Oof!"

Nick's jaw dropped when he got a look at her. It was the very beautiful, very naked, Kelly Moore.

What was worse, as he sat up, groping for his trousers, he saw the silhouette of another woman standing in the doorway, the door open and the early morning sunlight behind her. That woman was Marilyn Voight.

"Hey!" Kelly barked at Nick. "You pushed me."

Nick's mouth hung open.

"I got lonely," Kelly said indignantly, looking up from the floor. "I just wanted to be close. You didn't seem to mind."

"I do mind," Nick almost shouted. "Hi, Marilyn."

Kelly looked around and, for the first time, saw Marilyn Voight. She yelped, tried to scramble to her feet and cover herself with arms and hands at the same time. She ran on bare feet out of the living room, that delightful ass jiggling with every step.

Nick pulled his trousers on, giving Marilyn a wan smile.

"I can't let you out, can I, Nick?" Marilyn Voight said in amusement. "Really. A high school kid." She clucked her tongue in mock distaste. "I won't tell." Then she came all the way inside with a small carryall case and marched past Nick toward the bedrooms, the direction in which Kelly Moore had fled. "Bathroom back here?" she asked but didn't wait for a reply.

Nick finished dressing and had just wedged his feet into his shoes when Marilyn came back. She said, "You've got another naked woman in bed back there. Honestly, Nick, I think we underestimated you."

"I plead innocence," Nick said. He went to the open front door and peered outside. There was no sign of Clarence Bettis and his men, but that didn't prove anything. The sun was up, bathing the front of the house in its early morning, yellow brightness. Marilyn's van sat in the driveway, in plain view, with—Nick realized—a nice bright, Indiana license plate stuck on its rear that could easily be seen from the street side. "I gotta move your van. Give me your keys."

Marilyn produced the single key on a rabbit's foot chain and tossed it to him.

Nick backed the van from the driveway and found a space in front of Augusta Dick's vehicle a short way past the Christopherson house. He looked around but still didn't spot Bettis's old car or the Broncho that the Garcias had used.

Marilyn waited for Nick in the doorway. He handed her the key, which she squeezed into her pants pocket. He steered her inside, shut the door, and guided her to the chair. Marilyn took off her poplin jacket, dropped it on the floor, sat down and leaned her head back. Nick noted the lines of weariness on her face, along with a look of grimness, and again found it remarkable that, no matter how she looked when tired, she couldn't conceal her beauty.

"We have to talk," he told her. "Straight talk."

"I know," Marilyn said, stretching her legs out in front of her. Somewhere in the back of the house she had deposited her bag and purse. She was wearing pants and a short-sleeved blouse. She blew out her breath in a long sigh with her eyes shut. "Our friend's not here."

"You mean Frank? No, he hasn't been here since day before yesterday, but he's keeping an eye on us. He's expecting you, might even know you're here now if he's got somebody watching the house."

Marilyn opened her eyes. "I should have got here sooner, but I couldn't keep going. I stopped when I crossed over from Georgia for a couple hours sleep in the car." She gave Nick her weary smile. “I'm baggy under the eyes. You can tell me how terrible I look.”

Terrible? Nick shook his head. One thing she couldn't do was look terrible.

She went on, “I haven't been very good to you, Nick.”

Nick sat on the couch, facing her, seeing her turn her head to glance at the shotgun that was propped up. From his jacket on the back of the couch, Nick took out the beach photo and reached it over to her.

Marilyn stared at it a long time. A corner of her mouth twitched.

“Which one's Frank?” she asked.

“You're asking me?” He got up to step beside her and tap the image of the young man in the middle, the one with his arm around her waist. “He hasn't changed that much.” He resumed his seat, watching her look at the picture. “That is Frank, isn't it?”

Marilyn laughed softly, but without humor. “Why not? Sure, it's Frank,” she said, letting Nick take the photo from her and put it in his shirt pocket. “That was our gang. Did he tell you who the others were?”

"Martin Ruhle and Lenny Wilson," Nick said, resuming his seat on the couch. "He told me a story. You killed a man on the beach for a money belt."

"That happened," Marilyn said, tiredly. "I don't think it was intentional. It's something I've been trying to forget ever since. Larry would like to forget it, too. Of course, we never will. One of our skeletons, Nick." She sighed. "Martin Ruhle and the man fought over the belt. The man collapsed and died. It didn't bother Martin to go ahead and take the belt. Rest of us wanted nothing to do with it. But we didn't try to stop him. It was the first time I was ever truly scared. I tell myself some good came of it. It changed Larry."

"How?"

"It made him see clearly that he didn't belong with people like us."

"Us? You're lumping yourself in there?"

"Nick, you don't know what I was in those days—what I'd let myself become, or start to become. You would not have liked me." She gave him a bitter smile. "When I tell you, you won't like me now. You probably don't anyway after I practically tricked you into coming here."

Nick watched her shut her eyes momentarily again as she rested her head back. He wondered if she was recalling something from the past, replaying it in her mind. Finally, he said, "At the airport, I knew you were concerned about more than your son."

Marilyn raised her head. "No, my concern has always been for Mark. The card I told you about from Frank Carr, when Mark didn't come home from vacation, I was smart enough to suspect a connection. I should have told you that before you got on the plane."

"We didn't have a lot of time."

"Stop trying to make things easy for me," she said. "You deserved better. You could've gotten hurt."

Nick decided he'd better not tell about what had happened to his rental car, not yet, or about the guys hanging out with Frank. He said, "What you should've done is told Larry about Frank as soon as you heard from him."

"I didn't want my husband ever involved with that man again," Marilyn said. "Back after that beach incident, Larry spoke to me before daylight, told me he was leaving, that he wouldn't be coming back. I should tell the others after he was gone. He was afraid of what Martin and Lenny and Frank might do to him. I understood and said it was best. Then he said something that touched me." She hesitated, savoring it. "He said I was too good to hang out with those guys. He said he was too embarrassed to speak up before, but he thought I was the most beautiful person he had ever met. That he really liked me, and had from the start, but never planned to tell me. I looked at him, Nick, standing there with that pained expression on his face, hopeful, lost—whatever. And I thought to myself, this man's got all the decent qualities Martin could never have. Hell, I was nuts over Martin Ruhle, but I never trusted him. Everybody knew I was Martin's girl. Anyway, the last thing Larry did, he gave me his parents' address and his college address and said if I ever needed a friend, or wanted to get in touch with him, I could do it."

Nick interrupted her. "Larry's on his way here now, following you. Does he know this address?"

"Shit," Marilyn muttered. She squeezed her eyes shut and looked for a moment like she might start cursing. "I guess I'm not surprised. Why couldn't he just stay out of it?"

"Because he loves you."

Marilyn blinked back sudden tears. "I didn't tell him the address," she said, "but I did have it written down. He never goes through my things, but he might have this time. I should've destroyed the address. Nick, when he comes, you've got to look out for him."

"Him?" Nick said. "What about you?"

"First, did you find out about my son? Is Mark all right?"

"I saw him yesterday, briefly. He's all right but mixed up. Frank Carr told him he's his father. Is it true?"

"No." Marilyn's eyes hardened above her taut jawline. She said, "Martin Ruhle knocked me up. Not Frank Carr. I'd never have anything to do with Frank Carr."

Nick nodded. "Okay. Eighteen years ago Ruhle must have told his buddies you were pregnant. Frank's trying to capitalize on it. He told Mark he's his daddy to get him to stay. The purpose was to get you here, Marilyn."

"Of course," she said. "He thinks I have something that belongs to him. He doesn't give a damn about Mark."

"What do you have that belongs to Frank? Money? Like maybe a half million dollars?"

"He told you that?"

"I don't know what's true, and what's not," Nick said. "He spun a story about Ruhle and Wilson stumbling on the tail end of a holdup, and the money wound up in their hands. Ruhle and Wilson were murdered by the holdup men. Frank was on his way to Fort Myers when it happened. He said the money was gone, assumed taken back by the killers. Where do you fit in, Marilyn?"

She gave him the sad, friendly smile again. "Poor Nick, I've been so unfair to you. After we spoke on the phone Friday night, our friend called me. Called our house. Larry was asleep. He didn't say much, just that he wants me to bring his money. He told me to think of Mark. You, too. He intimated that something bad might happen to that big friend of mine."

"I'll worry about me. Frank's got a tough crew working with him," he told her, not keeping it from her any longer. "Guys that can kill people. They could decide to kill you."

"Maybe," she said, quietly. "First he wants the money back."

"Tell me about the money, Marilyn."

"It was a year after the beach thing," she said. "Martin Ruhle said he and Lenny were going to Fort Myers to do a deal. I'd just got a waitress job in Clearwater, so I didn't go with them. Besides, I needed money. I'd just found out I was pregnant. I figured Martin would be dumping me real soon. He wouldn't want to be shackled with a woman and kid. When I told him, before he and Lenny left for Fort Myers, I was afraid of what he might do eventually. He told me a lot of things might happen that could make me unpregnant."

"The money," Nick prompted.

"Martin said they'd be gone only a few days. Then I got a call from him to get down there, to meet them at a motel. Martin and Lenny lucked onto the tail end of the robbery, somehow had picked up the money. Probably just the way you heard it. They called Frank to come down, too. I remember how frightened I was, but I didn't dare not go. I got there the next day, before Frank arrived. Martin took me aside, away from Lenny, because he didn't want Lenny to overhear him. That's when he told me about the holdup."

Nick gave her time to catch her breath, time to pull the memory back into the forefront of her mind.

Marilyn said, "Martin said there would be a lot of heat on, and the best thing was to put the money away until later. He gave me the suitcase with a half million in it and told me to keep it for him, that I should take the bus back to Clearwater and wait. Lenny didn't know of the arrangement. Frank hadn't showed up yet, but they were expecting him any time. For the first time in my life, I did a lot of fast thinking, Nick. I knew if I kept the money, I'd be an accessory. But there I was, pregnant and afraid to say no to Martin Ruhle and yet scared to death of him. He left me off at the bus station."

"What did you do then?"

"Made the first big decision in my life," she said. "I hitchhiked south to Naples. There I stole a pickup truck and drove into the Everglades. I hid the money in an isolated spot where Martin and I had once gone on a joyride. I took the truck back to Naples and got on the first bus to Clearwater. All the time I was thinking, fretting. I knew Martin would be furious when he showed up and I didn't have the suitcase. A beating would be the least I'd get, and I had to think of my unborn child. By the time I got to Clearwater, I'd made up my mind. It took all the funds I had to buy my bus ticket north. All the way to Muncie, Indiana. To the only person I felt who might really be my friend. I had to beg change from a stranger to call Larry Voight."

"Jesus," Nick said. "Then Larry knew about the robbery."

"Nothing of the sort. I never told him. I wanted a safe haven, Nick. I wanted away from Martin Ruhle. I didn't know about the killings until I read it in a Florida paper. Then I was glad I got away."

Nick considered what she had told him and, finally, nodded. "Then you believe Frank Carr killed Ruhle and Wilson, chopped up their bodies and left them in the swamp." He waited, but got no response from her except a narrowing of her eyes and creasing of her brow. "Which means Martin Ruhle also told Frank that he gave you the money. Why didn't Frank follow you to Indiana? Couldn't he guess you were going to Larry Voight?"

"I doubt it," she said. "At least not at first. But I'm sure he searched for me all over Clearwater and the surrounding areas. He was always in trouble with the police. I imagine he got himself arrested and put in prison. Over time he probably figured it out. Locating us wouldn't be all that easy. All he knew was that Larry was somewhere in Indiana. Larry had never given the whole group of us particulars about exactly where he was from or where he was going to college, or even what he was studying to become. I'm sure our friend had never heard of Ball State University. As the years passed, I thought I was free of him."

"Why didn't you take the money with you to Indiana instead of hiding it in a swamp?"

"Conscience," Marilyn said, wryly. "Stolen money. If I'd got stopped or arrested anywhere along the way, and I had a half million dollars in a suitcase, I'd go to prison. There'd be no way I could keep the child."

"Right," Nick said. "I imagine Larry was surprised when you showed up."

"Very. He was glad to see me. I told him about the baby, and it didn't matter. He treated me better than I'd ever been treated in my life. Things were tough for us because he was finishing his first degree at Ball State. We borrowed money to get through and prepare for a family. I love him, Nick. And I mean that sincerely. He knows it, too. One of my happiest days was when we were married. I won't have anything happen to him, or Mark, if I can help it."

For a few moments, Nick sat silently. He said, "That's what we have to decide. What to do now."

"I've already decided," she said. "I'm going to see our friend."

"No way. I can't let you do that. Do you think the money's still where you left it?"

"Truthfully, I can't say. I've thought about it from time to time, wondered about it." Marilyn smiled sadly. "Many times I almost told Larry. Almost did. Once, I even thought about going back to find it. But when I weighed that against the home and family Larry and I have, I changed my mind. But you're right. It might've made things easier now had I told Larry. Mark might not have gotten himself in this jam."

"Spilt milk, Marilyn."

"But it never evaporates," she said. "I can tell you now all the things I should have or should not have done. But I was only a kid myself. I guess, after marrying Larry, I wanted to pretend none of my former life had happened. Did you know that after he got his first teaching job, Larry encouraged me to go to college and get my degree. Knowing what I had been, who would've thought I'd ever be a college grad. Life is funny, Nick. Sometimes good. Now the past catches up."

Nick said, "Well, goddammit, I'm not turning you over to Frank Carr. If I can stall him a little longer, that lady in the bedroom can help us. She's an ex-cop, now a private detective I hired for you, and she'll be able to find where Frank's staying. I need an edge to get Mark away from that guy."

"And if she can't find out?" Marilyn asked. "Nick, I brought this on myself, but it's got to finish. I'm in a bargaining position with our friend. I was thinking it out while I drove. I'll meet with him if he'll turn Mark over to you. That's what I want from you now. Take care of Mark. Get him home with my husband. You must look out for them."

"And you'll take Frank to where you hid the money?"

"Yes. At least we'll be going in the other direction."

"You'll get yourself killed."

Marilyn shrugged. "I hope not, but we'll see. If it should happen, do what you can to help Larry and Mark, and Monica, to understand. Assure them that I loved them."

There was a knock on the front door.

Nick palmed the pistol from the end-table, edged to the window, and looked outside. It was Christopherson, waiting.

Nick tucked the gun into his belt and opened the door. Christopherson looked around him at Marilyn, who was sitting upright now.

"Phone call, Indy. It's the asshole. Not for you. He said he wants to talk to Marilyn."

Nick looked around at her. "That does it. He knows you're here." He turned to Chris. "I'll be over, Chris."

"I have a cell in my purse," Marilyn said. "I'll talk to him."

"No, you won't," Nick told her firmly, "not until after I do. Promise me, Marilyn, or I'll tie you down."

Marilyn laughed. "I promise."

Nick went into the bedroom where Kelly was helping Gus Dick finish dressing. Kelly had put on white shorts and a slipover sleeveless blouse, shoes but no socks. Nick said, "Marilyn Voight's in the living room. Frank Carr knows it. There's no time span left. Kelly, you go find Marilyn's purse and get her cell phone. Now!"

Kelly scurried from the room, and Nick lifted Gus into her chair and wheeled her into the living room. He said, "You two can get acquainted, but stick close to her, Augusta. Will Sergeant Melton do you a favor?"

"If I ask," Gus said.

"Call him on the cell. Tell him where we are, who's here, and that we're in danger. He must know somebody on the Tampa police who can help."

"We can barricade the house, Nick."

"We might have to. But right now I'm going across the street."

"Is it safe for you?" Gus asked.

"Frank's waiting on the phone."

18

"Morning, Nick," Frank drawled into Nick's ear. "Seems like we got what we want, huh? Marilyn made record time. Or, what's more like it, you been stalling me."

"You've been misinformed," Nick said.

"She's with you now. It's her I wanna talk to. Didn't the old man tell you?" Frank made clucking noise of disapproval into Nick's ear. "What we'll do is this. You tell Marilyn to come to this phone and call me at the number you got. I'll tell her where we'll meet. You say to her she's gonna see her son."

"You'll see me, too," Nick said.

"No, ol' buddy, I don't think so. Clarence misjudged you. You should see the size of his nose now, like a goddamn balloon. When he tries to talk, he whistles through his nose. But you and Clarence got your own problems to work out. Me and you got nothing left to talk about."

"Fine. Goodbye," Nick told him.

"Wait a minute!" Frank barked into the phone. "Wait a goddamn minute! This gets nobody nowhere. I want to keep it from getting messy."

"I won't let you meet Marilyn alone," Nick said.

"<u>You</u> won't let? Nick, you're out. She'll be safe with me."

"And after you get the money?"

"What money?"

"The half million Ruhle and Wilson stole. It ain't here, Frank. It's back in Indiana."

Frank paused a second, then said, "I don't think so. She ain't stupid. I told her to bring it in order to get the kid. She said she's got it hidden down here. I can see her doin' that, then turning chicken and running to Larry Voight. She told me it's here, and I believe that part. I also believe she wants her boy back. We're talking a trade."

"You know I'll call the cops."

Frank laughed gruffly. "And say what? Spin a wild story 'bout a half mil stolen almost twenty years ago? Cops're busy people, Nick. They ain't got time to listen to crackpots. My probation officer will vouch for me. Or, in Clarence's case, whistle. You see, Frank Carr's got an alibi for when the robbery took place. He was working for a man who's still alive in St. Pete. Even called him when he got to Fort Myers that day to make sure the old fart remembered the date and time he left. We got to give Martin Ruhle credit for that idea. No, by the time anybody pays attention to you, I'll be long gone. I always wanted to visit South America. Maybe I'll send you a postcard."

"You forgot to tell me," Nick said, "that you're the one who killed Ruhle and Wilson and diced 'em into small body parts."

"And put 'em in the swamp," Frank said. "They'd 'a only been in the way. Ancient history, Nick. Look, neither one of us wants the woman hurt. Or the boy. You let things go, and I'll see what I can do about keeping Clarence off your ass. At least give you a head start home." He paused, for effect obviously, giving Nick a chance to think it over. "I'm giving you the best break I can, buddy. Where you are now, you got too many people to protect."

"A small army," Nick said. Really small. Practically non-existent.

"Army?" Frank laughed. "Neeves told 'bout the crip with the shotgun. That's two of you, Nick. What about the old fuck across the street, the guy whose phone we're using? What about that kid with the pretty ass? Paulo Garcia's got his eye on her. You wanna gamble with all of them? I don't see you that way. If it was just you, maybe you'd try us. The boys can shoot so many holes in that house, somebody bound to get killed." He paused to draw in an audible breath. "Tell Marilyn to call me. I'll give it fifteen minutes." Then he hung up.

Nick told Christopherson to lock all his doors and stay alert. He crossed the street to where his "army" was gathered in the living room. He told Marilyn Voight and Gus Dick what Frank had said.

"No bargaining, Nick," Marilyn said, calmly. "I told you what I'm going to do."

"You can't," Gus Dick snapped at her. "There's no guarantee he'll return your son. Nick, I got hold of Dave Melton. He woke up when I told him what's happening. He'll call the cops in Tampa." Looking steadily at Nick, she chambered a round in the Baretta. The shotgun was across her lap. "We'll be okay if we've got fifteen minutes."

"I don't want anyone getting hurt on my account," Marilyn said. "We have a child here."

"Child?" Kelly said with disgust.

"Then you can help," Nick said to Marilyn, "by taking Kelly to one of the bedrooms and bracing the door from inside. Move a dresser or something in front of it. Please stay there."

"I'm the cause of all this," Marilyn said. "Give me the number, Nick, and I'll call our friend."

"No." Nick took the cell-phone from Gus and held it out of Marilyn's reach. "We're going to use every second of that fifteen minutes. The police will be here by then." He hoped. "Frank's leading his little band of outlaws, but he's violated his parole. If the cops can take him, the others will give up Mark."

"We don't know that," she said.

"I think so," Nick said. "Bettis will have to do something to save his own ass. The Garcia brothers will be scurrying for cover. That leaves Kenny Neeves. He looks like he's been around, knows the score. He'll know when to cut his losses."

"Suppose they kill Mark first?" she asked.

"It would be dumb with no possible upside. Trust me, Marilyn."

"Hey," said Kelly Moore. "If we got fifteen minutes, why don't we all just get in the van and leave?"

"We're being watched, and they wouldn't let us get far. We're safer here than in a car chase."

"Nick's right," Gus said from the window, edging the curtain aside with a forefinger. "Somebody's coming toward us. It's that skinny one that was talking to you last night. He's waving a white hanky."

Nick peered from the window over Gus's shoulder.

He saw Kenny Neeves, the thin-faced man in the wrinkled tan suit. Neeves had a panama hat tilted back and to one side of his head.

"Maybe I should shoot him right now," Gus said, "and save us a hassle."

"I'll talk to him," Nick said. "You keep watching."

"I'll be behind you in the doorway. Tell him I'll drop him if he pulls anything else but that hanky."

Nick stepped out, leaving the door open behind him.

Neeves stopped a few feet away and grinned. "Hey, Mr. Cotton! Or can I call you Nick?"

"What do you want?"

The thin man nodded, keeping the grin in place. "Giving you guys a chance. Let the woman come out. Frank wants the woman. Then nobody has to get hurt."

"We got fifteen minutes," Nick said. Much less now, he thought.

"Frank lied," Neeves said. "Hector and Paulo and I'll come in and get her if necessary. Somebody bound to get messed up. Gotta tell you, Nick. I'm pretty handy with a gun."

"The cops are on their way."

Neeves chuckled. "Maybe, maybe not. It won't take us long. Know what I like to do? I did this a few years ago. Couple guys tried to rip me off, cop my share of a deal we had. I told 'em I was coming, and I did. I went right in through a door, and they had guns, too. I went in like you see in the movies, gun in each hand, blasting away. Not giving a shit. I nailed both of 'em, Nick." He snapped the fingers of his free hand twice. "Just like that." He grinned broadly. "Know why? It's adrenalin, Nick. I can feel it building up. When I feel like that, nothing can stop me. I'm getting that feeling now. When I get to the exploding point, I just go. Then I'm living hell."

"I'm impressed," Nick said.

"You impress me, too," Neeves said. "I watched you last night, saw how you levered that gun into your hand a split second after punching ol' Clarence. Pretty fast, Nick. Frank says you're just a school teacher, but I'm suspecting something else. Like maybe a cop, or an ex-cop?"

Nick shrugged. To hell with chit-chatting with Kenny Neeves. Nick was watching the man's eyes, not his hands. If he made a move, Nick would see it in his face first. Besides, he knew that Gus was behind him in the doorway with the shotgun primed and ready.

"It looks like," Neeves said, "we're at the point of you delivering the woman to me or making us do it the hard way."

"You don't get her," Nick said.

"Okay." Neeves shoved the handkerchief into his jacket pocket. "Thought I'd give you a chance."

"Where's Frank?"

"He ain't arrived just yet. This was my idea. One pro to another."

"The money won't be worth it," Nick said. "Frank will kill you, too. He wants it all for himself."

The slight change in the other man's expression, the cocking of one eyebrow, showed that he had thought about that possibility himself.

"He might try." Neeves shrugged and turned away.

Nick went back inside the house and shut the door.

"Where the hell are the cops?" he said irritably.

Gus, back-wheeling to give him room, shrugged.

"Nick," Marilyn Voight said, "I'm putting an end to this. I'm going out."

"No, you're not," Nick said. "Not if I have to sit on you."

"Somebody's pulling into the driveway now," Gus said from the window.

Nick rushed to her side and peered out. He hoped it was the police.

It wasn't.

Nick saw a new, mid-sized, Buick slowing to stop close to the house. He watched the neatly-dressed young man in the blue blazer bringing a clipboard from the car and heading toward the front door. The young man, smiling brightly, was the same Alamo rep who had surveyed the charred remains of the little car the day before. He raised a fist to knock on the door.

Nick opened the door first. "Go away!"

"Mr. Cotton." The young man's smile never wavered. "I have your replacement vehicle—"

"Go away," Nick repeated and started to close the door.

The energetic young fellow stopped it with his free hand. "Which you see is a more luxurious model. The good news is—"

"Will you get the fuck out'a here!" Nick stormed.

"—you won't be charged extra. It's the company's way of compensating for your inconvenience after—"

"You're in <u>danger</u>, asshole!"

"—yesterday's unfortunate incident. Of course, there are some papers—"

"What part of 'go away' don't you understand?"

"—after which you sign, I will hand you the keys. Now, let me get my pen, and you can sign where the X's are." The young man reached into the breast pocket of his blazer and took out a ballpoint that he clicked open with a flourish. "I know it's quite early in the morning, but I did want to get the car to you as soon as possible."

"Am I going to have to kick your butt to make you leave?"

"Oh? You wish to read the contract first. I understand—"

"Leave! Now!" Nick stormed at him.

"It's the standard contract, same as the one you signed for the other car."

"Have you ever been shot at?" Nick asked.

"You'll keep a copy also."

Nick pulled out Bettis's pistol and pointed it at the young man's nose.

The young man blinked, his eyes crossing, as he looked into the barrel. "That, sir," he said, "is a gun."

"By God, you <u>do</u> know something."

"Mr. Cotton, I can understand your dissatisfaction at having to wait, but I assure you we worked as quickly as possible to get you this car—"

"You are fucking hopeless," Nick moaned.

"—and this is still a busy season for us. We put you first on the list for a cancellation or a return. I hope you're not suggesting this vehicle is unsatisfactory."

Nick thumbed the hammer back, pointed the gun skyward, and fired a shot.

The young man levitated two feet back off the stoop, his eyes like saucers.

There was a metallic whang, followed closely by another single shot. From somewhere across the street someone had drilled one into the Buick.

The young man dropped the clipboard and pen and jumped back in Nick's direction.

Nick grabbed him, one-handed by the lapel of his jacket, and hauled him through the open doorway into the house. "Hell, come on in," he said, hooking the door with his foot to kick it shut behind them.

"I see him," Gus said from where she had parted the window curtain with the nose of the shotgun. "Two of 'em."

"Kelly!" Nick yelled.

"Nothing back here," Kelly called from the kitchen. "Wait! I do see something."

"If I were you, Mrs. Voight," Gus said to Marilyn, "I'd do what Nick said and get yourself and Kelly in a room and barricade the door." She looked at the young man in the blazer, kneeling with his face to the carpet and both hands clasped behind his head. "Who's he?"

"He delivered my rental," Nick told her.

"He's got his ass stuck up in the air," Gus noted. She looked out the window. "Two of 'em coming across the street—one with an Uzi, other with a handgun. They're zigzagging this way, move and cover."

"Get away from the window, Augusta," Nick told her.

The barking of the Uzi commenced. They could hear bullets striking metal and glass.

"There goes the rental," Gus said.

Her observation roused the young Alamo man. He sprang to his feet and rushed to the window. "My car!" he cried, woefully.

"Get down!" Gus hissed at him.

A round came into the house, high through the window. The Alamo man took two strides and dived headlong over the couch. The floor reverberated when he landed on the other side.

"Are they trying for us?" Nick asked.

"Intimidation," Gus said. "We'll know when those rounds start coming lower through the door and windows."

There was a noise from the back. Nick turned his head and shouted, "Kelly?"

"I'm okay," Kelly's voice called back. "They shot out the door window and a kitchen window."

"Nick, get Kelly under cover before she gets hurt," Gus said. She lifted a curtain from the side. "Those guys might not be tactically trained, but they're not stupid."

Nick, crouching, went into the kitchen where Kelly was huddled below the sink. She had had the foresight to tip over the table in the middle of the room and push it as close as possible to the rear door. Nick grabbed Kelly's wrist and pulled her with him. At the first bedroom, he shoved her inside.

"Crawl under the bed," he snapped at her, "and stay there. They don't want you."

Marilyn Voight appeared at the doorway. "You win. I'll keep her here."

"Nick! I see your friend," Gus called from the living room.

Nick hurried to her, bent low, and peered around her out the window. "Where're the goddamn cops?"

Striding up the driveway, holding an automatic pistol at his side, was Frank Carr. He was approaching warily, but not running.

"God, I hope they see him with a gun in his possession," Gus said.

"Right about now," Nick said, "I don't think he gives a shit."

Nick could see that one of the Garcia's had taken a position at the back of the riddled rental car. He saw the barrel of the automatic weapon over the trunk.

"Other one's to your left," Gus said. "Around the side of the house somewhere."

"Enough!" Frank Carr shouted. He peered at the house. "Nick! Hear me, buddy? Let's stop this shit! Send Marilyn out, and we'll leave."

"He got here pretty goddamn quick, didn't he," Gus said. "He's never been very far away."

"Why aren't the neighbors calling every emergency number in the book?" Nick grumbled.

"Nick, this is Florida," Gus said. "Only the tourists get excited about shootings."

"Hey, Marilyn!" Frank called.

"You ever shot at anybody?" Gus asked Nick.

"Once. When I was in the service."

"And—?"

"I hit him in the leg."

"You must be a helluva marksman."

Nick shrugged. "I was aiming for his shoulder." He looked at her and brandished Bettis's gun. "So?"

Gus shook her head. "Shit."

"And," Nick added, "I don't even know if this piece 'a junk shoots straight."

"Take my Baretta."

"No, you keep it."

Gus sighed. "Anybody watching the back of the house?"

"On my way," Nick said and scurried, running low, to the kitchen.

One of the Garcia's had his face close to the outside window, the palm of his hand shading his eyes as he tried to peer in.

Nick fired a single shot high through the window, and Garcia's head ducked down.

Then he had to hug the floor as short bursts from the automatic weapon punched holes in the wall, windows, and door. A shelf of designer plates and teacups on hooks flew to pieces. Chips from the overturned kitchen table showered Nick's neck and back. Fuck this, he thought.

The shooting stopped.

"Hey, mon!" Garcia called. "You almost hit me."

"Get the fuck out'a here!" Nick shouted back.

"Can't do that, mon! Clarence say he love you! Wanna get close to you!"

"Nick!" Gus's voice screamed from the living room.

Nick crawled to the hallway entry, jumped up and ran.

Gus, her face blanched, wheeled her chair back to spin around in front of the ruined window. "She's gone!"

"What?"

"Mrs. Voight! She ran out the front door. He's got her!"

Nick looked over Gus's shoulder. He saw Frank Carr, grinning, standing upright behind the rental, holding onto Marilyn Voight's arm, keeping her partially in front of him. She looked more resigned than frightened.

"Why didn't you stop her?"

"How?" Gus said. "You want me to shoot her?"

"Hey, Nick!" Frank called, tugging Marilyn with him as he paced backward. "It's okay now. Take care, buddy!" He turned his head. "Clarence!"

Clarence Bettis appeared from the side of the house, backing up toward Frank and the woman. Bettis held a pistol in each hand, both pointed at the house. His face bore a huge swath of homemade bandage, making it look like he wore a mask.

The three turned and headed across the street.

Nick yelled out through the broken window. "Frank! Call off your shooters."

Frank turned his head with a big grin. "They're gonna stay an' entertain you."

Gus cursed. "If I shoot him in the back, he'll kill her. What'll we do?"

"Not a thing. Can't right now. See if the others leave."

Gunfire opened up on both sides of the house, rounds slamming into the living room. Gus wheeled backward until she bumped into the couch. Behind the couch, doubled down with his arms over his head, the Alamo rep moaned. Nick, too, was prone on the floor.

"That answer your question?" Gus said.

From the bedroom, Kelly Moore screamed shrilly.

With bullets whacking into the walls around him, Nick scrambled in the direction of the scream, hoping he wasn't already too late.

Scooting around the corner into the bedroom, he saw her. She was face down near the bed, her legs spread apart, not moving. Nick's initial thought was: My God!—she's been hit!

"Kelly!" he shouted.

He threw himself down beside her. Where was the blood? Where was she hit? Thank God, he didn't see any blood.

Kelly turned her face, wide-eyed, toward him. Her lips trembled.

"Where're you hurt?" Nick rasped.

"A <u>bug</u>," she said.

On the floor, at her side, Nick looked under the bed. Staring back at him, wiggling its antennae, was the huge palmetto bug, or its twin brother or sister. Nick looked at Kelly.

"Ugh," Kelly said.

"You scared the shit out'a me!" Nick stormed at her.

Kelly made a face. "It's disgusting."

"Get your ass under the bed."

"Not with that thing there," Kelly told him. "It's bigger'n my miniture dachshund."

The blast of the shotgun from the living room jerked Nick up. He banged his head on the bed frame, dammed near knocking himself out. It hurt like hell.

Back to the living room he went. Still dazed, his senses reeling, he felt like one of those stupid targets at the arcade, running back and forth between the rear and front of the house, waiting to get shot.

The front door was open. Lying on his back across the front stoop, his twitching legs extended into the living room, was Kenny Neeves. His eyes were wide open, and he had a surprised look on his face, but he wasn't focusing on anything. He still held a pistol in each hand. The front of his jacket and shirt was mangled and soppy-red. His luck at bursting through doors, along with his adrenalin, had leaked out of him.

"Dammit! I had to," Gus said, wheeling halfway around to look at Nick. "He came in shooting."

Crouching, Nick kept his eyes on the open doorway in case another one decided to charge forth. Nobody was charging. The Garcia out front most likely had seen what had happened to Neeves.

"I got hit," Gus said, somberly.

Nick scampered to her side. "Where?"

She hitched her left shoulder to show him the tear in her flesh above the elbow. Her blood flowed freely, soaking her left side and dripping from the arm of the chair. "It's a nick, Nick." She tried to grin through her own paling features. "That's a joke."

"Seeing you bleed is not funny," Nick said. The bullet had made a ragged crease in the fleshy part of her arm and lodged in the back of the wheelchair. "Are you okay? You won't pass out?"

"I won't pass out," she said.

Again Nick hurried to the rear, looking in the bedroom for Kelly.

Kelly stood inside the doorway, back to the wall, staring at a spot where the floor disappeared under the bed. Both of her hands clutched the long handle of a stainless-steel skillet, holding it raised shoulder high like a batter stepping into the box.

"Where'd you get that?" Nick asked.

"In the kitchen," Kelly said. "I'm not staying in here, unarmed, with that <u>thing</u> under the bed."

"Stay the hell out'a the kitchen," Nick snapped at her.

"I think I will," Kelly said. "Somebody's worked his way in back there."

From the hallway, Nick couldn't see anyone in the kitchen, what part of it he could see into. He could see a portion of the back door that had been kicked or shoved open. He hadn't heard anything, but it would have been impossible to do so with all the shooting.

Risking a quick look around the doorjamb, Nick reached into the bathroom and grabbed a towel from the rack. He spun back around the corner into the short hallway toward the living room.

"Gotcha, mon," the voice said behind him.

Nick froze and turned slowly. The revolver he held in his right hand was at his side, pointed downward.

Coming from the kitchen, grinning, was Paulo Garcia, his automatic weapon held waist high and pointed at Nick.

"Clarence say to shoot you," Paulo said. "Where you wan' me shoot you?"

Nick realized that he couldn't get his gun up before Paulo could squeeze his trigger.

Kelly Moore, swinging the skillet, stepped around the corner from the bedroom. The flat pan of the skillet banged squarely into Paulo's grinning face. Instantly, Nick raised his gun and fired a shot, hitting Paulo somewhere in the middle of his body, driving him backward and down.

Kelly screamed and dropped the skillet.

Nick had the hammer thumbed back, ready to shoot again. But for the moment Paulo wasn't moving. Then his legs started to draw up as he writhed on the floor.

Nick bent down to wrest the Uzi from Paulo's grip. He found an automatic pistol tucked in the man's belt and took it. Paulo groaned with his eyes pinched tightly shut, blood pumping from both his belly wound and his flattened nose.

"You—you shot him," Kelly gasped.

"You hit him," Nick said. "Thank you. Now stay out of sight."

Nick tucked Bettis's revolver into his belt, did the same with Paulo's handgun, and took the Uzi and the towel into the living room. He nearly ran into Gus and the barrel of the shotgun as she was steering her wheelchair toward him.

"I was afraid you'd got shot," she gasped.

"Garcia," Nick said, and for some crazy reason found himself wanting to laugh. "He came in through the kitchen."

"Is Kelly okay?"

"She's fine. Scared to death of a cockroach."

Somewhere out front, the other Garcia started screaming.

Crouching, Nick scrambled to the window.

Hector Garcia, grimacing, clutching his ass, was trying to pull himself up by the fender of the shot-up rental.

His legs didn't want to support him, and he was swearing in Spanish at the top of his voice. He kept twisting his neck, trying to look over his shoulder at his backside.

Nick shifted his position and looked across the street. Standing on his porch with the .22 rifle to his shoulder was Christopherson.

"Paulo!" Hector screamed. "I geet shot in the butt!"

Another car had stopped at the mouth of the driveway. Getting out, coming forward, holding his pistol in firing mode, was Sergeant Dave Melton. Melton had thrown clothes on in a hurry, wearing a pajama top, jeans, and loafers without socks.

"Police!" Melton called to Hector. "Drop that fuckin' gun, you skinny son of a bitch!"

Hector, leaning against the rental, turned his head to look at him.

"I got you sighted," Melton warned.

Hector dropped his weapon and collapsed back against the car.

"On your face on the ground," Melton told him.

"Mon, I'm hurting."

"Now!" Melton snapped.

Groaning, Hector got down.

Nick went out the front doorway, careful not to step on the body of Kenny Neeves, and motioned to Melton.

Melton was looking both ways, ready for anything. "The others?" he shouted.

"Two down in here," Nick called back. "Nobody else."

"Dave!" Gus called from inside the house.

Melton's head snapped up. "Kid! You okay?"

"She's bleeding," Nick said. "She got hit in the arm."

Melton pointed his gun at Hector Garcia. "You sonuvabitch!"

"Not me, mon," Hector moaned. "I geet shot in the butt."

Melton relieved him of two weapons and stood up. "If you move, I'll kill you."

"I can't move," Hector protested. "It hurts."

By the time Nick tightened the towel around Gus Dick's arm, the woman's breathing sounded labored, and her face had taken on a gray pallor. She tried to smile a thanks at him.

Nick tossed the Uzi onto the couch and leaned close to Gus, his lips near her ear. "Augusta, I can't wait for the cops. They can't help us. I need to go after Mrs. Voight now, before Frank gets her out of town. Can you square it?"

"I'll think of something," she said.

Nick went into the hallway to collect Kelly Moore. He threw a glance at Paulo Garcia, drawn up on the floor, on his side, his eyes shut. Whether or not he was conscious, Nick couldn't tell. The belly wound pumped blood over both hands clasped to it. Nick was satisfied Paulo wouldn't be getting up and going anywhere. He helped Kelly sidestep the fallen man as he guided her into the living room.

Gus, slumped forward, had wheeled her chair to the front doorway, where Dave Melton was alternately comforting her and keeping his eye on the prone Hector Garcia on the driveway.

She backed her chair up a bit and looked at Nick. "Nick, get yourself and the kid away from here. We'll cover for you."

Melton frowned at her. "They can't."

Gus, her face paler, teeth clenched, looked straight back at Sergeant Melton. "Dave, these guys were coming after me. Trying to break in. We'll think of something. Nick, give Dave the gun you used."

Sirens could be heard. They appeared to be drawing nearer.

"Cavalry's coming, Dave," Gus said. "Let 'em go. Nick, take Kelly over to your friend's house."

"We are fucking up police work," Melton said. "They won't like it."

"They took their sweet time getting here," Gus snapped.

Nick pointed at Hector, who was lying prone and spread-eagled on the pavement. "I have to take him with me."

"No way," said Melton.

"Sarge, they've got Mrs. Voight and her son, and they've got a head start. I might need him." He handed Bettis's old pistol to Melton. "You got his brother and the other one inside the house."

"Please, Dave," Gus said. "Listen to him."

Melton bit down on his lower lip. "Goddammit! Go ahead. Make it fast."

"On your feet." Nick kicked Hector, who groaned again. "Up, or I'll drag you."

Painfully, Hector struggled upright against the rental. "It hurts to walk." He saw the pistol in Nick's hand that was leveled at him. "Hey, that's Paulo's. Where's my brother?"

"He's got a bellyache," Nick said. "Move it."

Nick took Hector's arm and, half walking him, half dragging him, headed toward the street. He turned and called for Kelly to hurry along with them.

Squeezing out of the doorway was the blanched Alamo man.

"Who's he?" asked Melton.

Nick nodded at the bullet-riddled rental. "That's his car."

The young man drew himself up as much as possible on his shaky legs and glared at Nick. "Mr. Cotton," he said, "next time, please call Hertz."

19

Once the shooting had stopped, a mixed group of residents had begun to creep out of their houses. Buzzing and gaping, they gathered on the street a fair distance from the McNally house. Nick Cotton saw several of them pointing in the direction of Sergeant Melton, who stood in the doorway with his gun drawn. He kept Hector Garcia moving so as not to draw attention to himself and Kelly, assisted the hobbling Hector across toward Christopherson, who was standing on his porch holding his .22 rifle.

"Get him closer, Indy," Chris called. "I'll take another whack at him."

Hector's tear-streaked, sweaty face showed his pain with every step. "You shot me in the butt, mon."

"Yeah, and I'll shoot you again."

"Hey, mon, I wasn't the one that hit you."

Nick told Chris to get everybody inside his house and away from the gatherers. Chris followed close to Hector, prodding him roughly in the back every other step with the muzzle of the rifle. He appeared to be taking a perverse pleasure in watching Hector wince.

"You better not bleed on anything of mine," Chris told him.

"What'm I supposed to do?" Hector protested. "You geeve me a second asshole."

At the window, Nick saw Tampa's finest arriving in two police cars. Four cops unloaded and swarmed into the McNally house as Sergeant Melton motioned to them from the doorway.

Chris had gone into his kitchen. He returned with a dish towel. "Stick this in your pants," he told Hector.

"It don't look too clean," Hector said. But, grimacing, he loosened his belt and wedged the towel down the back of his trousers. "Mon, I gotta lay down."

"Damned if you are," Chris told him.

Hector was eying Chris's sofa. "I mean on my stomach, mon. Only way." He looked at Nick. "Is Paulo dead?"

"I don't know," said Nick. He stepped back from the window. "Chris, I need your car. Hector and I are going after Mrs. Voight. Frank's got her."

"I saw him and the bald man put her in the van, the one with the Indiana license plate," Chris said. "I'll come with you, Indy, now that I got my shootin' eye back."

"No, I won't take that responsibility. This is Kelly. She'll stay here with you."

"Not," said Kelly. "I gotta help Mark."

"You've been lucky so far," Nick said to Kelly. "We're not pushing it. Hector and I'll go alone."

"What'cha mean?" asked Hector, shifting from one foot to the other while leaning against his arm on the wall.

"I mean," Nick told him, "that you're going to show me where you've been holding Mark Voight."

"Fuck, mon," Hector said, "Clarence's house ain't seex blocks from here. I can take you there, but they might shoot both of us. Clarence don't love you. I tell you where to go, and I stay here." He shrugged his skinny shoulders. "I can't seet in no car."

"I'll shoot you if you don't," Nick said.

"You theenk it's no painful to be shot in the butt? Can I draw you a map?"

"He'll run out on you," Chris said.

"I can't run," said Hector. "I can't even walk. Old man, you got sometheeng I can take for the hurt?"

Chris went to the rear of his house. Nick stood at the window watching the activity across the street. An emergency-aid ambulance had arrived and was parting the onlookers to get into the driveway. When Chris returned, he was carrying a double handful of pill bottles.

"Some 'a these are old, really old," Chris emphasized. "They were prescribed for my wife. She died of cancer ten years ago. I just never threw 'em out. The Tylenols're fairly new."

Hector squinted, trying to read the faded, peeled, or blurred labels and gave up. Leaning against the wall, he lined the pill bottles along the windowsill and started on the caps. "There's gotta be codeine in here," he said, dumping several from each bottle into the palm of his hand. "Got a cold beer I can wash 'em down with?"

Chris's expression showed that he couldn't believe this asshole. Nick was fascinated by way Hector was pouring pills into the palm of his hand, some from each bottle, until he had a handful in assorted colors. Hector wadded them into his mouth and started chewing. He squeezed his eyes shut as he swallowed.

"Jesus Christ, Indy," Chris said, "I don't know what's in those pills. He's gonna kill himself."

"My butt hurts," Hector explained. "I need a drink."

Shaking his head, Chris went back toward his kitchen and out of sight. In a little while, he returned with a bottle of beer. Nick went back to watching the uniforms and medical techs across the way, two cops in front of the house talking with Sergeant Melton, one staring down at the body of Kenny Neeves and scratching the back of his head. When Nick looked at Hector again, he saw the man tilting the bottle and gulping from it. Then Hector went to work dumping out another handful of pills.

"Heets the spot," Hector said, "but I feel a little funny."

"Can I get to your car without being seen?" Nick asked Christopherson.

"I think so," Chris said. "It's out back."

Nick looked out the window and said, "Oh, shit!"

"What's up, Indy?"

Something Nick didn't need, or want, was up. He watched a familiar-looking Chrysler cruise to a halt in the middle of the street. He could see the backs of the heads of three men inside the car, all of them craning to see what was happening at the McNally house. Two of the men were up front, one in the back seat. An irritated, uniformed cop came down the driveway and motioned them onward. Nick watched the car slide forward and halt again.

Once more, Chris asked him what he was looking at.

"We've got three more visitors. Chris, you're about to have a houseful of guests. Talk about your lousy timing." Nick turned and motioned to Kelly Moore. "Come here, Kelly."

Kelly had become fascinated watching Hector Garcia shoving another handful of pills into his mouth and chewing away. "What, Coach?"

"Go out and bring those guys inside. Don't—I repeat, <u>do not</u>—let them talk to the cops."

"Who?" asked Chris as Kelly went out the front door.

"Mrs. Voight's husband and two other clowns I didn't want to see," Nick said.

Chris pushed in beside him to peer out. Kelly was talking to the driver and gesturing. The car eased forward and into the space vacated by Marilyn Voight's van.

The three men who got out were Dr. Larry Voight, S.O.B.'s principal Sanford Wilcox, and assistant principal Hal Ryerson. Voight had on a polo shirt and jeans. Wilcox wore a white shirt, with necktie no less, the shirttail tucked into a garish pair of purple Bermuda shorts, his skinny legs resembling hairy spider's legs. Ryerson was even more colorfully dressed, in polka-dotted Bermuda shorts and a multi-colored shirt with its tail out. They looked like three misplaced tourists with everything but camera straps around their necks.

Nick watched from the window. Somehow, Kelly, talking rapidly though Nick couldn't hear what she was saying, managed to herd the newcomers onto the porch and into Christopherson's house. Looking across the street again, Nick saw the attendants sliding an occupied stretcher into the ambulance. He turned to face a confused and concerned Larry Voight.

"Nick! What's going on?" Voight asked. "Where's Marilyn and Mark?"

"They're with Frank Carr."

"Frank? I don't get it. Who's hurt?"

"Not them, Larry," Nick said. "I'll explain later. Soon as those cops are diverted, I'll go after them."

"Frank's got her?" Voight looked even more crestfallen. "Nick, I asked you to look after her."

"Don't blame him," Kelly Moore said. "There was all that shooting, and I was attacked by a giant cockroach."

Wilcox and Ryerson stared at her, evidently not sure if they had heard correctly.

"What are <u>you</u> doing here?" asked Ryerson.

"Helping Mr. Cotton get Mark," Kelly said.

"She's just a child," Wilcox said, stating the obvious. "She shouldn't be here."

"What shooting?" Voight, grasping Nick's arm, wanted to know.

"Your wife and son are not hurt," Nick told him. "Frank's got a partner, and they both have guns. Frank will have them driving south after some money. That is, unless I can catch them near here first, before they leave town. That's what I'm hoping."

"Let's go," said Voight.

"You're not going," Nick said. Gripping the man's arm, he turned Voight to face Christopherson. "This is Chris. You men and Kelly will stay here with him. Hector and I will take his car. Hector's the one standing there bleeding. Wake up, Hector," Nick snapped at him. Hector had been leaning back against the wall, his chin tilted forward, his eyes closed, the beer bottle tilted to spill some of its contents on Chris's rug. "We're leaving."

"Mon, I can't move," Hector moaned.

"You'll need somebody to watch this snake," Chris said.

"We're not staying behind," Larry Voight said. "I'm going with you, Nick."

"Don't do this to me, Larry," Nick told him. "We don't have time for a discussion or vote."

"I'll follow you if I have to. It's my wife and son."

"We're sticking with Dr. Voight," said Wilcox, indicating himself and Ryerson. "We came this far to help Larry."

Nick cursed and shook his head.

"I'm going, too," Kelly Moore announced. "I came here to help Mark."

"No way," Nick told her. "These guys are old enough to be dumb if they choose. You, Kelly, are definitely not going."

"Way," said Kelly. "If you don't let me, I'll go across the street to the police and tell them you're here and you know all about the shooting. I won't be left behind, Coach."

Nick stared at her, fighting the urge to spank her.

"Is Mark all right?" asked Voight. "Did you see him?"

Nick sighed. "He's okay. Frank will have to stop for him and take him along. It'd be the only way to assure Marilyn's cooperation." He motioned toward Hector Garcia, who had resumed gobbling pills and drinking the beer. "That one's gonna take us to a house to check out."

"He don't look so good," Hal Ryerson said. "He should sit down."

"Dude, I can't seet down," Hector told him. "I got shot in the ass."

"What're we waiting for?" asked Voight.

Nick peered from the window. "Those two uniforms across the street. They're looking at the houses on this side. We don't want to get stopped with Hector leaking blood. Do you know the license number of your van?"

"My van? Marilyn's?"

"That's the one they left in."

For a few seconds, Voight thought. He chewed his lip. "I know some of the numbers. But now—I'm not sure of the exact order. I can't think straight."

"Call the State Police and tell them it was stolen," Nick said. "The State Police," he emphasized. "Say your wife and son were kidnapped. Emphasize that. They'll contact the local F.B.I. Say you think they're headed south out of Tampa."

"Why south?"

"Naples is south, ain't it?"

Voight blinked. "Yeah. Why Naples?"

"That's the direction Marilyn will take them. They have to be stopped before they get there."

"Wait! Wait!" Voight protested. "I want to know what's going on."

Nick continued to look out the slit in the curtain toward the police activity. He saw one of the cops bring Gus Dick's wheelchair out the front door of the McNally house and place it on the sidewalk. Sergeant Melton came from the house carrying Gus Dick in his arms. The cop assisted

Melton in getting Gus onto another stretcher. Nick knew she would be all right. Sergeant Melton would see to that.

He flicked a look over at Voight. "Eighteen years ago, Marilyn hid something in the Everglades. Frank Carr wants it. You don't have to explain any of that to the cops. Now make that call. We need the backup in case we can't catch up to Frank."

"I never knew Frank to hurt anybody," said Voight.

"He's changed, Larry. If he gets cornered, he won't hesitate."

"Nick, there are cops across the street," Sanford Wilcox pointed out. "Tell them."

"We don't want those cops involved," Nick said. "They're local. We approach them, and we won't be going anywhere."

Chris took Larry Voight to the telephone. Nick jerked on Hector's arm to awaken him. Hector had been leaning against the wall with his eyes closed and had started to snore. Nick looked at Kelly Moore.

"Please, please, Kelly," he said, "don't fight with me on this. I told your parents I'd be responsible for you. You have to stay here."

"I'm going with you," she said.

Voight re-entered the room, too soon to have made any phone call. "I'm not calling the State Police," he said. "I can talk to Frank, reason with him. If we go now, Nick, we've got a chance to catch up to Marilyn and Mark."

"Six of you," Christopherson said with skepticism. "I don't know if you can fit in my car. I've got a little Honda."

"We'll take the Chrysler," Voight said. "We can squeeze in there. Let's go."

"I theenk you guys are pussies," Hector Garcia said, dribbling the last of the beer from the corners of his mouth.

"It's off," Nick said. "It's all off. I won't be part of this, Larry. You do what you want. I'll call the State Police and turn Hector over to the cops outside."

Voight grasped Nick's arm. "What happens if the police manage to stop the van? You imply Frank's a killer, and the guy with him is willing to shoot. What if they do get cornered? Marilyn or Mark could get killed. We're the best chance they got, Nick."

Nick suspected it probably was in Frank's plan anyway to kill Marilyn and her son, but he didn't want to tell

Voight. "Larry, the state cops have resources we don't. Especially if we don't reach them before they're on the road."

"I can't risk it," Voight said. "Listen. You said they're going to head for Naples. We know that much. If we can catch 'em, maybe I can talk sense to Frank. I want to try that first, Nick. It's worth a try. Let's walk out and get in my car like we're minding our own business."

Hector Garcia cradled the pill bottles. "I take these," he said.

"Your car is out front in plain view," Nick pointed out.

"You can bring it around to the alley in back," Christopherson suggested.

"Let me do it," Kelly offered. "They won't stop a teenager from leaving. Not a girl."

Larry Voight gave her his keys.

"Go to the corner and turn right," Chris told her. "Turn right into the alley. You'll see my car. It's a small black Honda."

Kelly went out the front door and to the Chrysler. A uniformed cop, standing near the middle of the street, looked at her. From the window, Nick saw her give the cop a wave and a little hip-twitch before she got in the car. She fastened her seat belt and waved to him again. The cop didn't wave back, but he made no move to intercept or stop her, and he was grinning lasciviously.

Kelly pulled away and disappeared from Nick's view.

Nick tucked the gun into his belt at the back and took Hector's arm. "You walk straight. I don't care how much it hurts." He nodded to Chris. "Leave your rifle here. Go out the back way and take a look, Chris. We'll be at the back door. Motion to us when it's clear."

They lined up at the back door as Chris walked into his back yard. He looked around, looked at the sky, and stood with his hands in his hip pockets. The Chrysler stopped in the ally, and Chris turned and nodded.

Out they went, not hurrying, but moving in nearly a straight line toward the car. Nick kept hold of Hector's arm, letting him limp along. Kelly was out and had all four doors open.

Nick looked over the situation and shook his head. "This is gonna be tight. Sanford, you and Hal and Kelly get in back with our prisoner. Put him on the floor. I'll drive. Dr. Voight can ride up front. Hector—" he nudged the wounded man, "—you direct us straight to the other house. Screw with me, and I'll take away your pills."

"Aw, mon," Hector said, but shrugged.

Wilcox, Ryerson, and Kelly Moore climbed into the back seat and, with Nick's help, maneuvered Hector Garcia inside so that he was kneeling on the floor across their knees. Nick took the driver's side, and Larry Voight climbed in the passenger's door.

From a bad dream two days ago to a nightmare was how Nick felt. He had a whole bunch of people here, including a wounded man gobbling painkillers, who had no idea of what they were getting into. He didn't even know what he would be letting himself in for. Smart thing would be to turn it over to the local cops and hope they could handle it. Weigh the safety of three school administrators and a teenager against the very likely danger to Mrs. Voight and her son, then play the percentages—four versus two. But Marilyn and Mark were friends, the family of a close friend, and, regardless of what would be logical or smart, Nick could understand Larry Voight's feelings.

Kelly Moore, from the back seat, said, "We're all in. See? We're doing fine."

Nick craned around to see her. "Kelly, why won't you listen to reason?"

"Hey, I'm a blonde," she said. "You know we're stubborn."

"You would've called the cops, wouldn't you?"

"Bet your ass, Coach."

Between the time spent shoveling pills into his mouth, chewing, and swallowing, Hector Garcia raised his head on command to peer forward and give directions. They hadn't been riding a full three minutes before he tapped Nick's shoulder, squinted his eyes, and announced that the house was in the next block. Bettis's car, Frank's Ford, and the Broncho were in the driveway, but Marilyn Voight's van was not.

Nick stopped at the mouth of the driveway, behind the Ford, left the engine running, and took the pistol he had tucked beside his seat. "Everybody stay in the car except Hector and me." He leveled his gaze at Larry Voight. "You, too, Larry. Your van's not here. It means Frank and Marilyn are on the road. If anything bad happens, you drive these people away from here." He tilted his gun back over his shoulder to touch the muzzle to Hector's nose. "Back out, Hector. You're walking in front of me."

Nick got out and went around, realizing he was showing his back to anyone inside the house, opened the rear door and assisted Hector by dragging him, ass first, by his belt.

"Sheet, that hurts," Hector protested. "Take it easy, mon. My peels—?"

"Leave 'em."

Hector pushed the bottles into Ryerson's arms. "Hold my peels," he said.

Nick got Hector reasonably straightened up at the end of the driveway and gave himself a moment to look at Clarence Bettis's abode. It was a smallish, pink, stucco house with overgrown front yard. He gave Hector's arm a tug. "Right in front of me, Hector, in case Bettis is watching us."

"Not heem," Hector said. "It takes two to handle the woman and the boy. Clarence's ol' woman might be there. She won't be no trouble."

They were nearly to the stoop when a fat woman in a kimono-styled bathrobe opened the door. She saw the gun in Nick's hand but didn't look alarmed.

"He ain't here," she said without being asked. "They done took off."

"Where?" asked Nick.

"I dunno. Clarence don't tell me nothin'. Who're you? And what's wrong with him?" She nodded at Hector Garcia.

Hector twisted around and showed her the bloody seat of his pants. "I geet shot in the butt."

"He's a mess," the woman said. "He ain't comin' in my house. Donnie Ann!"

The freckle-faced, red-haired girl appeared at her side and peeked around at Nick.

Donnie Ann said, "Yeah, that's him, Mom. He's the one that come after Mark."

"He ain't here neither," the woman told Nick. "Clarence come in an' got him. Him and the kid and Frank drove off with some woman in a van." She frowned at Hector. "Where's your buddies?"

"Dead, I theenk," Hector replied and shrugged.

"Christ!" the woman said. "You an' your guns."

Nick realized that someone had come up behind him and saw that it was Kelly Moore. Kelly and Donnie Ann looked straight at each other.

"Where're they going?" Nick asked Mrs. Bettis.

"I dunno. Clarence just said not to expect 'em till they git back."

"You can do better than that."

"Go to hell," the woman said. "Believe me or not."

Nick chewed his lip. Threatening this woman wouldn't get him anywhere, and she probably knew from looking at him that he wasn't going to shoot her. He remembered what Marilyn had told him. She had gone down someplace into the Everglades from Naples. But she hadn't told him where—she hadn't divulged any highway or town names. And, Nick realized, the Everglades is one big place. So, whether he believed this woman or not, he wasn't going to get any more out of her. Unless—?

He asked her, "Did Clarence tell how they're going to split the money?"

That got her attention. "What money?"

"Hey, mon," Hector said to Nick. "Ixnay on the moolay."

Nick said to Hector, but for the woman's benefit. "You mean he didn't tell his wife he's gonna be a millionaire?"

"Hey, what?" she said. "My Clarence? A millionaire?" She glared at Hector. "Hector, if you bums are holding out on me—"

"Don't let 'er hit me," Hector cried to Nick. "I can't run."

"If you want your share," Nick said to Mrs. Bettis, "you better tell me where they're going."

"God, don't I wish," the woman said. "All Clarence tol' me is, the woman's gonna take 'em someplace. I got no idea where."

That settled it. She really didn't know. Nick said to Hector and Kelly, "Back in the car."

"What the hell, mon?" Hector protested. "Lee' me here. Clarence got a hammock in his backyard. I'll flop there."

Nick tightened his grip, digging his fingers into the nerve along Hector's forearm, making Hector wince. "I like your company too much."

"Hey, wait!" Mrs. Bettis shouted. "What's this money Clarence is gonna get?" Angrily, she shook her head. "That fuckin' Frank Carr. I knowed him and Clarence was cooking up some big deal. That's why they had that boy here. Clarence come in the house an' got him a little while ago."

Nick looked at the redheaded girl. "How about it, Donnie Ann? You got any idea where your daddy's going?"

"He come in and took Mark. He didn't say nothing to me." She had edged around her mother at the mention of money, and now took another step forward. "You'll look out for Mark, won't you?"

"You!" Kelly Moore snapped at Donnie Ann. "Did you touch Mark?"

The redhead's eyes glinted. "Mark's my fella."

"He is, huh?" Kelly said.

Kelly turned her back on her, then, with no hesitancy whatsoever, wheeled around and landed an uppercut with her right fist under Donnie Ann's chin. Donnie Ann popped erect and fell backwards onto the grass. Her eyes rolled. Mrs. Bettis gasped.

Dragging Hector, Nick kicked out with one foot and booted Kelly in the butt. She yelped in surprise.

"Get in the car," he snapped at her.

Rubbing her posterior, Kelly followed to the car. "Coach," she said, "let me beat on that skinny tart. I'll get some answers for you."

"Hell, no," Nick said. "You'd enjoy it too much."

20

"Larry," Nick Cotton said, "what the hell are we doing?"

"We'll catch up to 'em," Voight said.

They were barreling south on I-75 with no regard for the speed limit. Voight was driving, having switched positions while they were at Bettis's house. Nick, in the passenger's seat up front, tightened his seat belt. Behind him and Voight, the other four were wedged in back.

Kelly sat against one back door. Hal Ryerson took up most of the center space, and at his other side Sanford Wilcox scrunched against the other door. Hector Garcia had draped himself face down across their legs, saying he had to have his hands free to take his "peels."

Nick craned back to see Hector's butt in the air and his face pressed down on Kelly Moore's lap.

"Coach," Kelly said, "if this asshole puts his tongue on my leg again, I'm gonna gouge his eyes out."

"She means it," Nick said to Hector. "Keep your tongue off her legs."

"Aw, mon, I'm just tryin' to geet some balance."

With reckless abandon, Voight passed a line of cars and weaved back into the right lane to avoid another car passing ahead of him. "What does Frank want from us?" he asked.

"Money," Nick said after he had managed to catch his breath. "Marilyn hid a lot of money."

"When?"

"Eighteen years before she went to Indiana. Your Florida buddies picked up a bank robbery bundle in Fort Myers. Martin Ruhle gave her the money to keep for him. She hid it instead."

"I don't believe it," Voight said. "Marilyn wouldn't rob a bank."

"Not her." Nick threw his hands against the dash to brace himself as Voight weaved them in and around interstate traffic. "She was called after the fact. So was Frank Carr. She thinks it was Frank who killed Ruhle and Lenny Wilson and then started after her. But he got himself sidetracked, like in prison." He blew out his breath as he saw the speedometer needle waggling above ninety. "Slow down, Larry, before you kill us. Listen to me. Let's call the state cops. They can stop the van."

"No!" Voight snapped. "You know what happens if we do. We're shuttled off someplace to wait. I can't wait around for a police report. I know what I need, Nick. I need a chance to talk to Frank Carr." He gripped the steering wheel so tightly that his knuckles showed white. "How much money, Nick? I can give Frank money."

"You got a half million lying around?"

"God, no! Maybe—maybe if it means Marilyn's and Mark's lives, I can raise it."

"I doubt if Frank's gonna be patient enough to wait while you liquidate assets and borrow what you can."

"Jesus," Voight said softly, his brow furrowed. "Marilyn never told me."

"That's right, Larry. She didn't even want the money for herself. She wanted a life, and you helped her get it. That, plus the fact she loves you and didn't want you to know."

"And that's what Carr's after?" Voight shook his head, keeping his eyes on the highway. "That's what shook her up when she read about the double murder. I wondered why she insisted on subscriptions to the Miami Herald and Tampa Tribune when we couldn't afford it. She told me Ruhle and Lenny had been killed. But there wasn't anything about Frank Carr."

Nick nodded. "Apparently Ruhle told Frank that Marilyn had the money. Frank killed Ruhle and Wilson, but then got in trouble with the cops and didn't know how to locate her. He's been thinking about it all these years, Larry. I'm afraid he'll kill Marilyn and Mark when he gets his hands on what he wants. That's why we have to get the police involved."

"But you said she told you she hid the money somewhere in Naples."

"No, she stole a truck in Naples. She hid the money in the Everglades. Last time I looked at a map, the Everglades is a big place. She didn't tell me where."

Voight stayed quiet for several minutes as they sped along. They had blown past Bradenton and had reached the first Sarasota exit. Nick hoped that Voight was at last getting reasonable about calling in the state police.

Voight said, "Maybe I can find it."

Nick looked at him. "What?"

"Two years ago, we brought Mark and his friends down here on spring break. We drove down the Keys to Key West. When we got back to Miami, we had another day before we were to start home. The boys wanted to stay in the city, but Marilyn asked if I wanted to take a ride with her into the Everglades. I could see she wanted to, so I agreed to drive. We came west on Forty-one, and she gave me directions. We turned off onto a state road, I don't remember the number. After awhile there was another turnoff and a bridge over a culvert, I remember that. That's where she told me to stop the car. I had no idea what she was doing."

The car rocked as Voight weaved around two more motorists who were doing a slow seventy. Nick shut his eyes and breathed.

Voight said, "She told me I could wait in the car, she wanted to talk a little walk. I couldn't see anyplace to walk. It looked like all jungle to me. I wasn't going to let her go off by herself. We went along a little trail that I, by myself, couldn't have found and came to the edge of a swamp. She stopped and stared at a cabin built on stilts out on the water. Told me it used to be a place used by poachers. Said she'd been there when she was a kid. The thing looked like it was about ready to crumble. I had no idea what she found interesting about it."

"You didn't ask?" Nick queried.

"When Marilyn's not in a mood to communicate, she won't. I didn't nag her. She looked at it a long time and looked at the water. She told me the water wasn't deep along there, she was thinking of taking her pants off and wading out. I asked her not to, afraid there might be snakes and alligators and God knows what else in that filthy water. But she looked like she was considering it. Finally she just laughed and said she didn't really mean it. We went back to the car and left. On the ride back to Miami, she was a lot more chipper, like maybe she'd settled something in her mind."

"And you honestly think you can find this place again," Nick said.

"I have to try," Voight said. "I'm trying to think. We were going west on U.S. Forty-one, almost to a little town called Ochopee. A few miles east of it was where she had me turn off the highway. But now we're coming from the other direction."

Nick shook his head. "Are you willing to bet their lives on it? That you can find it?"

Voight's expression clouded again. "Whatever choice I make is bad, Nick. You want the cops, and I say no. I don't trust if, or when, they'll try to do anything for my family. Or what will, or won't, work. I feel fucked no matter which way I go. But it's got to be my choice."

"Larry, we need help. Look at us. Even if we find the place, do you think we're qualified to go after armed men in a swamp?"

"I hope the money's still there," Voight said. "That was a long time ago. I want my chance to reason with Frank Carr. I used to be able to talk to him. I didn't like him, but I talked to him. I'll make arrangements to get him some money if he'll let my family go. Not a half million all at once, but Marilyn and I can work something out with him. I'll offer him a certain amount every year, like a retirement fund. I'll give him my word, and I'll keep it."

"I know you'll keep it, Larry," Nick said, "but that won't carry much weight with Frank."

"Marilyn's smart," Voight said. "She might be telling him that right now."

"I just hope she's smart enough not to let herself and Mark get taken on a one-way ride if she can help it. Dammit!—watch that car!"

Voight weaved in and around more traffic. "If he hurts them, I'll kill him."

"He's a big man, tough and hard. You won't scare him, Larry. I don't know if you're capable of killing anyone, but I know he is."

"When I knew him," Voight said, "he wasn't so tough and hard. He was the weenie of the bunch. Always sucking up to Martin Ruhle, sucking him off too, I bet—oh, sorry, Kelly."

"I know what sucking him off means," Kelly said from the back seat and then smacked Hector Garcia on the ear when he looked up hopefully at her.

"Larry," Nick said, "if he could murder Ruhle and Wilson, that proves he wasn't a weenie. On top of that, prison can harden a man more."

"Frank ain't no queer," Hector Garcia said. It was the first time he had spoken since they'd departed Tampa.

"Hell he ain't," Voight snapped over his shoulder.

"I know he ain't," Hector said. "I got a couple girls for him."

"That I can believe," Nick said.

"You don't know him, Nick," Voight told him. "I spent three summers with those guys. Only good thing out'a the whole experience was Marilyn."

Nick took the beaten old photograph from his shirt pocket. It was folded in half and sticky from his perspiration. He put his finger under the face of the young man in the middle, the one with his arm around a young Marilyn's waist. "That's not a gay look he's giving Marilyn. I'd call it lewd. That is, if we're looking at Frank Carr."

"Let me see that." Voight shifted his eyes between the road and the photo. "He's not even looking at Marilyn. The one you're pointing to is Martin Ruhle." Voight used his finger to point at the one standing next to himself in the picture. "That's Frank there."

Nick stared at the photo. All right, why wasn't he surprised? It made more sense now. What was it Frank—or Martin Ruhle—had said, bragging about himself, "tough," "leader," "a cut above" the others? Much more sense. A man who could kill another on a beach over a money-belt—right. But Marilyn should've told him.

It dawned on Voight. "Christ," he said, "are you saying Martin Ruhle's alive, and he's got my family? God help us. Marilyn didn't know."

"Of course, she did," Nick said. "She knew it when she left Indiana because he called her."

Voight was shaking his head, not wanting to believe it. "Why would she trust him? Why would she let herself be taken in like that?"

"For Mark," Nick said. "She's gambling that this man won't kill her and the son he fathered after he gets what he wants."

Voight's features turned crestfallen. "She told you that, too?" Then he had another thought. "The money? What if it's not still there? He's a son of a bitch, Nick. He's capable of murder."

"I know. He practically bragged about it. He killed Lenny Wilson and Frank Carr, cut them up so the cops wouldn't have fingerprints or dental records to compare, and switched identities with Frank. At the time he thought it was a cutesy idea because Frank Carr had an alibi when the robbery occurred. Frank was working in St. Pete and probably had never gotten himself arrested. When the real Martin Ruhle was sent to prison, nobody thought to compare past fingerprint records, and he slipped through the cracks. He's been living as Frank Carr ever since. I doubt if his parole officer knows the difference."

"You lost me," Sanford Wilcox said from the back seat. "Who killed who, and who fathered who?"

"Whom," Kelly said.

"It's a long story," Nick said.

"We got time," Sanford Wilcox said. "Take our minds off how fast Dr. Voight's driving."

Hector Garcia raised his head. "Yeah, mon. I'm interested."

Nick gave them the story as Marilyn had told him. Voight nodded occasionally as he alternately mashed the accelerator and hit the brakes. When he was finished, Nick squeezed his eyes shut in exasperation. How the hell could he convince Larry Voight that they had to bring in the state police?

"Coach," Kelly Moore said, "he's slobbering on my knee again." The sound of her striking Hector Garcia's head could be heard by all. "Wake up, you asshole. Spit on somebody else."

Hector raised his head, his eyes bleary. "Mon, I'm out'a peels. My belly hurts. I might geet sick."

"You're out'a luck too," Nick told him.

"Goddammit!" Voight said, and Nick asked him what. "We gotta stop for gas."

"Good thing," Hal Ryerson said, "cause I gotta pee."

"And I'm hungry," Kelly announced.

"I need more peels," Hector slurred.

"What?" Voight said. "You think we're on some leisurely trip here?"

"They're right," Nick said. "You have to stop anyway."

Voight cursed the fates in general and the Chrysler Corporation in particular for building a car that needed its gas tank occasionally refilled. Nick wondered if there were any possible way, short of knocking the man out, that he could take the keys and do the driving himself.

At the next auto-service-and-food sign, Voight took them off the interstate and looped around to a full service station-convenience store. Everybody in the back seat assisted Hector, none too gently, in inching backward to get out. Nick took him by the arm from there. Hector couldn't straighten up. He appeared to be permanently bent forward. This incited a little girl in a rental convertible at the parallel pump to lean out the window and ask her father what was wrong with the funny looking man.

"Hush, hon," her father said. "The man's physically impaired. It's not nice to stare."

Hector turned around in little pigeon steps and pointed to his stained backside. "Bullet in the butt," he said to the little girl.

The father's eyes popped open. Evidently he had heard about Florida. He jammed the nozzle back into the pump, made sure he was clutching his credit card in hand, jumped back into the rental and gunned the engine. The mother, on the other side of the little girl, was seriously pretending to study a road map. They screeched off.

"Somebody gonna help me to the li'l boy's room?" Hector asked. He pigeon-stepped around to leer at Kelly.

"Not me," said Kelly. "I wouldn't touch your pee-wee if your life depended on it."

"I theenk it does," Hector said.

"You take him," Nick told Ryerson.

"Why the hell me?"

"Do it, Hal," Wilcox said. "I'm still the principal, and you're the assistant principal. I'm your boss."

"Down here, too?"

"Hal!"

"Yes, sir," Ryerson said.

"We'll all go," Nick said. "I don't trust Hector's hurt as much as he claims." He turned to Kelly. "You too, Kelly. Go to the bathroom."

Voight was busy at the pump with the gasoline.

When they were gathered again on the tarmac, waiting for Larry Voight who was the last to use the restroom, Hector Garcia pleaded for somebody, anybody, to go inside the store and buy him all the painkillers available. At that moment, Hector didn't appear to be feeling much pain. He rocked unsteadily, and his eyes had glazed over.

"You brought him," Wilcox said to Nick. "What do you think?"

Kelly wrinkled her nose. "He's a mess. Why don't we just leave him here?"

Nick gave it some thought. "I don't see that we can do that. He'd scare off all the tourists."

"Well, I'm riding up front with you," Kelly said. "I'll sit on your lap, Coach." She grinned at him. "Unless you're afraid you'll get another hard-on for me like this morning."

"Another?" said Hal Ryerson.

"Just shut the hell up, Kelly," Nick told her.

"We're all hungry," Ryerson said. "Let's grab something while we're here."

Larry Voight, coming back from the restroom, said, "Fuck that. Let's hit the road."

"Hal's right," Nick told him. "We've still got a long trip."

"I'm going after my wife and son," Voight snapped.

"By yourself?" Nick asked, pointedly.

Voight considered, scowled, and finally said, "Okay. Make it snappy."

It was decided that Kelly and Nick would do the shopping while Voight, Wilcox, and Ryerson kept Hector Garcia surrounded outside the car. Not that Hector was likely to go sprinting off anywhere. Every step he had taken had produced groans and perspiration. He reminded Nick, again, to not forget the pain pills.

"An' the beer," he called. "Gotta have that, mon!"

Inside the store, Kelly and Nick separated. Nick looked over the available non-prescription medicines. He selected Tylenol, Advil, and two bottles of codeine cough syrup, rounded a short aisle and said, "Son of a bitch!"

He had come face to face with Martin Ruhle, alias Frank Carr, who was equally surprised. Ruhle had been withdrawing pre-made, cold salad sandwiches from the refrigerated section.

The two of them stood and stared at each other. They were eight, perhaps ten, feet apart.

"Damn, Nick," Ruhle finally said. "I can't get rid of you, can I?"

Ruhle used his forearm, his hands full with the wrapped sandwiches, to part the front of his light jacket just enough so that Nick could see the butt of the pistol in his belt.

He said, "You got one, too. Right?"

"Sure," Nick replied. He didn't. He had left the gun on the floor mat in Voight's car. Where the hell was the van? he wondered. He hadn't seen it out on the tarmac.

"What are we gonna do?" asked Ruhle. "We gonna fast-draw each other in this public place?"

"Up to you," Nick said. His brain computed two choices. Could he drop what he had in his hands and close the distance to Ruhle before the other man could draw and shoot? Probably not. Not a good choice. His other option, if Ruhle dropped the sandwiches and his hand moved, was for Nick to hit the floor rolling. He saw Ruhle start a slow grin. "Well?" he said.

"You don't wanna do what you're thinking, Nick. You won't make it." Ruhle's grin faded, turned to a thoughtful expression. "How'd you follow us? It was Marilyn, right? She told you where we're going. I should'a guessed."

Nick responded with a shrug. Fuck him.

Ruhle nodded. "My girl lied to me. She said she didn't tell you. Well, we know she's full'a surprises. Who's with you? The crippled lady?"

"She couldn't make this trip," Nick said.

"The young kid? One Clarence says has got a cute ass? Clarence got his eye on her, Nick. So has Paulo." Ruhle cocked an eyebrow. "By the way, how'd you get away from Kenny and the Garcias?"

"Kenny's dead. Paulo couldn't make the trip either," Nick said and watched Martin Ruhle's eyebrows rise higher. "I'm alone."

"Gotta hand it to you," Ruhle said, sounding like he meant it. "You got the cajones. What I gotta figure is what I can do with you now to end this standoff."

"Give it up," Nick said. "Let Marilyn give you directions, or draw you a map, and you can let her and the boy go. That's all I want. I don't give a fuck about your money."

Ruhle smiled. "Don't like that plan."

"Where's Marilyn?"

"In the van with Clarence. He's got a gun in the boy's ribs. She won't try nothin'."

"Mark still think you're a fine man?"

Ruhle shrugged. "Kid's kind'a confused right now. His mom keeps telling him not to worry. Keep smiling, Nick. People will think we're two old buddies having a nice conversation. I'm walking out. Be smart, turn around, and go home. Clarence <u>wants</u> to kill you, and I'm willing to."

"Where's the van?"

"At the pumps out back. Don't follow me out, Nick. Clarence sees you, he will shoot you, and we will drive away before anybody can do anything."

"I can make you pull that gun in here," Nick said, knowing he didn't want to do that. "Would you, Frank? Here I am calling you Frank, and that's not your name."

"Marilyn told you quite a bit. You can call me Martin since we're buddies. Yeah, Marilyn's a great girl." He tilted his head at Nick. "You're gonna chase after us. That adds an element of chance. I like it. I like games of chance." The man sounded like he meant it. "But for now, you just stay where you are."

Nick took a step forward. A bold move, under the circumstances, but he had no plan in mind other than to see what Ruhle would do. Besides, he had heard some voices in the aisle behind him. He said to Ruhle, "You're not going anywhere."

Ruhle laughed and, with a single sweep of one arm, that hand dropping the sandwiches, caught a stack of cola cans at the corner of the aisle. The triangular stack flew apart and went crashing toward Nick.

Nick tried to sidestep, did a little dance as the cans tumbled toward him, and wound up stumbling ankle-deep in canned soft drinks. He had to balance himself, kick cans aside, and create the semblance of a lane before he could move forward.

Martin Ruhle was gone. A few other shoppers peered around corners toward Nick. An aproned woman with a scowl hurried toward him, looking alternately from him to the cans littering the floor.

"What'd you do?" asked Kelly Moore, approaching from his back.

"An accident," Nick muttered.

The aproned woman showed Nick a disapproving glare. "Why do people always have to pull a can from the bottom? Get away, get away. I'll straighten up." She gave him another disgusted look.

Kelly raised the paper sack in her arms. "I got the food and drinks," she announced.

Nick was in motion, starting to run, heading for the entrance at the other side of the building. The store employee yelled at him, "You gotta pay for those things. I'll call the manager!"

Nick hadn't even realized that he still had an armload of Hector's pain medicine. He dumped his purchases on the check-out counter and ran through the rear door to the outside.

Marilyn Voight's van was pulling away.

Martin Ruhle grinned at Nick from the dirver's side.

21

Larry Voight rammed the heel of his hand against the steering wheel, exclaiming, "I can't believe it. You let him get away!"

"Shut up, Larry," Nick said with equal disgust. "He had a gun, I didn't. We were too far apart. He's capable of doing what he said. And maybe I didn't think fast enough."

"He'd shoot?" Voight asked. "In a public place like that?"

"At that particular moment, I thought he might," Nick said. "And he'd probably walk out untouched while everybody else sheltered down."

Voight scowled through the mirror at a car that was trying to pass him, stepped on the gas and sped ahead of the other motorist. "Why didn't you tell him I'd make him a deal?"

"Larry, I don't believe Martin Ruhle's gonna be interested in your retirement plan. He wants his half million dollars <u>now</u>."

"I'd manage it somehow," Voight said, not letting go. "He's got to understand that. I'll make him understand."

"Slow down, Larry." Nick cringed as Voight sped even faster. "You'll make him? You don't know this man. Whatever he was twenty years ago, and he sounds like a bastard then, you don't know what he's become since. You expect people to be as reasonable as you. It doesn't work that way."

"You let him just walk out'a there," Voight repeated, testily.

"We had no idea. None of us saw the van because it was around back."

"How much of a start does he have?" asked Voight.

"Five, maybe ten minutes."

Kelly Moore, from the middle of the back seat, leaned forward over Hector Garcia's stooped back and tapped Nick on the shoulder. "Guess what? This turkey's already opened a second bottle of cough syrup."

When Nick craned around, Hector Garcia raised his head enough to give him a stupid grin. Hector obviously was feeling no pain.

"If he throws up on us—" Sanford Wilcox started.

"You'll sit in it," Voight snapped. "I'm not stopping."

Nick rolled his eyes to take a look at the speedometer. "You don't have to kill us on the highway. Ruhle and Bettis are willing to do it for you. For Chris'sakes, Larry, slow it a little."

Voight appeared to grit his teeth. "Fucker's got my wife and kid."

"What's your plan? Run 'em off the road? They'll riddle this car with bullets."

"You've got a gun," snapped Voight.

"You take it," Nick said, "if you think it's gonna do you much good."

"Sounds like you're scared, Nick."

Nick knew he was. Scared, angry, frustrated, helpless, and pissed off at himself for getting brain-lock and allowing Kelly Voight to be anywhere near this group, he gritted his teeth. "I admit it," he said after a moment. "Martin Ruhle scares me. Clarence Bettis scares me, too, because he's unpredictable. And you're scaring the shit out of me. I'd like to live long enough to stop them."

"You are driving awfully fast, Dr. Voight," Kelly offered from the back seat.

"Great," Voight muttered. "News bulletin from the peanut gallery."

"Only person in the car who's not scared is Hector," Hal Ryerson said. "And he's in another galaxy."

Voight stomped harder on the accelerator.

"I think I know where they're going," he grumbled. "I might be wrong. I can't see the van. We don't know if they're still on the interstate."

Nick said a silent prayer that the state police would stop the van somewhere along their route.

"What did we get to eat?" Hal Ryerson asked from the back seat. He rattled a sack, could be heard opening it and pawing into it. "Take my mind off how low we're flying."

"That's it," Kelly said.

"Nothing here but potato chips and Cokes."

"What else do you need but chips and Cokes?" asked Kelly.

"Shit," Sanford Wilcox said.

"Next time I'll do the shopping," Ryerson said, handing a couple bags of chips toward the front seat.

"What wrong with these people?" Kelly asked. Nick looked around to see her using her teeth to rip into a bag. "Here, Dr. Voight. I opened one for you."

Hoisting his right arm and crooking his elbow, Voight took the bag and put it on the console between him and Nick. He took out a single chip and bit into it. He said, "They might be on a different road, maybe cut over to Forty-one South. Where the hell are they?"

"This is the fastest way south," Nick said. "They're still ahead of us."

Voight weaved them into the passing lane, whipping around two other cars that were going a slow seventy-five or eighty. Nick saw the speedometer waggle above ninety again, shuddered, and said, "This won't help, Larry, not even if you pull up behind them. Ease up, man. You want to out-think him, not out-race him."

"Nick's right, Dr. Voight," Sanford Wilcox said. "Last thing you want is to get stopped by a highway patrol."

"I haven't seen any cops," said Voight.

As if on cue, Nick heard the siren. He turned his head to look through the rear window and saw the approaching blue lights. The patrol car was bearing toward them.

"No!" shouted Voight, looking into the rearview mirror.

"Pull over, Larry," Nick said.

"Maybe we can outrun him."

"Fuck that. Don't even try. We'll all spend time in jail, and you won't see your wife and boy again. Pull over and be nice."

"Hey, mon," Hector said from the rear, "don't let me geet arrested. I go to jail an' they forgeet about me."

Cursing, Voight brought the Chrysler to a halt on the shoulder, and the patrol car pulled in behind. As he watched through the mirror, Voight tapped his fingers nervously against the wheel. "What's taking him so long?"

"He's calling your license plate in," Nick told him. "See if there are any outstanding warrants on this car and if he'll have to shoot us. Everybody keep cool."

Voight tapped the steering wheel and muttered curses for what seemed a long time.

Finally, the highway patrolman appeared just behind Voight's window and tapped it with his knuckles. His right hand was down out of sight near his hip.

Voight lowered the window and said, "Yes, yes, yes."

"Registration and driver's license please." The young cop wore mirrored, blue sunglasses. He peered in at the passengers. "You're packed in like sardines."

Voight drew out his billfold and extracted his license. He lowered a visor to unclip the car's registration slip.

Kelly leaned forward, over Hector Garcia's back, and gave the officer a bright, friendly, smile. The cop was looking at her from behind his reflector glasses all right. Nick saw a slight twitch at the corner of the young man's mouth.

The cop peered a little closer, realizing there was someone hunched down in front of Kelly. "What's wrong with him?" he asked.

That tears it, Nick thought.

"He lost something," Hal Ryerson said, his own body hunched forward to shield Hector's bloody ass, which, fortunately, was opposite the cop's view.

"Yeah, his earring," Sanford Wilcox said, and gave the impression of peering hard at the floorboard.

"He's wearing his earring," the cop announced.

"Hey! You're wearing your earring," Wilcox told Hector.

"My other earring, mon," Hector said.

"Sit up on the seat," the cop told him.

Hector forced a grin and, with Ryerson's and Wilcox's assistance, eased and squeezed himself onto the back seat between them. His grin was frozen in place as the sweat popped out in huge drops on his forehead.

The cop stared at him for a few seconds, then leaned down to look in at Kelly again. She gave him another smile and a little wave. Trying not to be too obvious about looking at her, the cop backed away, taking Voight's license and registration slip with him.

"What now?" asked Voight.

"We wait till he tells us what," Nick said.

"I can't handle this."

"You better handle it, Larry."

"Jesus," Hector groaned from the back seat. "I can't seet here."

"Sit!" Wilcox and Ryerson snapped at him in unison.

The cop returned and handed Voight the speeding ticket along with the registration and license. He peered in at Kelly, who was smiling back at him. "How old are you?" he asked.

"Eighteen," Kelly said. "In a few days," she added.

"Is one of these men your father?"

"He is," Kelly said, tapping Nick on the shoulder. "He's a helluva daddy. We're on vacation."

Nick could tell that the cop didn't know whether to believe her or not, but Kelly kept giving him that disarming smile.

"Know how fast you were going?" the officer said to Voight. "I clocked you at ninety. I could arrest you and impound your car. But since you're tourists from Indiana—" he shrugged a little, tilting his head toward the smiling Kelly, "—I'll put it down as eighty. Anyway, it's going to cost you. You can pay in court or mail the payment in with this envelope I'm giving you. You have seventy-two hours to pay the fine, or there'll be a warrant issued on this car. I suggest you don't try to leave the state without paying the ticket."

"We'll pay it. I promise," Voight said between clenched teeth as he stared straight ahead.

"Yeah, well, you slow down." He looked in at Kelly again, and this time he did smile back. "Where you headed?"

"Naples."

"We like our tourists to get to their destinations safely." The officer looked in at Kelly, who smiled back and gave him a little finger-waggly wave. The cop's smile widened in return. He tipped his cap before returning to his patrol cal.

When they were on the move again, Kelly said, "He was kind'a cute."

"Cute, my ass," Voight grumbled.

"Well, my ass is keeling me," Hector said from the rear. He had groaned and wiggled himself off the seat to resume his kneeling position on the floorboard.

"What else can go wrong?" muttered Voight.

"I'd keep it under seventy-five," Nick suggested, watching the speedometer indicator make its way to eighty-five with no signs of backing off.

"Hell with that," Voight said.

The sound of a siren drew upon them again.

Nick twisted around and looked back. The flashing blue lights of the state car were pulling up close arrears.

Voight looked in the mirror. His mouth dropped open, and his eyes glazed over. He pounded the steering wheel with one fist. "No!—no!—no!"

"You are one stupid mon," Hector Garcia said.

"Ditto that," Nick said. "It's the same cop." He saw the blanched look on Voight's face but also the pinched-lip anger. For a second, he was afraid Voight might try to floor it this time. "For God's sakes, stop for the man."

"Maybe he'll arrest us," Ryerson said, sounding a bit hopeful. "I understand prisoners get decent meals."

Voight expelled a long breath as he finally stopped once more on the shoulder. He appeared about ready to cry. Nick looked around again.

Yes, it was the same, young, highway patrolman in his same, reflective sunglasses. He slammed the door of his own car and strode purposefully toward them.

"I don't think I'm cute enough to get you out of this one, Dr. Voight," Kelly said in earnest.

"Out!" the officer snapped, his hand hovering near the grip of his holstered weapon. "Everybody out of the car—now! Line up on the other side. You—!" He jabbed a finger at Larry Voight. "Bring your registration and driver's license. This car's being impounded."

"Can't you just give me another ticket?" asked Voight.

"Your second violation in six minutes, I don't think so," the cop told him. "I want all of you to line up out here, and I want to see everyone's I.D. Then you can wait in your car for the tow."

The cop stood at the rear as everyone managed to unload. He looked at Ryerson and Wilcox in a peculiar way as they assisted Hector Garcia backward and out. Hector still couldn't straighten up.

"That man's stoned," the cop said.

"On cough syrup," Nick said, keeping his own hands apart where the cop could see them.

"I geet shot in the butt," Hector moaned.

The young cop recoiled perceptibly, his hand hovering closer to his holstered pistol. "You got <u>what</u>?"

Hector turned around and showed him.

This was almost too much for the cop. Here he had unloaded a bunch of touristy-looking people from Indiana, including one good-looking girl, along with one skinny Cuban with a bullet hole in the ass of his bloody pants. He appeared ready to draw his gun.

"Don't move," Larry Voight's voice croaked.

Nick realized what had happened and shut his eyes.

Voight had slid over and stepped from the car with the registration and license in one hand, his other hand momentarily out of sight behind him. When he brought that hand around, shaking, it held Paulo Garcia's pistol and was pointed at the cop.

"Jesus Christ!" the cop said.

"Put your hands up."

The cop thrust both hands up in the air.

"No," Nick snapped. "Put 'em down."

The cop lowered his hands.

"Up," Voight said.

"Don't shoot," the cop said, "but make up your minds."

"Larry," Nick said to Voight, "we're standing here on a highway holding a gun on a patrolman with his hands in the air. Won't that draw some attention?"

"Okay, okay," Voight said. "Down."

"But please don't reach for your gun," Nick said to the patrolman. He was more worried about one of his party getting shot than for the cop's safety.

The officer, bug-eyed, was staring at Voight's shaky hand holding the gun. "For God's sakes, can you point it down or up?"

"Just—just shut up while I think," Voight snapped.

"You are in big fucking trouble," the officer said.

"I can't argue that," Nick said.

"You don't have to do this. You're making a big mistake."

"Wow! This is radical," Kelly Moore said.

Ryerson and Wilcox looked at each other. "Radical?"

"Stupid is more like it," Nick said. Hell, he was resigned now. They all were going to jail.

"I better take hees gun," Hector said.

"You move one step, Hector," Nick told him, "and I'll kick your sore ass."

They couldn't simply stand there like that, so Nick had to make a move. He stepped around and a little behind the young man to remove the 9mm service pistol. This he held down along his pants leg. "Okay, Larry," he said. "You got us into this. Now what?"

"I don't know," Voight said, lowering Hector's weapon to keep it out of sight from passing motorists. "I guess we get back in the car and go."

"Not that simple," Nick told him. With his free hand he patted the cop down. He stooped and patted around the cop's ankles. The young man was not wearing a holstered back-up piece. "Take off your belt slowly and carefully," he commanded.

"We're wasting time," Voight said.

"Be careful with that gun," the cop said. "Your hand's shaking."

"I guess you better take off your shoes too," Nick said to the officer. "Larry, open your trunk."

Voight looked incredulous. "We're taking him with us?"

"What else? We're looking at ten years anyway. If we handcuff him inside his car, he'll use his radio. Handcuff him outside somehow, and somebody else will see him and call highway patrol. Either way, we'll be hunted down before we get much further. We have to take his car, too."

"Come on," the cop pleaded. "Not in the trunk. You know how goddam hot it is here. What do you want—fried highway patrolman?"

"He's got a point," Wilcox said.

"He can sit next to me," Kelly offered with a smile. "He's cute. But ask him if he's gay."

Nick considered. "If we put him in the trunk, we'll have to stop every few miles to give him air."

The cop said, "I like the young lady's suggestion better. And, for her informatioin, I am not gay. I think she's cute, too." Then, apparently for the first time, he looked closely at Sanford Wilcox. "Hey, I know you. You're Ichabod!"

Wilcox stared in astonishment.

"From S.O.B.," the cop said. "In Indianapolis? I graduated there ten years ago. You're Ichabod, the principal."

"I hate that name," Wilcox groaned. He watched the patrolman carefully remove his sunglasses. "I don't remember—"

"Nyles. Richard Nyles," the young officer said. He looked at Ryerson. "And you were the assistant principal. I can't recall your last name. Fat Hal Something."

"Fat?" Ryerson retorted. "Jesus, that what you guys called me? Yeah, I know you now." He extended his hand toward the young cop but then, on second thought, withdrew it. "Dickie Nyles—with a 'y'."

"Pul—leeze, not Dickie." Officer Nyles slipped an embarrassed look at Kelly when she giggled.

"Oh, this is a dandy little reunion," Voight said, sourly. "We don't have time for this. Get in the trunk."

"That'd kill me," the cop said. "You wouldn't do that to another S.O.B. grad."

"Here's a better idea," Nick said. "He'll drive his own car, and I'll ride with him. Hector in back in handcuffs."

"Hey, mon—" Hector started to whine.

"You follow us, Larry," Nick continued, "until we get to Naples. We'll cut off to U.S. Forty-one, and then you take the lead."

"Follow you? I don't like it."

"Either that, or you go the rest of the way without me, the officer, and Hector. Kelly, too. And I'll keep the guns. You and Hal and Sanford can do what you want."

"Nick! My wife and son—"

"I know," Nick said. "I want 'em back safe. But we've stepped over the line of serious criminal activity. If we live through this, I see a lot of years ahead of us in a Florida prison. That's if you don't kill everybody on the road first. You'll get ten, maybe twenty miles further before you'd wind up with a state police escort straight to jail. That's the deal, Larry."

"Dammit, Nick, I'm holding a gun."

Nick calmly reached out and took it from his hand. Voight didn't resist.

"Now you're not."

Voight cursed, turned to stride away, and came back. "I don't have a choice. Promise me you won't bring any more cops into it, and let's get the hell on our way."

"Okay," Nick agreed. "As long as you follow us."

"This mean I can keep my shoes on?" Nyles asked, hopefully.

"Can I ride with you, Mr. Cotton?" Kelly asked.

"No, you stay with these guys," Nick told her. "I don't want too many in the police car." He turned to the officer. "Now you can put your cuffs on this skinny prick and we'll go."

A half hour later, Richard "Dickie" Nyles looked around at Hector Garcia handcuffed in the back seat of his patrol car. Hector had made himself as comfortable as he could by drawing his legs up and lying on his side. Officer Nyles kept both hands on the steering wheel as directed. He glanced in the rearview mirror at the Chrysler behind them.

"You don't have to keep the gun pointed at me," he told Nick.

"I don't know how much you believe, or what you might try," Nick said. "I know it sounds crazy, but that's exactly what happened. Everything since I arrived at the airport."

"I believe you," Nyles said. "Let me call it in. We'll get some guys after that van."

"I'd like to. It would be the one smart thing I've done, but I promised Larry. He's about nuts over this, and I can't blame him. I don't want him breaking too many more laws."

"Kidnapping a police officer. Holding him hostage. Fleeing with a wounded felon. You got a pretty good list going."

"I'm hoping you'll decide to help us."

"Let me see if I got it," said Nyles. "This guy Frank is not Frank, he's the other one named Martin—?"

"Ruhle," said Nick.

"And he murdered the real Frank and another buddy a long time ago over money, hid the money—"

"Voight's wife hid the money," Nick said, "before she was his wife. Then she ran away. The money's what they're going after."

"But is she or isn't she in it with this Frank—I mean, Martin Ruhle?"

"Negative," Nick said. "That's where the son comes in."

Driving in silence for several seconds, Nyles appeared to be mulling it over. He said, "You think they'll kill the woman and the boy."

"I'm afraid of it," said Nick. "If Martin Ruhle gets what he wants, he won't need them anymore. Without your help, we don't have anybody who's a match for Ruhle and Bettis."

"What's your plan if we catch up with them?"

"Plan?" That made Nick laugh without humor. "I haven't a clue, Dickie. But I know Larry Voight. He'll try reason first, even pleading for his family's lives. He has some crazy notion of ransoming them. Ruhle's not interested in whatever money Larry can raise, and certainly not in waiting for it. He's going all the way. It's that simple."

"Let me call it in, Mr. Cotton. It's your only hope." He looked over at Nick. "Think about that young girl—Kelly. You said she's your responsibility. You could get yourself killed trying to save her."

"That's where you come in, Dickie. That's where you can help. Once we find them—if we find them—I want you to take Kelly away in your car. I'll keep your gun, but I'll trust you to get her out. Then you can call all the buddies you want."

Nyles sighed, checked his rearview mirror again, and said, "Break your promise to Mr. Voight."

"That would be the smart thing," said Nick. "But it's his family, and he feels it's up to him to do something. I don't agree, but if we cut him out and something happens to his family anyway—? You know the police can't guarantee their safety."

"Nobody can."

"And if I were in his place, right now, I'd be doing the same thing," Nick said. "I'd do anything to help them and blow over anybody else in my way. So would you."

"If I reach for my radio, I don't think you'll shoot me," Nyles said.

"I'll shoot the radio," Nick told him. "The bullet might ricochet and hit you. Neither of us would like that."

"I can't go on not responding to calls."

"Yes, you can."

Nyles puckered his lips and sighed. "We'll be in Naples soon."

In the back seat, Hector Garcia snored.

22

Outside of Naples, the two-car procession exited the interstate to get onto the Tamiami Trail and head eastward. Dickie Nyles had slowed the cruiser down to allow Larry Voight's Chrysler to pass and take the lead. Voight made some indecipherable hand signals to Nyles and Nick Cotton as he went around.

"He's a dammed fool," Nyles said. The highway patrol tactical-band's dispatcher's voice broke in, peppered with static as it had been for some time. "They're gonna wonder why I don't answer. Mr. Cotton, we need to utilize all possible resources. You know I'm right."

He was right, Nick knew, but it didn't alter the circumstances. "Just drive, Dickie," Nick told him. He looked over his shoulder. "You still alive, Hector?"

"I need a doctor," Hector moaned. "I theenk I'm creepled. Stop for more peels."

Nyles glanced in the rearview mirror. "What's he been taking?"

"About three bottles of pain-killer," Nick said. "I don't see how he's conscious."

"You fucks don' care if I'm creepled," Hector said. When that brought no response, he put his head back down and started humming.

The highway was surrounded by swamp. They passed ranger stations and some beat-up looking Everglades country stores with battered tin signs, miles of sawgrass and islands of palms, even spotting a few gators sunning on banks next to the road.

Nyles peered ahead at the Chrysler. "That man's gonna try to find a turnoff he's only seen once, and from the other direction?"

"That's what he says. How about it, Dickie? You'll take care of Kelly for me?"

"Sure. You can give me my gun. I'll go along."

"Later, maybe." Nick smiled at him. "You're still the idealistic young cop."

"We catch up to those guys, I'll need my gun."

"Got to hand it to you, Dickie," Nick said. "You didn't panic when Larry pointed the pistol at you."

"Pissed me off," Nyles said, "but I'm not stupid. I was scared he'd shoot by accident."

The two cars weaved around and into the lines of traffic on the highway. Most other motorists slowed when they saw the police car following the Chrysler. In both directions there was a steady stream of RV's, campers, rental cars, SUV's, pickup trucks, many of the vehicles towing boats. But, so far, Nick hadn't been able to spot Marilyn Voight's van.

"Tell me about Kelly," Nyles said. "Is she a cheerleader? She looks like one."

"Captain of the cheerleading squad." Nick raised his brows at the young officer. "Forget it, Dickie. She's seventeen years old."

"She said eighteen."

"She said in a few days. A few days to her is actually a few months."

Nyles grinned from the side of his mouth. "Hell, I'm not thirty yet."

Nick liked the young cop. Nyles was smart enough to grasp this odd situation and not be too big an ass about it. And Nick sincerely believed that Nyles would look out for

Kelly. He also believed that the officer sympathized with Dr. Voight's plight. He wished he could hand over the gun and simply ask for Nyles's assistance. But the first thing he would do, as a cop, would be to stop the leading car and put everybody under arrest. And that would leave Marilyn and Mark Voight in Ruhle's hands.

They rode without speaking for the next several miles. Ahead of them, Voight left the highway when they got to Ochopee and found a service station. Dickie pulled his patrol car in behind the Chrysler and stopped. Nick and he watched the occupants up ahead unload and trek to the restrooms.

Hector raised his head and announced, "I need to peese."

Nick looked around at the man, who was trying to push himself up on the back seat. Hector raised his manacled hands and stuck them between Nick and Dickie Nyles.

"We'll have to walk him between us," Nick said.

Dickie nodded. "He stays cuffed."

"Aw, mon—" Hector moaned.

"Hey, Chico," Nyles said to him, "it's the only way you go anywhere. Or else you hold it."

Nick and the officer eased Hector from the car. Nick tucked the gun in his belt and looked at Nyles. Nyles, reading the question in Nick's mind, said, "Okay, I won't try for it."

They supported Hector, one on each side, to the men's room. Then they flanked him, supporting him at the urinal, as he dawdled with his dick. Finally they propped Hector against the wall and took care of their own business. Keeping their eyes on Hector, they washed their hands. Back outside, they walked Hector, groaning with every step, to the cruiser and got him inside it.

Nyles caught the eye of one of the station attendants who was gawking from inside and motioned to him. The young attendant came out.

Nick described Marilyn's van as best he could. He told the young man there would be three males and one female in it and tried to describe all of them. The attendant pursed his lips and shook his head.

When Dickie and Nick walked to the Chrysler, Larry Voight was replacing the pump-handle and motioning for Kelly, Wilcox, and Ryerson to get inside.

"Nick," he said, taking Cotton a little away from the others, "I'm so scared I got the shakes. I don't know if I can find that turnoff. Not from this direction."

Nick had never seen Voight in this condition. The man actually <u>was</u> shaking. He said, "Maybe we'll have to go past and double back. Can you find it that way?"

"I don't know," Voight said, miserably. "It'll be dark in a couple hours. I was following Marilyn's directions, and that was two years ago. I turned when she told me to turn. As I recall, I don't think there was a sign. She had me drive real slow before we got to it."

"Can you remember any kind of landmark?"

Voight appeared to be thinking hard. "We were coming westward. I stopped at a gas station to take a leak. I remember because I got out of the car and Marilyn didn't. She looked thoughtful, and I asked her why. Then she came alive, gave me a smile, and said, 'Go take care of business, honey.' See, I remember that real clear, but afterwards—" He stopped to inhale, furrowing his brows. "I remember we came on a little ways after that, not too far. Five miles? Ten?" He shrugged.

Nick looked toward the sun lowering in the western sky and swatted a mosquito. An hour or less until dark, he figured, maybe less. If night fell, Martin Ruhle would be doubly hard to locate. Nick shook his head. "Larry, it's time to bring the police in on this."

"No!" Voight snapped. "I won't take that chance. I have to talk to Martin myself. I'll look for anything familiar. If that doesn't work, I'll find that gas station, Nick. We'll double back from there."

Nick got into the police car where Dickie Nyles waited behind the wheel. Hector Garcia, handcuffed in back, lay on his side humming softly. Nyles looked at Nick.

"He's not sure he can find the turnoff," Nick said.

Nyles nodded, looking up at the Chrysler pulling out. He started the engine and followed. "If it gets dark, we've lost 'em," he said, echoing Nick's thoughts. "What will he do then?"

"The man's desperate, Dickie," Nick said. "I'm letting him make the call because it's his family."

"Give me back my gun, Mr. Cotton."

"No."

Nyles leaned forward and reached down alongside the left side of his seat, his eyes locked on the road and the Chrysler ahead of them. When he straightened up, he showed Nick that he held a snub-nosed revolver in his left hand, not pointing it at Nick, simply showing him.

"You could have pulled that on me anytime," Nick said.

"Yeah," Nyles said. "I keep it under the seat as back-up. Reach over carefully and slip mine in the holster. Make sure the safety's on."

Nick did, saying, "The safety's always been on. Are we giving Dr. Voight a chance?"

"It's against procedure and even common sense."

But Nick noted that Dickie didn't hit the flashers or siren. "However it turns out, he'll thank you. I thank you now."

"I'm probably screwing up," Nyles said. "We'll play it Dr. Voight's way a little longer."

For the next several miles they followed as the Chrysler cut off of the main highway onto one access road after another. Voight would travel four or five miles each time, attempting to locate yet another isolated turn-off. Then it would be turning around and heading back to the highway.

Nyles motioned toward his radio. "This isn't getting us anywhere."

Nyles was right, of course. They could be out there all night chasing ghosts. It was past time to call in the cavalry, and Nick knew it. He said, "Next time he stops, tell him you're calling it in. Focus the search on the van only, not on us. Tell your guys why they should stop it and approach it carefully."

Nyles nodded. "I'll report it as a kidnapping, say I'm attempting to follow and approximately where we are, and they must radio me soon as there's a sighting." He started to reach for his radio until Nick touched his wrist.

Nick pointed ahead. "Let's see what's he up to."

At one, short, access road, the Chrysler pulled over and stopped, and Nyles eased the patrol car in behind. He and Nick got out.

Larry Voight was out of his car, peering toward a mangrove swamp. Dickie Nyles opened his trunk and brought his binoculars out for Voight to use. The forlorn-looking passengers from the Chrysler stood outside the car. In a few seconds, they all were slapping at their bare skins.

"Dammed mosquitoes," Hal Ryerson said. "Million's of 'em."

Kelly Moore was emitting little yelps while swatting her bare knees, legs, neck and arms. Nick Cotton smacked the back of his own neck.

Dickie Nyles brushed some of the insects away from his face. "Better get your bug repellent. Fast."

They all looked at each other.

"You came down here without repellent," Nyles said.

"We never thought about it," Sanford Wilcox said, doing contortions to keep the bugs off of him.

Nyles rummaged in his trunk and found a used can. He shook it and told them there wasn't much to go around. Single quick shots on the bare arms, legs, and necks of everyone and, hopefully, that would work. It was decided to start with Kelly. Nick noted that Nyles, bending down, was taking a long time spraying that so-called, 'single, quick shot' on Kelly's shapely legs. Then the can was empty.

"Oops," Nyles said and shrugged.

"I hope these mosquitoes bite your dick," Nick whispered to him.

"Everybody back in the car," shouted Wilcox, but by then the cars had been invaded too.

Nick saw the shine of tears welling in Larry Voight's eyes. "I thought maybe—" Voight started miserably and stopped. "I thought there was something familiar—"

"Dickie's calling the state police," Nick said. "We have to have help."

Voight shook his head stubbornly, blinking back tears of frustration. "Please don't," he pleaded to the officer. "Give me one more chance at it. Just one. I'll go to the gas station where Marilyn and I stopped and turn around. It can't be more than a few minutes from here."

"That's too much of a longshot," Nyles told him as he smacked a couple more feasting mosquitoes.

"Fifteen minutes," Nick said, and looked at Nyles. "Give him that, Dickie." He turned to Voight. "Fifteen minutes, Larry, then Dickie uses his radio."

"Oh, hell," Nyles said. "But that's it."

It wasn't more than another three or four miles eastward on the highway before the Chrysler swung off at another gas depot and turned around. Nyles used his blue lights until he could maneuver his cruiser in behind Voight's car. The only daylight left now was a thin, pink line visible through occasional breaks in the trees. Another ten minutes, and it would be pitch-black out in those swamps.

Following the Chrysler, they picked up speed. Bugs whacked off the windshield, and Nyles used his washer and wipers, smearing crème-colored streaks across the glass. They had their side windows down to blow the mosquitoes out of the car. Hector Garcia was quiet in the back seat.

Voight's taillights showed just ahead of them. Every so often, Voight would tap his brakes to slow down. Nick knew he was peering at turnoffs.

"It's time to make the call, Mr. Cotton," Nyles said.

Up ahead, Voight slowed, stopped, then eased into a right turn off the highway. A couple of slow miles further he hesitated at the mouth of a graveled, access road that led onto a wooden bridge over a black-water culvert. Voight would stop and start forward, then jerkily stop again. Nick had seen a number of unpaved access roads branching off this one. What little he could tell from their headlights, they weren't roads at all, more like beaten, tire-rutted pathways that went back into the forests and God knew where. Up ahead, Voight stopped at another one. Apparently, something had caught his attention. But after a few seconds, he started to pull forward again.

Nyles braked sharply.

"Keep going," Nick said, watching the Chrysler's taillights.

"Wait a minute. I saw something. A flash of something that might'a been metallic, maybe chrome." Nyles honked his horn and blinked his headlights. Farther up, Voight's brake lights glowed red. Nyles backed up and turned onto this access road. "It might be a vehicle."

"Might be?" Nick asked.

"Hell, for all I know it could be a snowy egret wearing a bracelet."

They eased over the old, wooden bridge that Nick couldn't even see and, on the other side, found the roadway considerably dark and overgrown. To Nick, it looked like a wilderness of mangrove and scrub. Through the open windows he could hear the marsh noises. In seconds, moving as slowly as it was, the police cruiser filled with buzzing mosquitoes. Then the headlights picked up the rear of the van with the Indiana license plate.

"There it is," Nyles said. "Is that the van?"

"That's it," Nick said.

Nyles switched off his headlights and eased forward slowly with his parking lights. Behind them, the headlights of Voight's car approached. Nyles waved his arm out the window until Voight slowed and stopped several feet behind the cruiser.

The van had been stopped on a very narrow shoulder, nearly nonexistent, and turned nose-first into a mass of shrubs and vines.

Before Nick opened the door, he said, "Dickie, I want you to get Kelly into this car and get the hell out'a here. Then call for help."

"I'll do that," Nyles said, "but you keep your friends right here. Don't try to be a hero. And don't go off into that swamp."

"We're not heroes," Nick said. He heard car doors slamming from the Chrysler in back. "Take Hector with you. I don't want him yelling to his buddies."

Larry Voight, illuminated in the headlights of the Chrysler, was already on foot, scampering past the police car toward the van.

"Stop that idiot," Nyles hissed. "Somebody might be hiding in the van ready to shoot."

"Larry!" Nick called as he leaned out on his side with his door open. The seat belt restrained him until he managed to unfasten it.

Nothing was stopping Larry Voight. He ran to the van and started scurrying around it, trying to see inside. Apparently nobody was waiting in ambush. At least, he wasn't getting himself shot.

Wilcox and Ryerson, swatting in futility at flying insects, were now beside the cruiser. Nick got out and caught Kelly Moore's arm as she started past. "I want you in the car with the officer, young lady," he told her. "You're getting out of here."

"Not," Kelly said, firmly. "Mark's here somewhere, and I came to help him."

"Kelly, I'm giving you an order."

"Is that a fact?" she said.

"Your parents told you to obey me."

"My parents tell me lots 'a things."

It made Nick grit his teeth in exasperation. "I'll handcuff you to Hector and lock you in the police car."

"Brute," Kelly sniffed.

"Nick!" Sanford Wilcox tugged at his arm. "We gotta catch Larry. He's gone off down the path."

"Shit!" Nick took two steps to the front of the car and peered. Voight was nowhere in sight, but he could hear his fading voice calling out, "Martin!" and "Marilyn!" The man had no light and was running into the swamp in pitch darkness. Nick turned to Wilcox and Ryerson. "You guys better wait in the car."

"And turn off those goddam headlights," Nyles added, getting out of the cruiser. "We're advertising our presence."

Ryerson reached in through the open window and switched off the Chrysler's headlights.

Nick was astonished, again, at how dark it suddenly was in this jungle. He shut his eyes and opened them, waiting for some semblance of night-vision to assert itself.

"Hey! Don't!" he heard Hal Ryerson's voice shout. Nick turned, confused by Ryerson's warning call, and looked around.

Kelly Moore was gone. The last sound of her voice was her shouting Mark's name.

Ryerson pointed off road. "She ran—that way. I couldn't grab her. I can't see her. I can't see anything."

Nick stared into the darkness, hearing her crashing out there. "Why didn't you stop her?" he flared at Dickie Nyles.

Nyles was leaning inside his car to replace the hand mike. "I called for back up, gave 'em the best directions I could. I'll meet 'em on the road. Where's the girl?"

"That's what I'm telling you. She ran into the swamp."

"Oh, shit," Nyles said. "Alone? Jesus Christ!"

Nick felt his shoulders sag. "I've never hit a woman in my life, but I swear to God I'm going to spank that kid."

"I'll go after her," Ryerson said and plunged off into the scrub before anybody could stop him.

"Hal! Goddammit!" Nick shouted.

"That wasn't too bright either," Nyles said. "There's alligators, rattlers, and moccasins in there, to say nothing of the sawgrass and quicksand."

"He's better off not knowing it," Sanford Wilcox said in dead earnestness.

Nick had had it with these people. He felt ready to sit down, cross his legs, swat mosquitoes, and give it up. This was fucking hopeless.

Instead, he went back to the cruiser and withdrew Garcia's pistol from under the seat where he had placed it. He said to Nyles, "You got your flashlight?"

"In my hand."

"Find Kelly."

"On my way," Nyles said. "You guys stay put. Don't go running off anywhere. Take my word for it, and I'm nowhere near being a skilled swamp-rat. People die in places like this." He clicked on his flashlight. "Soon as I find the kid, I'm calling for help again. Maybe we can get a helicopter out here with searchlights."

It got very quiet, as well as very dark, around the three vehicles.

"Nick," Wilcox said softly, "what're we gonna do about Dr. Voight and Hal? God knows where they are."

"Exactly," Nick said. "I sure as hell don't."

"Looks like just the two of us, Nick," Wilcox said, looking in the direction Nyles had taken after Kelly and Ryerson.

Nick sighed. Hell, he couldn't stand here, getting eaten alive by mosquitoes, and not do <u>anything</u>. He felt his way alongside Voight's Chrysler and opened the door. The interior light came on. He rummaged under the seat and in the glove box, looking for another flashlight. He didn't find one. The key had been taken from the ignition, probably habit, by Larry Voight. The small interior light was no help in seeing anything outside the car. The Chrysler was several yards behind the cruiser which was parked in closer behind the van. Nick decided he had no choice so he turned on the Chrysler's headlights again.

"I'm blinded," Wilcox yelped.

"Shut your eyes, Sanford."

Guiding himself by the direction of the headlights, Nick tried the van and was relieved to find it unlocked. There was no flashlight on or around the front seat, but, when he felt the ignition, he was surprised to find Marilyn's rabbit's foot key-chain in it. That could be Martin Ruhle's mistake. Nick took out the key and pocketed it. Then he went to and searched the police cruiser.

He removed that key which Nyles had left in the ignition. He looked at Hector Garcia's silhouette, Hector sitting up straight now in the backseat with his wrists cuffed in front of him. Nick took Dickie's key to open the trunk. The Chrysler's headlights were a help here. In the cruiser's trunk, Nick found another, larger, box-shaped, battery-operated light with a wire handle. He also felt and withdrew two road flares and tucked them into his belt.

The box-lantern worked.

Nick added Dickie's key to Marilyn's in his pocket. The only vehicle key he didn't have was the Chrysler's, which would be in Larry Voight's pocket. If he could get hold of that one, it might just mean stranding Martin Ruhle and Clarence T. Bettis. They wouldn't be driving out.

"I want you to stay here, Sanford," Nick told Wilcox. "Get in the car and wait. You can keep an eye on Hector. I might have to move fast."

"Where you going?" asked Wilcox.

"I'll take the path Larry followed."

"Screw Hector, and I'm not waiting here in the dark," Wilcox said. "These bugs are killing me. I'm right behind you."

A hundred feet further on, the road became nothing more than a slightly beaten-down trail, indiscernible in the dark and barely discernible by the lantern light. Deep ruts in the pathway, probably long-ago tire marks, showed soggy and soft. Every grunt, rustling of brush, and bird call gave Nick a start. This was totally insane. Worse, he and Wilcox were probably lost, too. The lantern was useful on the path, if they still were on the right path, but the thick jungle on all sides looked impenetrable.

Behind Nick, Sanford Wilcox got his feet tangled in vines and fell with a curse. Nick had to go back and help him to his feet.

"Yuk!" Wilcox said.

"Stop wiping your hands on me," Nick whispered to him. "Try being quiet."

"I heard something," Wilcox whispered back.

"I hear lots 'a things," Nick replied softly, "and I can't tell one goddam noise from another." He paused for a moment, listening to the buzzing of the insects, and then the hooting of an owl. "Sanford, we're crazier'n hell. We're in the wrong playground, and it's in somebody else's backyard."

"I'm swallowing bugs, too," whined Wilcox. "Every time I breathe, I inhale the little suckers."

"Keep your mouth shut. Blow little puffls of air to clear 'em from your face."

Wilcox remained silent for only a few seconds. "Where do you think Larry is?"

"Lost—like us."

"Nick, you think there's really poisonous snakes out here?"

"I'd bet your salary on it," Nick said. He raised an arm to shut Wilcox up, and Wilcox bumped into him from behind. Nick listened intently. He shined the light in all directions. "Sanford, you're slowing me down. You should turn around and go back."

"I don't much like that idea," Wilcox said.

"Take it slow and easy between the trees and you can find your way back to the car."

"Without a light? No way, Nick. I'm right behind you."

Well, hell, he was a grown man. But Nick could feel their situation, which was bad now, deteriorating rapidly.

A few minutes later, sliding, pawing their way through creepers, brush, and sawgrass, Nick heard Wilcox say, "This is awful. I'm itching all over. This stuff's cutting my legs to pieces."

"You wanted to be here," Nick reminded him.

"Nick! I think I'm sinking in quicksand. I think I'm going under."

Nick clambered back to him and shined the light. Wilcox was ankle-deep in muck, probably a peat quagmire. The ground had looked solid, but that was deceptive. The light also showed that Wilcox's legs, bare below his touristy shorts, looked badly bitten. Nick took the man's arm to help him pull himself free. Each foot that Wilcox freed made a loud, slurping noise.

"Okay now?" Nick asked him.

"My shoes are ruined."

"Hold it right there!" a voice said.

Nick and Wilcox froze. Nick inched his fingers toward the gun in his belt.

"Don't touch it, Nick." The voice belonged to Martin Ruhle. A flashlight beam played along Nick and Wilcox. The next time Ruhle spoke, he was closer behind them. "Thumb and fingers only, Nick. You know what I mean. Hand the gun back slowly. In case you're wondering, I got mine pointed right at your spine."

Carefully, Nick removed the gun and extended it between thumb and forefinger out to one side. It was taken from his hand.

"What'cha got in your belt there, Nick? Dynamite sticks?"

"Flairs," Nick said.

"Hand 'em back. Same as the gun—one at a time."

Nick did.

"Okay. Set down your light an' turn around." Nick did, and the flashlight beam was in his face. Ruhle said, "I was half expecting you, Nick. But who the fuck's this character?"

Wilcox tried to square his drooping shoulders. "My name is Sanford Wilcox. I am principal of Sylvester Overton Barton High School."

"You don't say," grunted Ruhle.

Wilcox actually started to explain. "Sylvester Overton—"

"Don't repeat it," snapped Ruhle. "Once through that's enough. Am I missing something, Nick? What's this guy supposed to do for you?"

Nick shrugged.

Ruhle laughed. "I been hearin' you turkeys at least a quarter mile. Well, now that you're here, let's join the others."

23

"Joining the others" meant being prodded along an almost non-existent pathway through the heavily wooded, ebony swamp, Sanford Wilcox, carrying the battery lantern as ordered, up front, turning, slowing, moving according to Martin Ruhle's instructions, Nick Cotton right behind Wilcox, keeping his hands, fingers laced, on top of his head as warned, with Ruhle and his flashlight bringing up the rear. They trudged forward in the darkness, often tripping, stumbling, except for Martin Ruhle, who seemed not only more adept but more confident in the jungle surroundings.

As well as keeping close as possible to Wilcox, Nick concentrated on trying to estimate distance covered from the point where Ruhle had intercepted them. Somewhere in his guesstimate, between a hundred and two hundred yards, the path widened again and freed itself from the trees. A splashing of water caught Nick's ear.

At the water's edge, another flashlight beam welcomed them, and Nick heard Clarence Bettis's curse that sounded both surprised and triumphant. The lantern light illuminated some of the clearing.

"Don't shoot him," Ruhle told Bettis. "But I hope you learned enough to keep your light and your eyes on him."

Turning sideways and slowly lowering his arms, Nick got his first look at Ruhle in Bettis's light. The man's clothes were soaked and pasted to his skin, his hands and nails blackened with sticky dirt, his face streaked.

Bettis waved his light over at Wilcox. "Who he?" he asked, thickly, making a slight whistling sound through his damaged nose.

"He's the something of something or other. You—whatever you are," Ruhle said to Wilcox, "set the light down and stand over there. Keep your mouth shut."

"I can thy him," Bettis offered.

Nick looked at Bettis's face in the lantern light. Clarence had removed the bulky bandage. His nose was terribly swollen, multi-colored, and slightly flattened. When he breathed, he sucked air through his mouth. His clothing, in contrast to Ruhle's, appeared to be dry except for the dark perspiration stains under his arms and on his upper chest.

"Later," Ruhle replied in response to Bettis's suggestion. "He ain't going nowhere, and he's not dangerous. But Nick here—" he chuckled, "—I just ain't sure. So tell me, Nick. Is this it? I doubt if you got the crip out here in a wheelchair. What about the little girl?"

Nick didn't answer him.

"You're parked back by the van," Ruhle said. "Have to be, am I right? So, either you didn't bring her, or you left her there. Smart either way."

In the dim lighting, Nick Cotton saw the others. Larry Voight, Marilyn Voight, and Mark, hands bound behind them, were propped in sitting positions against the bases of cypress trees. Larry Voight had bled from the corner of his mouth and showed a discolored lower lip. The blood had run down from his lips to his chin and dripped onto his shirt. Marilyn Voight, her clothes also wet and clinging, her hair stringy, her face grimy, stared hatefully at Martin Ruhle. Mark Voight, dry except for his sweat-soaked shirt, his hair matted, was sobbing. Insects darted around all of them, making them turn their heads and spit the little buggers away from noses and mouths.

Clarence Bettis glared at Nick. He said to Ruhle in his high-pitched nasal whistle, "Wanna know where he lef' that l'il girl? I'll make him tell uth."

"Really?" Ruhle said with some slight amusement. "What you will do, Clarence, is not get close to him."

"I can thoot him in the knees."

"Not yet. Let's make sure the party's all here before we start popping guns." Ruhle poked Nick with the barrel of his weapon. "But if you make any sudden moves, Nick, don't think I won't shoot you."

Nick hadn't the slightest doubt of that.

Bettis waved a swarm of insects away from his head, careful not to touch his nose. "Why you mething with thith thon of a bith?"

Ruhle looked at him. "You can't get it, can you, Clarence. We got two people here, Marilyn and Nick, who ain't cryin' or beggin'. You don't appreciate how I like that. Look at her." He turned his single light beam onto Marilyn. "She's a fucking mess, but she's still beautiful. She hates me, but you won't see a tear. If I offered her a chance to fight me, single-handed, she'd jump at it. That's the kind'a woman she is, Clarence. It's why I love 'er. I could cut her tits off, and she won't tell us where she hid the money."

"I told you, you asshole," Marilyn said.

"I don't think so, kid. How's the finger, Mark?"

Mark groaned between sobs.

"Clarence broke one of his fingers," Ruhle said to Nick. "His mother still won't talk. 'Course, he's got seven more fingers and two thumbs. We'll take 'em one at a time. You can hear how they crack when Clarence breaks one."

"Don't hurt him anymore," Marilyn said, her voice catching. "I can't tell you anything else."

"That's what we'll find out. I figure if we go through each of the boy's digits, and you ain't changed your story, you tol' the truth. Disappointing, but—" Ruhle let the thought drop.

"I take it you didn't find the money," Nick said.

Ruhle cast his flashlight beam briefly out toward the swamp. Out a ways, on the calm, black water, Nick detected a silhouette that could have been a shack on stilts. "Nothing there. That's how we got so fucking wet and dirty."

"Somebody else found it," Marilyn said. "Or it got washed away. Who knows? That was a long time ago, Martin."

"It's what we'll find out," Ruhle said. "Here's another idea for you. Maybe we'll make the skinny guy over there wade out in the water and splash around a little. Stir up a gator or two." He turned his light on the ashen-faced Sanford Wilcox, who had been brushing at insects. "Like to see that, Marilyn? Gator take his leg off? Maybe drag him under and hold him down till he drowns? That's how they do it. Am I right, Clarence?"

"You're rith," Bettis whistled.

"Nick—?" Wilcox moaned.

Nick gave him a look and a shake of his head to shut him up. At the moment there wasn't a thing Nick could do to help poor Ichabod, who was petrified with fear. Wilcox had stopped swatting bugs and had begun shivering. What interested Nick more, at the moment, was their location. It appeared that they were situated on a jetty, surrounded on three sides by water. One way in, the trail they had come, and the same way out.

Ruhle took a stick of bug-repellent from Bettis and stroked it on his forearms and neck. The others were not so fortunate. Insects buzzed around their faces and in their hair. Even in the dimness, Nick could discern the welts on Marilyn's and Mark's faces. Ruhle turned his flashlight onto Larry Voight. "Or how 'bout Larry there? That do it, Marilyn? Send your precious husband out as bait? You could listen to him scream."

"Do what you want with me," Voight said. "Let her and the boy go, Martin. You can't be that cold-blooded."

"Hey, that's good. Beg some more. Appeal to my sympathy."

Nick nodded to himself. The son-of-a-bitch was enjoying this. The man was truly sadistic. Larry Voight just didn't get it. Reason wasn't going to work with Martin Ruhle. Nick had tried to tell him that.

He looked from one of their captors to the other. Both had guns pointed, both kept their distance from him. If it got down to it, and it looked like it might, Nick would have to go for Ruhle. The knowledge that he would certainly be shot, probably several times, was not appealing, but—if he was strong enough to stay on his feet—strong enough to grab hold of Ruhle, maybe drag the man down into the swamp water with him—? Oh yeah, one hell of a good plan. Of course, that would leave Bettis to murder the other witnesses.

"Clarence," Ruhle said, "break another one of Mark's fingers."

"No!" cried Marilyn.

Mark Voight choked out a sudden racking sob and cried, "No! No! Please!"

Bettis waggled his light in Nick's direction. "Lemme break hith fingers."

"And how do you propose to do that, Clarence?" Ruhle asked, mildly. "Without getting close to him? Twice you got close to Nick, and twice you got your head handed to you. You ought'a see yourself. Think you'd learn something. But if you wanna try, I'll take your gun and you can go over and break all his fingers you want." He paused in the silence. "What's'a matter, Clarence?"

"I am gonna thoot the thonuvabith," Bettis said with his nasal whistle.

"Sure, you can. When I say so. First, break another'a Mark's fingers."

"Frank?" a croaking voice called from the jungle. The call was repeated: "Frank? Where chew at?"

"What the hell—?" Ruhle said.

Nick knew whose voice it was. It belonged to Hector Garcia. Hector had somehow got out of the police car and was fighting his way through the swamp. In pitch blackness yet.

"Over here!" Clarence Bettis shouted back.

"Smart move, Clarence," Ruhle grumbled.

Presently, a crashing and cursing preceded Hector's stumbling from the thicket of mangroves into the clearing. His clothing was ragged, and he was covered with insects, his hands still manacled.

"Hector?" Bettis said with some concern in his voice as he shined his light on him.

Hector saw Nick and, forgetting his damaged ass, tried to take a kick at him. He missed when Nick sidestepped and he fell, rolling over and groaning.

"Wha' th' hell happened to you?" asked Bettis.

"I geet shot in the ass," Hector moaned.

"Better question," Ruhle said, "how'd he get here?" He looked at Nick. "Those're handcuffs on his wrist. Nick? Belong to your crippled girlfriend?"

"Cop—'nother guy—young beetch." Hector struggled onto his knees and spit the muck from his mouth. "They out here somewhere."

"Cop?" Ruhle asked in a different voice. "Talk to us, Hector."

Hector, rolling onto his side, squirmed his shoulders and arms. "Geet these goddam things off me."

"What cop, Hector?" asked Ruhle.

"Highway cop. They kidnapped heem, brung heem along."

"Is this cop armed?"

"Course he is," said Hector. "He's a cop."

"Where thee others?" Bettis asked. "Wherth Paulo an' Kenny?"

Nick spoke up. "They didn't make it, Clarence. Your friend Kenny's dead. He ran into a shotgun. Paulo's either in the morgue or in a hospital in Tampa."

"Thit! I don' fuckin' beleaf it," Bettis growled.

But Martin Ruhle merely looked at Nick and nodded. He said to Garcia, "So you, Hector, got shot in the ass. Know what that tells me? You were running the other way."

"Chew crazy, mon. I got ambushed," Hector protested, jerking his wrists against the restraints.

"Right," said Ruhle. He placed a foot on Hector's shoulder, pinning the man to the ground. "By a school teacher and a crippled woman. Where'd you get these dumb fucks, Clarence? These tough sons of bitches you bragged about."

"Non my fault," Hector said. "Mon, I'm hurting."

"Frank, we better do thomethin' for 'im," Bettis said.

"Yeah? Like what? You got a saw handy?"

In the dim light, Bettis looked perplexed. "We'll haf'a shoot the cuffs off."

"Your tough boy's gonna have to wait." Ruhle kicked Hector sharply in the ribs. "With his mouth shut. Hear that, Hector? Shut your fucking mouth. I want ever'body quiet."

Marilyn Voight let out a shrill cry for help.

Ruhle glowered at her. "My smart girl."

Marilyn glared back at him. She opened her mouth.

Ruhle took a stop closer to Mark Voight, whose eyes were bright with fear. "You yell again, Marilyn, and I'll kick this boy's teeth down his throat. Wanna try me? You know I will."

Marilyn closed her mouth, and her shoulders sagged.

"For Chris'sakes, let them go, Martin," Larry Voight said. "Everything's finished. There's no money. Cut your losses and get out while you can. That cop's never seen you. We won't identify you."

Ruhle grunted a short laugh.

"Martin," Voight said, "you want money. I can arrange some for you. Tell me where to transfer it. I'll give you my word."

Ruhle sneered at him. "Your word? Oh, you're a prince, Larry. I still owe you. You fucked my girl."

"I married her," Voight said.

"I know you didn't see nothing in him," Ruhle said to Marilyn. He squatted to talk to her, his voice almost gentle. "You were desperate, kid. I know how that feels."

"You don't know a fucking thing," Marilyn said. "He's a <u>man</u>."

Nick had to hand it to her. The woman was a fighter. He appreciated that, but she didn't know when to stop needling Ruhle. He watched Ruhle slowly rise, looking down at Marilyn, a harder look now. Nick was suddenly afraid that Ruhle was about to kick Marilyn in the face.

"Ruhle!" he said, to get the man's attention. "Larry's right. He'll keep his word. It gives you a chance to get away."

Nick was watching Ruhle closely. Since the mention of the cop, the man appeared to be losing assurance, maybe losing control. And that worried Nick. Ruhle could bounce from flashes of anger to moments of calm. Anything could happen at any moment. Where the hell is Dickie Nyles? Nick wondered.

"Not bath idea, Frank," Bettis told Ruhle, "if we pack it in."

Ruhle squared his shoulders and turned on him. He said, "Don't start on me, Clarence."

"Yeah, but if we geth thumpthin' out'a this—?"

"Oh, I'll get something out of it," Ruhle said.

Some animal grunted now far away, and Nick saw Sanford Wilcox jump and look around. The jungle noises had quieted somewhat, except for bird calls and the incessant buzzing of mosquitoes and flies.

Ruhle kicked Hector Garcia in the ribs again. “Hector, you said another guy. Who?”

Hector craned his head from his fetal position until he could blink and focus on Larry Voight bound against the tree. “Come with heem. That one there.” He nodded his head vaguely at Sanford Wilcox. “An’ that skinny one wit’ the necktie. ‘Nother crazy mon.”

Ruhle spoke down to Hector, but his eyes flitted toward the dark jungle. “My question is, does he know what he’s doing?”

“No,” Hector said. “He dumber than that one.”

“But the cop will know,” Ruhle said over his shoulder at Bettis. “Rotten fucking luck.” He looked at Nick. “I’ve had nothin’ but bad luck since you showed up, Nick.”

“I know, shit happens,” Nick said.

“So you keep telling me. What we’re gonna do—ever’body that wants to keep their teeth—is this. We’re gonna be quiet, and we’re gonna listen. That goes for you, too, Marilyn. We’re gonna douse the lights and not make a sound. And, Nick—" Ruhle said to Cotton, "—don't make me shoot you yet."

"Give these people some of your bug repellent," Nick said. "They're hurting."

Ruhle uttered a short laugh.

"Wha' the plan, Frank?" Bettis asked. The whistling sound he made was louder than his voice.

"I don't have a fucking plan," Ruhle growled. "I wasn't expecting a cop."

"He might not find uth."

"Maybe. Larry practically found us, and he's a total asshole. Hector found us."

With the flashlights and lantern turned off now, it was dark on the jetty but not pitch black because there was no overhanging foliage to block the night sky. Nick's eyes had adjusted so that he could see the others in silhouette. The moon was mostly obscured behind drifting clouds since the wind had picked up. Some birds flapped their wings nearby. That sound lasted a few seconds before fading. The insects maintained their noisiness.

Hector Garcia couldn't take it anymore. "Somebody geet these cuffs off me!" he shrilled.

"Keep your gun pointed at Nick," Ruhle told Bettis and stepped over to drop to one knee beside the squirming Hector.

"What'cha gonna do, mon?" Hector asked loudly. "Geet these cuffs off? Hey!"

Nick heard an ugly popping sound. All he could see was Ruhle's stooping, broad back.

He saw Ruhle's silhouette straighten up, saw the momentary glint of the gun back in his hand, now moving back toward him.

"Thit, Frank! Whath you do?" asked Bettis.

"I convinced Hector to shut up," Ruhle replied softly.

"Thesus, you broke hith neck."

"He shut up, didn't he?"

"Tha' thmell," Bettis said. "He's thitting his panth."

At the edge of the jetty, Sanford Wilcox made a slight, gagging sound.

"Everybody quiet," Ruhle said. "You too, Clarence."

Now the question in Nick's mind was, how many more minutes would Martin Ruhle wait before he decided to kill Sanford Wilcox and him.

24

For the next few minutes, the passage of time became illusionary as the humans attempted to keep silent according to Martin Ruhle's instructions. Nick Cotton had no idea how long they stood in the dark on the jetty. He concentrated on restraining himself from slapping at the stinging bites of insects on exposed skin. The others, with the exceptions of Ruhle and Bettis who had at least some repellent smeared on arms and neck, had to be equally miserable.

He could hear their breathing, occasional spitting sounds as they sought to chase mosquitoes away from their faces, and an occasional choked off sob from Mark Voight. The surrounding swamp noises alternately picked up and receded, the rising and falling shrillness of the cicadas, another owl chucking, bird wings flapping, splashes somewhere on the dark water, and the interminable buzzing of insects. No noises that sounded like a person or two coming through the bush reached them.

Sweat dripped from Nick's nose. He wiped his nose with his upper arm.

Clarence Bettis finally broke the silence by saying softly, "Therth nobody out there, Frank."

"Maybe," Ruhle said. He stepped closer to Nick. "Did the cop use his radio?"

"Why don't you ask Hector?" Nick said.

Ruhle struck Nick with a backhanded swipe of his pistol barrel against the cheekbone. Nick stumbled backward and nearly fell. He blinked off the searing pain and shook his head. Ruhle was smart enough to step back quickly, out of Nick's reach.

"Nick's a smart-ass, Clarence," Ruhle said. "Go ahead and break Mark's finger."

"Yes," Nick said, feeling a drop of blood track down his cheek. "He called it in." He gave Ruhle a second to consider that. He had asked Dickie Nyles to find Kelly and get her out of there. Had he taken Hal Ryerson also? If not, poor Hal was lost somewhere. The man would be a nut case by this time. "The highway patrol will be here soon."

"Thit," Clarence Bettis said. "Leth go, Frank, while we can." From nearby in the swamp came a noisy flurry of bird wings. "Thith thit's making me crathy." Bettis said in a voice loud enough to carry.

"Hang on, Clarence," Ruhle told him. "I'm thinking how we do this."

From the ebony jungle came the weirdest sound. Everyone on the jetty froze to listen.

"Who? Whoo?"

Nick's mouth dropped open in surprise and disbelief.

It was a <u>human</u> voice. What's worse, it was a human voice doing a very bad imitation of an owl call.

"Whoo? Whoo?"

Shit, Nick thought. It had to be Hal Ryerson. Certainly not Dickie Nyles, the cop. Nick doubted if anything like a very bad bird call was taught at the academy. No, it was Hal. The man had somehow found them and, probably imitating something he'd seen in a movie, was trying to alert Wilcox and Nick to his presence.

The only problem was, it was goddamn ludicrous.

Even Martin Ruhle stifled a laugh.

"Whoo? Whoo?"

"Should we answer him, Nick?" Ruhle said softly to Cotton. "Or should we just invite him to join us? He knows we're here. We know he knows we're here." He flicked on his flashlight and waggled the beam in the general direction of the sound's origin. "Tell him to come into the light and nobody will hurt him. Not too loud now."

"Hal!—get the hell away from here!" Nick yelled.

"Fuck, Nick—" Ruhle started.

A rushing, crashing sound came from the darkness.

Clarence Bettis cursed and fired off a shot. The report clapped loudly in the night.

Into the clearing, barely visible under the night sky, a shape charged onto the jetty. If the noise it had made in the woods was ludicrous, the charge was even more so. For a split second it was caught in Ruhle's flashlight beam, and the second one that Clarence Bettis clicked on. Nick saw that it was indeed Hal Ryerson. The man looked like a wild, frightened animal, mouth open, eyes bulging, hair askew, the colorful shirt and shorts shredded.

Bettis fired again, wildly.

The charging Ryerson, arms waving out in front of him, grabbing for anything or anybody, barreled past Ruhle, past Nick, past Clarence Bettis, who emitted a little whistling scream in surprise and confusion, and—as luck would have it, instead of driving headlong into a Cyprus tree and batting his brains out—collided with Sanford Wilcox, who hadn't budged from his place at the edge of the jetty. At the impact, the breath whoosed from Wilcox.

By the time Ruhle got his light on them, Ryerson and Wilcox were going head over asshole into the dark water. Nick was so fascinated with the bizarre scene himself that he missed his opportunity to go for Martin Ruhle.

"Don't move, Nick," Ruhle hissed. "Clarence! That will bring the cop. If you shoot again, I swear to God I'll kill you. I should anyway, you stupid fool."

The sound of thrashing in the water was receding.

"But they're gething away," Bettis protested.

"To where?" Ruhle said. "And so what? Okay, we gotta move now. Untie the boy. He won't try anything."

"Why?"

"Because—" Ruhle said and stepped toward Nick.

Nick didn't see it coming, and he felt stupid for not expecting it, but Ruhle had already started his swing. This time he used the butt of the gun, and it connected solidly with Nick's head, just in front of the temple. A bright light exploded in Nick's brain, and his knees went limp. He didn't comprehend that he was falling until his face was flush with the wet ground. He was struck again, this time on the back of the head. His whole body filled with a nausea such as he had never experienced. If he wasn't dead, or dying, he wished he were and that it would hurry up.

He heard Ruhle's and Bettis's voices, but the words sounded choppy. One thing Nick knew for certain. He wasn't getting up right away.

"Now I can thoot 'im," Bettis said, the sound of his voice drifting as though from a great distance.

Nick's weak vision was brightened by Ruhle's light shined into his face. "Do what I told you, Clarence. Untie the boy and untie Marilyn. When we're ready to move, you can shoot Nick."

"But thit—" Bettis started.

Ruhle cut him off sharply. "Clarence! Shut the fuck up and do what I tell you. Argue with me, and I'll leave you here like Hector."

There was a mumbling from Bettis that Nick couldn't catch. The light moved away from his face, but his eyes still refused to focus. He wanted to shut them, let the sickness swallow him, and maybe he could peacefully slip out of consciousness. But he fought it, turning his head with an agonizing effort in the direction of the choppy voices, struggling to keep his brain functioning. He wished he had some strength left in his body.

Martin Ruhle popped one of the flares and dropped it, illuminating the clearing again, brighter this time. His back was to Nick.

"Frank," Clarence Bettis said, down on his knees behind Marilyn, tugging at the knot on her wrists, "whath the fucth's going on?"

"The cop," Ruhle told him. "If he's out here searching, you know he heard your shots. Now he might see the light and find his way here. We won't be here. Hurry it up, Clarence."

Nick willed consciousness and effort into himself. With a forced, painful concentration, he made the supreme physical effort to roll over, then rolled over again, away from Martin Ruhle. Ruhle still had his back to him. The moist earth concealed any sounds Nick made. He forced himself to roll over again—toward the edge of the jetty.

One more roll—and then Nick felt gravity taking hold of him. His fuzzy brain told him that he was falling.

"Frank!" Bettis shouted.

Nick splashed into the water. It filled his nose, mouth, and throat. He thought he heard sounds but could not decipher them. Then a gunshot, from a long way off, or maybe his brain had cracked—he didn't know. He didn't feel anything as the black water dragged him down. He willed his arms and legs to move but couldn't tell if they were responding.

Whatever consciousness he had clung to was snuffed out in the blackness.

25

Nick Cotton woke up coughing great gobs of water from his burning throat and sinuses. His head felt on fire. He had the scary realization of a great weight on his back, pressing down, and wondered what creature had hold of him before he realized it was a person straddling him, pumping him out.

"He's okay, he's coming to." Hal Ryerson's voice sounded far off.

"Nick, don't move," Sanford Wilcox's voice said. "Lie still till we can get some help."

Nick's ears rang. "Get off me, Hal," he managed to gasp.

The weight lifted. Painfully, Nick accepted assistance to roll onto his back. He coughed more water and stared upward into the black night sky. Shapes hovered over him that gradually took form. There was light from somewhere. But where? Then he remembered the flare Ruhle had popped. Nick realized that he was back on the jetty.

"Larry?" he asked, weakly.

"I'm here." Voight knelt beside him. "I'm okay."

"Good," Nick gasped. "I thought he might'a killed you."

"Worse," Voight said. "They took Marilyn and Mark. The bastard knew that'd hurt me more than shooting me. My family's gone, Nick."

"Help me up," Nick said, lifting his arms.

"Better not," Wilcox told him. "You've got a gash on your head. Police should get here soon if Dickie Nyles did his job."

Nick had to get up to see if he could handle being on his feet. "Hal!" he snapped at Ryerson.

Ryerson took his arms and hauled him to a standing position. Nick staggered until Ryerson and Wilcox caught him.

"Dammit, Nick, you might have a concussion."

"Who pulled me out?"

"Hal and Sanford did," Voight said. "They saved your life."

"We were in the water," Ryerson explained. "We didn't know what to do except keep quiet and keep our heads down as low as possible. They were pissed off when you went in. The bald one took a couple shots at you. We had to wait till they left before we could come after you."

Nick gradually felt his equilibrium returning. He tested it and was able to stand without assistance. "Gone how long?" he asked.

"Five to ten minutes," Larry Voight said. "We were so close."

"Yeah, close to getting killed," Nick told him. He looked at Ryerson. "Hal, that was a gutsy move—charging in and grabbing Sanford."

"All by accident," Ryerson said, humbly. "I didn't know what to do to help you guys. I was being eaten up by bugs, then something brushed against my leg and scared the shit out'a me. I just panicked and started running."

"Now we're stuck here," Voight said, miserably.

Think, Cotton, Nick told himself. His mind worked to focus on something, something that had fleeted past while he attempted a few steps to see if he could manage walking. His balance seemed fair when he concentrated on it, but his body still had the urge, giving him the fear, to collapse. He shook his head, making it ache more. It was another couple of seconds before his vision cleared.

"They know where they're going," Voight said. "We don't even know if we can follow the trail. The flare's burning out, and it's pitch black in that jungle."

Then Nick remembered what had been nagging his brain. "Larry, did they take your car keys from you?"

"No. They're still in my pocket. But they got the van."

"Not unless they find an extra key," Nick said. "I got Marilyn's. Dickie Nyles' too."

Voight shook his head. "She's got a key for the Chrysler in her purse."

"Yeah, but she don't have her purse. She didn't take it from the house." Nick was getting it straight in his head now. "I've got her van key."

"Then maybe they're not gone," Voight said, this time with a touch of hopefulness.

"Unless Ruhle knows how to hot-wire, and that I don't know. There's a possibility he might not."

Voight gripped his arm, the suddenness of it almost toppling Nick. "When we were kids we swiped a car to take a joyride. But we had to find one with the key. Martin didn't know about wiring then."

"Without transportation, they'd have to get out on the road and stop somebody," Wilcox said.

Voight's hopefulness faded. "Yeah, but how can we catch up to them? We'll get lost out there."

"Think," Nick said, talking more to himself than anyone else and squeezing his fevered forehead between thumb and fingers. He turned to Wilcox. The flare had almost burnt down, and in a few moments they would be enveloped again in total darkness. "When he brought us here, we veered to the left. Right?"

"No—left," Wilcox said. "I mean, yes, you're right. Left."

"How about it, Hal?"

"Don't ask me," Ryerson said. "I was wandering around, bumping into trees, falling in bushes. I might'a gone in a dozen circles before I heard voices."

Nick was busy calculating. "A distance somewhere between a hundred and two hundred yards. That was my guess. Sanford?"

Wilcox shivered violently. "Distance I don't know about. We did some veering from one side to another. I don't know how much ground we covered before that, Nick. They took the lantern and flashlights. If we leave this spot, we'll be in the dark."

"Sorry I'm no help," Hal Ryerson muttered.

Again, Larry Voight grabbed Nick's arm. "All we can do is head out and feel our way along."

"Too slow," Nick said. He shook his head, trying to clear it, succeeding in only making it hurt more. He raised a shaky hand to point across the water. "Look at that tree line out there. See it? It looks like it curves to the right."

"Nick, I can't even see the trees," Wilcox said.

"That darker mass over there. If they're making their way along that goddamn trail, we might cut 'em off."

"How?"

"Take the water," Nick said. "We'll wade and swim. That way."

"The water?" Ryerson said. "Are you nuts? That knock on your head put you out of your mind. There's crocodiles and snakes, to say nothing of all the diseases we can pick up in that swamp."

"What's the alternative? We won't find our way anywhere before daylight."

"We gotta try," Larry Voight said. "Hell, there's a chance."

"I won't argue with Larry, but you guys stay here," Nick said to Wilcox and Ryerson. "When it gets light, you might be able to find that trail. And if Dickie did what he said, somebody will come before then."

"We'll be dead," Wilcox said. "All these mosquitoes. We'll do what Dr. Voight does. I'm not much of a swimmer. More like a flounderer."

Nick peered at the dark water and turned to Voight. "Water's probably not that deep in most places if we stick close to the shoreline."

"Let's get going," said Voight.

"Oh, hell," Ryerson said in resignation, "I can't stand getting eaten by these bugs. Count me in. But what if we're wrong? Only going deeper into this swamp?"

"Then we're in trouble," Nick said.

With Nick leading, they eased into the water, sinking at once as far as their chests, in Voight's case to his chin. The tepid water felt slimy. Wading became cumbersome, dammed near impossible as their feet sank above ankle deep in the bottom muck.

First, testing the depth, they made their painstakingly slow way around the side of the jetty. Then they were in among trees and crawlers. Occasionally, the footing hardened, and they rose to waist deep before stepping into more goo and sinking back to their armpits. It was treacherous going, slogging around roots, getting entangled in weeds, sinking in muck. Twice, plunging ahead in the blackness and trying to sight on the darker shadow of the trees at shoreline, Larry Voight went totally under and had to swim back to the surface with the aid of the others.

"Don't rush it," Nick told Voight. "Let me go first."

He moved in front and plodded on, his feet being sucked into the bottom muck. Behind him, Nick could hear Hal Ryerson's labored breathing as the man fought to keep up. He hoped Hal wasn't working himself into a heart attack. Also, from somewhere behind, he could hear the mutterings of Sanford Wilcox.

"Larry!" Nick called back to him in a low voice. "We'll do better time if we swim and then take rests."

"Anybody here not know how to swim?" Voight asked softly.

"I'm not much good at it," Wilcox whispered. "I'll try."

"Larry, fall back and try to help Sanford," Nick said.

"Just don't let me drown," Wilcox whispered.

In a few moments, Nick, probably the best conditioned swimmer in the group, struck out. His nausea was passing, but his head still throbbed, and his arms and legs felt leaden. At that, it was easier to swim than to wade. He had to remind himself to stop after a couple of minutes to give the others a breather.

"All these trees around us," Wilcox gasped. "I can't see a thing."

"Little longer," Nick urged. "Then we'll cut to our left toward the shoreline."

"I hope we didn't get turned around in the wrong direction," Ryerson wheezed. Then he exploded with "Shit!" when there was a loud splash off to his right.

The next moment Wilcox and Ryerson were frantically churning the water to froth, outdistancing both Larry Voight and Nick Cotton. They thrashed forward for a full ten seconds before stopping. Nick had lost sight of them, but he could hear their wheezing inhalations.

When he caught up to them, he said, "I thought you couldn't swim, Sanford?"

"What the hell was that?" asked Wilcox.

"Sounded like something big to me," Ryerson gasped.

Nick gave them a few seconds to calm themselves as Larry Voight swam up and planted his feet. Here they were, Nick thought, four guys up to their chests in a swamp. One, himself, with some conditioning and training, the other three with zilch. It did not make him optimistic.

Nick pushed off and settled into longer strokes. Since they had started, his saturated clothing had been trying to drag him down, and he had battled it hard every inch of the way. He knew it was the same for the others. He couldn't hear a sound from Larry Voight except splashing as the man was trying to stay close arrears.

When they rested again, Ryerson asked, "How long we been doing this? Feels like an hour."

"About ten minutes," Nick whispered. "You guys okay? Can you keep going a little longer?"

"We can keep going," Voight said.

Moving toward what he perceived as the shoreline was Nick's next challenge. Bumping into mangrove trees, tripping over underwater roots, getting entangled and then having to free himself, he found their progress even slower. It required all four men grabbing and helping each other. Nick wondered if he had led them into a worse situation than they would have encountered had they tried to plow through the jungle in total darkness.

"If we get out'a this goddam water," Ryerson wheezed, "where will we be?"

"God only knows," Wilcox muttered.

Nick said, "We'll try a straight line when we reach solid ground. Main thing is not to get separated."

"And how do we do that?"

"I'll go first. Line up and take hold of the guy's belt in front of you."

Nick's silent prayer was answered when he slopped up a slippery slope and slid to his knees, but was free of the water. He crawled further before trying to get up on his feet. On solid ground he stood and bent forward, catching his breath, with his hands on his knees. He heard the others gasping and cursing as they clambered after him.

"Question, Nick," Wilcox said, sucking air.

"Shoot."

"My point. What happens if we do catch up to them? Those two guys have guns—"

"And we don't," Hal Ryerson finished.

"We'll ambush them," Nick said.

"What? With sticks?" asked Ryerson.

"Yeah, with sticks. Or anything else we can get our hands on. We can't let one of 'em get us in his light while the other one pulls his gun. That's the main thing." Not much of a plan, Nick realized.

"Let's go. Hurry up," said Larry Voight.

"We can't go running," Nick told him. "We have to take it slow and hope we intersect that path." He looked up, dejected at the cloudiness. But under the trees, they wouldn't have gotten much light with a full moon. "Line up and take hold of the belt in front of you."

Nick, leading, tried to bead on an imaginary straight line inland from the water. It was immensely tough and slow going. After a few minutes he halted, and the others ran into him from the rear. Feeling, groping, ahead of him, he had come upon a tangle of impenetrable vines and brush.

"Detour," he whispered to them.

Voight squeezed past him and tried to attack the barrier with both hands.

"Give it up, Larry. It's tougher than you are."

"We can't stop now," Voight said.

"These goddam bugs are all over us," moaned Ryerson. "I think I got a leech stuck on my ass. I'm afraid to feel for it."

"We gotta keep moving," Larry Voight insisted.

"Okay," Nick said. "Take hold of my belt. We'll go left till we find a way to cut back to the right."

"You're guessing, Nick."

"Of course, I'm guessing. It's all I can do."

They detoured until Nick could feel a way through an opening, and then he guided them back in what he hoped was the right direction. The problem with trying to travel at night in a forest, without a light or compass, and no clear view of the stars, was that he couldn't really know where they were headed. Another eerie thing about it were the night noises all around them, mostly distant, some closer. What was really close was the never-ending buzz of the insects. Nick realized they were a battered group of men, totally out of their realm. Bug bitten, poked by branches, hacked by sawgrass, tripping over roots, sinking into syrupy muck, probably infected with a number of alien organisms, and not able to see a foot in front of them, he had no idea where they actually were.

"I'm still hungry," Hal Ryerson, bringing up the rear, announced.

Nick almost laughed. It probably was a good thing, a good tension-breaker. A laugh might inspire hope, and they needed something inspirational. It was better than fumbling around out here in mortal danger with a serious mind. Nick wished Larry Voight could find something humorous, but he knew that wasn't possible.

"Hal, you're pulling my pants off," Wilcox grumbled.

"Right now," Ryerson went on, "I'm thinking of a thick ham sandwich and a cold iced tea."

"You would be thirsty," said Wilcox. "I swallowed half of that black lagoon."

"Maybe a piece of key-lime pie for dessert," said Ryerson.

"Shut up about it," Larry Voight snapped.

"Sorry, Dr. Voight," Ryerson said. "Thinking about it takes my mind off how fucking miserable I am."

"We're all fucking miserable," Sanford Wilcox said, surprising all of them with his use of the "f" word. "And quit pulling back on my pants."

"You know, I think my shirt's ruined," Ryerson said. Fact was, it had been in tatters the last time Nick had seen it. "And my shoes, too."

"Nick," Voight said behind Nick's shoulder, "can we dump these two morons?"

"Wouldn't be humane," Nick said, then stumbled forward and fell.

All four of them went down in the brush in a heap. Nick hadn't had time to warn anybody about the root that had hooked his toe.

"Everybody okay?" he asked.

"Wait a minute," Ryerson gasped. "I got stabbed by something."

"We'll tend to it later," Voight said. "Get up."

"Maybe I got snake-bit. It's burning." There was more than a touch of panic in Ryerson's voice. "Oh, Jesus."

"You got stuck in the brush," Voight told him. "On your feet, or we'll leave you here."

That got Ryerson up. When they were standing and reasonably assembled again, Nick said, "Line up. Let's go. Don't turn loose of the guy's belt in front of you."

He felt Voight take hold of his belt. He couldn't bear to tell Larry Voight that he was feeling some panic himself. Falling down, getting up, trying to work around this brushpile, Nick had no idea in which direction they had turned. All he could do was put his faith in blind luck and hope for the best.

"Are we going in the right direction?" Voight finally asked.

"Sure," Nick said. But he didn't know. If they fell in the water once again, they'd know they had got turned around.

"Tell me we still got a chance," Voight said between rasping breaths.

"We got a chance, Larry. How much of one, I don't know. Hang onto that. Following that trail was not easy. Now Ruhle and Bettis have to drag along a bound woman and a young man. And they'll be watching and listening for our cop buddy. I think Ruhle's gonna be careful and move as slowly as we are."

Nick had no idea how much more time passed before he brushed a mass of wet, tree webs away from his face and almost fell forward again. It came as a shock when he realized he was in an opening, a break in the forest. He stopped and the others jammed in behind him. There was still no light through the overhead branches, but Nick could barely discern that the next wall of jungle was a few feet in front of them. At least it gave them a chance to collect their breaths.

"Is this it?" Voight asked eagerly. "This the trail?"

"I don't know. Maybe. Maybe just a break."

"How can we be sure?" whispered Wilcox.

"We can't."

"Can we follow it?" asked Voight.

"We can try," Nick told him. "We can turn right here and see how far it takes us."

With Nick in the lead, taking it slowly and cautiously, the others a few inches apart behind him, they stepped along the narrow opening. Branches and fronds brushed them, cutting them, but at least they were moving now without clawing their way through jungle. Their pace picked up, Nick groping with his hands out front, reaching for anything that might block them. He came up against a tree, and it took him a few seconds of feeling around with hands and feet to realize that the little trail curved here.

He tried to remember the turns when Wilcox and he had been taken to the jetty by Ruhle. But Ruhle had had a flashlight, and the lantern, and had moved them along quickly. It was useless now to try to outguess the night and the jungle. Stick to the opening, Nick told himself.

Suddenly he thrust out his right arm, and Voight ran into it, almost clotheslining himself. Wilcox ran into Voight, and Ryerson bumped into Wilcox.

"What—?" Ryerson started.

Nick shushed him. He had heard something, but he didn't know what. He knew it wasn't a bird or an insect. He stood, listening.

"What, Nick?" whispered Voight.

"Voices, I thought," Nick whispered back.

They stood in the thick silence, listening to the insects and birds.

"I hear noises but not voices," Ryerson said, softly.

A cracking of brush sounded somewhere to the left front of them, not far away.

Friend or foe? Nick had to assume the worst and get his companions off the trail. It could be Ruhle or Bettis doubling back to check, and each of those men had guns. Nick felt pretty sure that this time they would simply commence shooting. But, for the moment, he kept his invisible hand up, keeping the others bunched and quiet. He was waiting for another sound, either nearer or farther.

A quick flickering of light showed and then disappeared. It had to be a flashlight.

"Get off to the sides," Nick whispered. "Behind something. Stay as low as you can and quiet."

Nick worked his way around the base of a tree, careful not to make noise. He felt somebody edge in beside him.

"Me," Voight's voice whispered.

From this position, if it was Bettis or Ruhle, not both of them, Nick figured he might be able to jump the man. Wrestle him down until the others came to help. Get hold of the gun if he could. It might be the best chance he would get at disarming one of them.

"Larry," Nick whispered to Voight, "if there's more than one, I'll take the first one. You tackle the other one. Both of these guys are right-handed. Try to keep a gun away from you and hold on."

"Okay," Voight whispered.

No doubt about it now. Another flicker of light, the way a flashlight is waved from side to side, but still mostly obscured by the foliage. Whoever was coming this way was not trying to be quiet. A sound like branches being moved aside reached Nick, followed by a bird screeching and fluttering of wings.

Closer.

Any moment now.

Then, for an instant, Nick believed there were <u>two</u> people coming. Not hearing voices, but just by sounds. Yet only one had a flashlight, or so it seemed. It was impossible to make out anything in this darkness. He would have to wait until the guy was very close.

His gun will be in his right hand, Nick reminded himself, his flashlight in his left. Angle the attack to grab the right arm. Then do what he had instructed Larry Voight to do. Hang on.

It just didn't make a lot of sense that both Ruhle and Bettis would be doubling back. If they were, what had they done with Marilyn and Mark? Tied them up again? Nick hoped he was wrong about two people approaching.

As soon as the first figure, uttering an audible sigh of relief, stepped onto the trail, Nick launched himself headlong. He smashed into the person with a head-butting tackle, his right hand grabbing at the other's right arm, his fingers digging into a muscled, bare forearm, dragging down on it, the weight of his assault driving both of them off-balance. They crashed down into the brush, and Nick started flailing with his free fist at the guy.

He hit him in the body, in the neck, all the time squeezing the arm he gripped with his other hand, forcing it between the two of them. The flashlight had been jarred loose somewhere. The other's left arm crossed over his body with a palm heel strike at Nick, catching him beneath his already cut right eye, stunning him, but still Nick held onto the arm and kept jabbing with his other fist. Both of them grunted with the exertion.

"Goddammit!—you're under arrest," the voice of the other man gasped.

Nick disengaged and rocked back on hands and knees. "Dickie?"

The other man relaxed his struggle also. "Who's on top of me?"

"Nick Cotton."

"Shit," Officer Nyles said. "Get off."

Stumbling in the tangle of undergrowth, Nick got up. He reached, fumbling in the dark, for the other man's arm and partially lifted him until Nyles got his feet under him.

The flashlight was picked up and waved at them. Kelly Moore's voice said, "What're you doing, Coach? You're beating up the wrong guy."

Nick couldn't have described the feeling of relief that filled him at that moment. "Am I glad to see you," he said. "Though I can't see you. Get the light out of my eyes."

26

"I got lost out there," Dickie Nyles explained softly as the little group of would-be rescuers huddled on the trail. "Don't know how much time passed. This dammed flashlight wasn't doing me much good. I never would've found Kelly if she hadn't stopped and started cussing the bugs."

"I found <u>him</u>," Kelly said. "And I stopped because I broke another nail. My legs are all scratched, too. He was talking to himself."

"I don't talk to myself," said Nyles.

"Do so," Kelly insisted. "And he was the one cussing, not me. Then this brave policeman here tries to drag me back to the car, and we get lost again. Look at me. I'm a mess." She sniffed. "My hair's ruined, I broke three nails, and I'm chigger-bit all over."

"We heard gunshots," Nyles said to Nick Cotton and Larry Voight. "I couldn't tell from what direction. Anybody hit?"

"We were lucky," Nick said. "Ruhle and Bettis have all the guns."

"Except mine." Nyles patted his hip. "We decided to move in widening circles, looking for a path or a sign of you guys."

"We didn't decide anything," said Kelly. "He read that in a book somewhere."

"Is she always so goddamn critical?" asked Nyles.

"We can't stand here and chit-chat," said Larry Voight. "They're getting away."

"They took Marilyn and Mark Voight," Nick said to the cop. "They'll go for the cars. You're the one thing they're worried about."

"Come on," Voight whispered. "Let's go. We got a light now, and Dickie's got his gun."

"Slow, Larry," Nick said. "They could be waiting to ambush us anywhere along this trail." He turned to Nyles. "They'll be able to see our light coming. Did you have an extra key in your car?"

"Extra?" Nyles said. "Hell, I left the key in the ignition."

"I've got it," Nick told him. "And I've got Marilyn's van key. Larry's got his in his pocket. They might be stuck without transportation."

"That's good," Nyles said. "But they're still armed, it's two to one, and that's their advantage."

"Give me the goddamn light," Larry Voight snapped. "You can stay here and discuss it all you want. I'm going after Marilyn and Mark."

Nyles kept the flashlight out of Voight's reach. "Not by yourself, you're not. We'll do this together, but we need to know what we're doing."

"He's right, Larry," Nick said. "We have to use the light a little at a time, on and off, only enough to follow the path. And we have to go slowly."

"If you hear or see anything," Nyles said, "duck into the brush and keep low."

Kelly cursed loudly and swatted a mosquito biting her leg.

"And it's better if we're quiet," Nyles said to her. "Single file."

Nyles took the lead, gun drawn and in his right hand, flashlight in his left at shoulder height and a little away from his body. He flicked the light on and off just enough to keep a bearing on the path, stopping every few feet to plot position and direction.

Nick noted that the ground was becoming firmer underfoot. The pathway appeared to be widening somewhat. Ahead of him, Nyles switched off the light and turned. Even though the cloudy night was quite dark, emerging from the blacker jungle behind them, Nick could make out his companions' shapes and silhouettes.

"Trail's widening," he whispered to Nyles. "It can't be much further."

"Why're we stopping?" Larry Voight wanted to know. "I don't see anything."

"Sir, they'll be watching for us," Nyles told him in a whisper. "We need to get off this path and into cover." He raised his voice only enough to carry to the others. "We'll split up to both sides. Kelly, Ichabod, Fat Hal, you three get behind some trees. Mr. Voight, Mr. Cotton and I will take the other side and move ahead. No more flashlight. I don't want to draw any shots if we can help it."

"Kelly, where are you?" Nick asked.

"Back here, Coach."

Nick pushed his way back to her until he could grab one of her hands. "Young lady, you get behind a tree and stay put. Make no noise."

"Forget it, Coach," she said. "I'm not standing still to get eaten."

"She's got a point," Hal Ryerson whispered. "I'd rather get shot."

"Shit," Nick said, shaking his head. "Okay. You can keep moving but real slow. Don't get ahead of Dickie and me." He turned and groped for Sanford Wilcox, getting his mouth close to Wilcox's ear. "Sanford, you take charge of Kelly," he whispered. "Don't let her do something stupid."

"What're we waiting for?" asked Voight.

"Don't go charging out there, Mr. Voight," Dickie Nyles said. "I know you want to, but don't. We got to find out exactly where they are and where your family is."

"Maybe we can trade. The car keys for my family."

Nick had moved back to the front close enough to catch Voight's suggestion. "That's what they'll want," he said softly. "But Ruhle won't make a trade like that. He'll threaten first." He touched Nyles' sleeve to get his full attention. "We might have another small advantage. They don't know I'm alive. And they don't know where you might be. But they left Larry alive. If he goes in from the front—"

"Yeah, a diversion," Nyles said. He seized Voight's shirt front. "But you've got to keep a distance from them. Close enough to get their attention but far enough away to run into the trees if you have to."

"Let's do it," Voight said. "I'm willing."

At Nyles' direction, the group split, Wilcox, Ryerson, and Kelly moving into the thick brush to the right of the trail, Nick, Voight, and the cop slipping in among the trees to their left. With excrutiating slowness they moved forward, close enough to the pathway to be able to follow bends. Despite their efforts, bushes rustled and branches snapped under their movement. Nick felt the burning scrapes from brush mixed with his sweat and bug bites and could only imagine the pain the others were suffering.

Suddenly a light came on ahead of them, a bright glare that was still mostly obscured by the trees.

Nick got his lips close to Nyles' ear. "Dickie, if we can see Ruhle and Bettis, I want you to shoot Ruhle. Don't give him any warning. Don't play cop and ask him to freeze. He'll be the big man with the full head of hair. If you can take him out, Bettis might be scared enough to give up the hostages."

"They're waiting for us," Nyles said.

"I know. If Larry can get Ruhle's attention, I'll try to work around to the side. You better stay in line where you can get a shot at him. Dickie—" Nick gripped Nyles' arm, "...don't miss. It's all or nothing for Ruhle now. He's cornered. He will kill the hostages."

"I've never shot at a man," Nyles muttered. He turned to Voight. "Dr. Voight, you'll be exposed in the light."

"I'll get him talking," Voight said. "He'll want the key in his hand before he kills me. If I can get him in the open, you'll have a chance."

"Great," Nyles said with sarcasm. "I'll probably have only one shot. If I can light him, you hit the deck. You ready?"

They moved ahead in the dark. It was pointless now to try to be silent. Every step rustled brush or cracked fallen branches. Nick didn't think Martin Ruhle would scare and shoot at noises. Dripping sweat, holding up a hand to shield his face from tree limbs and high bush, he inched forward with Dickie Nyles right behind him.

Time passed, now much Nick couldn't guess, as they wound their way through the jungle close to the main path. The brightness increased through the foliage. Nick and Dickie came to a stop and held their position, panting and peering toward what they now knew were high-beam headlights pointed toward the trail.

"Hey! Whoever you are!" Martin Ruhle's voice called. "Whoever's stumbling around out there? Who am I talking to? Speak up, or I'll throw a shot at the next noise I hear."

Wherever the man was positioned, there was no seeing him beyond the glare of the headlights.

"It's me, Martin," Larry Voight shouted back. "I'm coming in."

"Larry? Goddamn, man! How'd you find us? Who's with you?"

"Nobody! I want my family, Martin."

"I bet you do." Ruhle laughed. "Where's Nick?"

"I don't know. I think he's dead."

"So you're alone?" Ruhle said. "That's hard to believe, Larry. Hey, Nick!" His voice rose. "If you're out there planning something, forget it."

"I told you I'm alone," Voight said.

"How 'bout those other two guys? Those friends of yours?"

"They're trying to find their way back," Voight called. "Martin, I know what you want."

"Yeah, I want one 'a the car keys," Ruhle shouted. "Yours will do. It was dumb of me not to take it from you. Come out in the light, Larry. I won't shoot you."

"Not yet," Nyles whispered to Voight's back. "Don't walk out there. I can't see shit."

"Come on, Larry," Ruhle's voice boomed. "Don't be scared. I got Marilyn and the kid here. You know that already. What if I pop one 'a the kid's kneecaps? You won't like hearing him scream."

Nick could hear the exchange as he edged carefully around to the side, deeper into the bush, praying that he wouldn't make a sound to alert Ruhle or Bettis. He thought he detected another questioning voice, but low, coming from somewhere beyond the headlights. That had to be Clarence Bettis. Nick couldn't hear was Bettis was saying.

After a silence, Ruhle called again, his voice tenser. "Larry, is the cop with you? If he is, I got a message for him. Listen, I got two hostages here. Woman and her kid. All I want's your car key. Throw it out here in the light, and stay where you are. Then I'll let my hostages go."

Nick was glad that Dickie Nyles didn't answer.

"Listen!" Ruhle shouted. "If I'm talkin' to a highway patrolman, you listen to me. My partner's got a woman and her kid here, at gunpoint. If you try anything, they'll die. Understand? Forget that cop bullshit. We'll take your car and leave the hostages."

"I'm alone, Martin," Voight called back to him. "Trade with me. My key for my family."

Nick concentrated on moving as quietly now as possible, hoping the constant noise of cicadas, bugs, and birds covered his steps. From a break in the brush, he could tell that it was the police cruiser's headlights that were on. He was practically alongside it, but still in the bush felling sharp branches dig into his face and scalp.

He heard Bettis's voice, some panic in it. "Frank! Maybe it ain't the cop. Git the fuckin' key an' leth git out'a here."

"Am I talking to the cop, or not?" shouted Ruhle. "If it's the cop, I know you're armed. Goddammit, I'm telling you these people I got—their lives depend on you. If it ain't the cop, then you better step out in the open, Larry, where I can see you."

Nick heard Voight's voice call back, "Let either Marilyn or Mark go first. Then I'll come forward and give you the key for the other one."

"What you'll do is throw it out here in the light. Do it, Larry, and I'll give you the kid. Do it now!"

Don't do it, Larry, Nick prayed silently.

Faintly, from his angled location away from the headlights now, Nick could see Ruhle's dark silhouette. He was still too far away to rush him, and he didn't know where Bettis was. It would turn into a suicide mission if he made the wrong decision. He moved toward the rear of the cruiser, sighting on the nearest red taillight.

"Look!" Ruhle shouted again, agitation in his voice. "If it's you, cop, say something. Or throw one'a the goddamn keys. I'll count to three, and then my partner's gonna blow a knee off the kid."

Marilyn's voice called out: "He means it. Somebody do what he says."

Nick had made it to a spot behind and outside the cruiser. There was still a fifteen or twenty foot open space to cover. But now he could detect another silhouette standing outside on the passenger's side of the Chrysler. It had to be Bettis. Nick hoped that Dickie Nyles was getting into position to take as good a shot as possible at Martin Ruhle. When Nyles fired, he would make his move. He was gambling that Bettis wouldn't start shooting right away.

The downside of the gamble was that Nyles might not take Ruhle out with his first shot. If Ruhle was conscious enough to snap orders, Bettis would follow them—Nick was certain of that.

He continued to move slowly forward.

"One!" shouted Ruhle.

Nick was beside the Chrysler now, working his way around behind it, still several feet from Bettis whose back was practically to him.

"Two!"

"Don't shoot!" another familiar voice called, and Nick froze in horror.

It was Kelly Moore's voice.

"Don't shoot!" she called again. "I'm scared!"

Nick leaned his body to one side to follow the beam of the headlights down the pathway. Dammit it to hell, he thought. There was Kelly coming tentatively forward into the lights. She had a hand up, shielding her eyes from the direct brightness.

"What'a we got here?" said Ruhle loudly.

"I got lost," Kelly cried plaintively. "I'm so scared. Please, please don't shoot me."

"No problem, honey," Ruhle called to her. "Keep on comin'."

Nick heard Bettis's nasally-slurred voice: "It's tha' kid they had in the house with 'em."

"The one you said's got a cute ass. What'cher name, honey?"

"Kelly!" Kelly replied. She had stopped her forward progress.

"Where's your buddy? Where's Nick Cotton?"

"I ain't seen him," Kelly called back. She sobbed loudly enough that Nick could hear her from where he was. "I tried to find him, but I got lost. It feels like I been lost for hours. I thought something was gonna eat me."

"This is even better," Ruhle said and laughed. "Hey, Larry! Looks like I got myself another kid. That little girl is right in my sights. I's you, I'd walk out here with your hands up where I can see you. I tol' you, all I want's a key."

Nick was in position now to see Larry Voight step into the headlights. The look on Voight's face showed that he was as stunned and confused as Nick that Kelly had run forward.

Kelly sobbed and cried, "Please—don't shoot me!"

"Where's the cop?" Ruhle snapped at her.

"I don't know. Out there somewhere." Kelly sobbed twice more, harshly. "I'm so scared."

"You wouldn't be lying to me, would you, girl?"

Kelly wailed and dropped down onto her knees.

"Run, Kelly, run!" Mark Voight's muffled voice called from inside the open-doored Chrysler.

"No, don't run," Ruhle said. "I'd hafta shoot you down if you do. Come on up here to the lights. I won't hurt you."

Kelly's head bowed forward as she wept loudly.

Ruhle's voice rose. "Cut out the goddamn crying. I tol' you to come here!"

Kelly screeched and rolled in the dirt, drawing her legs up into a fetal position.

"Jesus Christ!" Ruhle grumbled.

Kelly wailed louder and beat at the ground with her fist.

"Thee's scared to death," Bettis said.

"Don't be scared'a me," Ruhle called to her. "Get up and come here."

Nick slowly moved up behind Bettis. The man's attention was focused on the hysterical girl.

"Goddammit!" Ruhle said and started forward. He stepped in front of the headlights, striding toward Kelly.

The night was shattered by the explosion of a gunshot.

Ruhle bucked backwards, slamming into the front of the patrol car, his body seemingly pinned for an instant. He tried to raise his own gun in his right hand, turning sideways as he did, his body jarring as another shot blasted and rocked him. Then he was stumbling away, out of the lights.

Nick was close behind Bettis, who stood transfixed.

"Clarence," he said.

Bettis turned his head and put his already ruined nose squarely in the path of Nick's fist.

Nick's punch was short and hard. The instant pain and shock turned Clarence Bettis as limp as a rag doll. He collapsed, fell down, and lay still.

Two more shots exploded, but Nick had no way of knowing who was shooting at whom. He heard a crashing off in the brush to the right side of the vehicles. At that instant the primary thought in his mind was Kelly Moore's safety. He ran in front of the headlights toward her.

Kelly was still on the ground with two men huddled over her. Not only huddled, but across the top of her, shielding her. A scared face raised into the headlights. It was Sanford Wilcox. The other man was Larry Voight, who had dived onto Kelly when the shooting started. Voight scrambled to his feet.

Nick heard Kelly's calm voice say, "Get off me, Ichabod."

Wilcox rolled away and rose to his hands and knees.

Kelly got to her feet, ineffectually brushing herself off, unhurried in her motions. Her face looked grim and filthy, but not weepy. She looked quite composed.

Nick reached her and pulled her off to one side, out of the main light-beams. "Christ!" he said, "I was afraid you'd got shot."

"Nope. I'm okay," Kelly said. "Ichabod about crushed me. I might'a broke another nail."

"I saw you collapse, and I thought—"

"Hey, Coach, it worked," Kelly said. "You wanted him out where Dickie could see him."

She grinned at Cotton and tilted her head.

"Holy shit!" Nick found it hard to breathe normally. "You were acting?"

Dickie Nyles, gun in hand, appeared beside them. "Are you okay?" he stammered at Kelly.

"Of course," Kelly said, like it was a dumb question.

"How 'bout you?" Nick asked.

"Yeah," Nyles said. "He got off one in my direction but missed. I don't know if I got him with my second. I know I hit him, pretty good, I think."

Nick pointed. "He went off over there. That direction."

"I'll look. You guys stay out of the light. Where's the other guy?"

"Back by the car. Out cold." Nick helped Wilcox to his feet and hugged him. "You're a fucking hero, Sanford. You risked your life to save Kelly."

"She got away from me," Wilcox shrugged.

Larry Voight had made a dead run toward the police car and the Chrysler. Nyles' attempt to shout him down, get him out of the glare of the headlights, was fruitless. Nothing was stopping the man. Finally, Nyles used his flashlight to assist Voight around to the side of the car, to the open door.

When Nick got there, he saw Clarence Bettis still prone on the ground, moaning and showing some signs of movement. Voight was leaning into the backseat, his arms around Mark, pulling the kid close to him. Mark sobbed with relief.

Voight turned his head toward Dickie and Nick. "She's not here." His voice caught. "He's still got her."

"No," Mark sniffed, making a vague gesture at Clarence Bettis. "Mom—took his gun. And his flashlight. She went that way." He pointed in the direction that Martin Ruhle had taken.

Nick straightened up and looked around at the dark jungle. "Shit," he muttered.

He and Dickie Nyles exchanged a look. Gun still drawn, Nyles went into the bush after Marilyn. Nick followed, trying to keep up.

Less than a minute later, Nick found himself separated from Nyles and trying to push his way forward in a reasonably straight line.

He heard voices ahead and stopped.

27

Marilyn Voight caught up with Martin Ruhle deep in the underbrush. The flashlight in her left hand picked up Ruhle's broad back as he stood in a small clearing, slightly spread-legged, his head bowed forward. He appeared to weave a bit. His own flashlight, in his left hand, pointed downward at his side. His right hand held his gun.

"Hello again, Martin," Marilyn said, her voice eerily calm.

Ruhle made small shuffling steps as he turned to face her light. He blinked into it.

"That you, kid?" he said. "Hey, babe, would you look at this? I got shot."

"I see," Marilyn said. "It looks bad, Martin."

"No kidding." A coughing laugh came from Ruhle as he rocked a bit.

Marilyn's right hand raised the pistol she had taken from Clarence Bettis. She had both light beam and gun pointed at Ruhle. In the beam of her light, Ruhle sagged back against a tree for support. His own weapon had been partially raised, but not to point directly at her.

"Shitty thing to happen," Ruhle said. He coughed again, this time trickling blood from his mouth. The front of his shirt looked wet and dark in Marilyn's light. "Damn it all." Ruhle took in a raspy breath. "Who the fuck shot me? Was it the cop?"

"I don't know," she said. "I don't care."

"But you came anyway, didn't you?" That brought no response from her. "Well, I'm glad. Always glad to see you." His voice had become patchy now, the words coming with obvious difficulty. In the light beam, his face grimaced suddenly and his head lowered. Slowly he looked up again. "Just can't stay away from me, can you?"

"I was doing fine for eighteen years," she said.

The tip of Ruhle's tongue came out, pushing more blood with it over his lower lip. "Naw." He bubbled a small laugh as he shook his head. "Not him. Not Larry."

"Him," Marilyn said.

"Tell me 'bout the money, kid. It's okay if you took it for yourself."

"There's no money, Martin. I told you the truth."

Another short, pain-racked laugh came from Ruhle's mouth. "Know what? I believe you. Hell, you can't blame a guy for tryin'."

"You hurt my son," Marilyn said. "I blame you for that."

"So what now?"

Marilyn laughed.

"I know," Ruhle said and coughed. "We can git out together. We can do it, girl. I need your help."

She didn't respond, kept the light beam squarely on him.

"Baby, a couple bullets can't stop me. You can nurse me."

Marilyn didn't say anything.

Ruhle coughed blood, raised and lowered his head. "You an' me. We can start a new life. Like it always should'a been."

Marilyn didn't respond.

"Babe," Ruhle said, "I ain't goin' back to prison."

"You got that right," Marilyn said gently. "I've got your friend's gun pointed right at you, Martin."

"You'd shoot me? I don't think so." Ruhle tried to push himself erect from the tree, showing his weapon now, bringing it around, wavering, toward the light. "I don' wanna shoot you." For a second his teeth bit down hard on his bloody lip. "Okay, babe, if that's how you want it. Stay where you are. I'll leave."

"Martin!"

Ruhle's hand was steadier, through an effort of will, as he pointed the gun at the light. "Hey, babe," he said.

Marilyn squeezed the trigger. The gun bucked in her hand. Ruhle slammed back into the tree. She fired again as he started to slide down, not knowing if she hit him. She was not frantic, not hurried, not even with a look of hatred. She fired a third time.

Then Nick Cotton was beside her, wrenching the gun from her grasp.

"Christ," he said, softly.

The light beam started to waver, and Nick took the flashlight from her as well.

28

"Is—is he dead?" Marilyn whispered.

Nick pointed the pistol and flashlight at the crumpled figure. He raised the gun slightly and fired a shot into the brush. "He is now. I killed him."

"Nick—" Marilyn started.

"I killed him," Nick said firmly. "And you better believe that."

Another light beam poked out from the brush behind them, and a moment later Dickie Nyles was there. He flashed his light on Martin Ruhle.

Nick handed the pistol to Nyles. "I killed him, Dickie."

"I thought I did," Nyles said. "You okay, Mrs. Voight?"

"Don't listen to him," Marilyn said. "I'm the one who shot him."

"She shot <u>at</u> him," Nick said. "She might'a wounded him some more, but she didn't kill him."

"Time out," Nyles said. He tapped Marilyn's shoulder with the back of the hand holding his service pistol. "Go back to your family. Go with her, Mr. Cotton. You got a flashlight."

"We'll make it from here," Nick said.

He brandished the flashlight and took Marilyn's arm, partially supporting her as they made their way through the forest toward the sound of voices.

Larry Voight came thrashing toward them and embraced his wife. They cried in each other's arms.

Nick stepped into the glare of the lantern light that someone had fired up and felt himself stumble. All at once, like a tidal wave, the weariness and pain washed over him. He had to grope to and lean against one of the police cruiser's fenders. He looked to his left and saw the side doors of Voight's Chrysler open. Sanford Wilcox and Hal Ryerson had slumped, half hanging out, into the front seat on each side. They looked totally spent as well.

What Nick wanted more than anything else right now was a place to lay his aching head, put up his feet, and shut his eyes. He looked in the other direction when he heard Kelly Moore's voice speaking to Mark Voight: "Maybe I'll just stay here, or come back after graduation, and go out with Dickie."

"Please, Kelly—" Mark said, his voice pain-racked and choked. His injured hand he cradled to his chest as he stood in front of her, slightly hunched forward with the pain. "Don't do this."

"Why not?" said Kelly. "Dickie looks pretty good in his uniform. I don't mean now when it's all dirty. He told me he doesn't have a girlfriend."

Mark's voice broke. "But—you're my girlfriend."

"What? You're tired of the redhead? Is that what happened? Did you get tired of me?"

"I—I was wrong," Mark stammered. "Did Dickie make a pass at you?"

"So many times I lost count," Kelly said.

"But—but Kel—" Mark whined, "I love you."

"Sure. I bet you said that to your redheaded slut, too."

"I was all mixed up."

As weary as he was, Nick Cotton almost laughed.

Kelly said, "That mean you'll get mixed up again the next time somebody wiggles her ass at you?"

"No, you're the one I love. Oh God, my hand hurts. Kelly, we made plans."

"I'll think about it," Kelly told him. "I broke four fingernails over you."

Now Nick did utter a small laugh.

"Don't do this to me," Mark pleaded. "I'm hurting."

"Good. Serves you right."

Then Nick gave a start as another shot blasted not too far away. Now what? He looked toward the jungle. At its edge, Marilyn and Larry Voight had turned to look. In a few seconds, a light flickered toward them.

Dickie Nyles came out, holding the flashlight and cradling both Ruhle's and Bettis's pistols in one hand against his chest, his own weapon holstered. His face bore a hardened look in the lantern light as he stopped beside the Voights.

"He still had a gun—tried to use it," Nyles said without emotion. "I had to shoot him again." His eyes rolled over toward Nick, and he shrugged. "So, Mrs. Voight didn't kill him, and neither did you, Mr. Cotton. I did. That's what I'll put in my report. I had no choice."

Nick wanted to say something, by way of thanks, about taking Marilyn Voight off the hook. But he could see in Nyles's expression that it wasn't what the deputy wanted.

Nyles, his expression bland, came to the cruiser. "I'll call again. Cars are probably on the road now, looking for this place." He looked at Nick, then at Larry Voight. "Where's the other guy, the bald-headed one?"

Both Nick and Voight were as unaware as he. They shook their heads. Clarence Bettis was nowhere to be seen.

Sanford Wilcox roused himself from the Chrysler. "He got up and went off into the bush. We didn't feel like chasing him."

"Okay," Nyles said. "We'll let somebody else dig him out. He can't get too far."

"He might get away," Larry Voight said.

"To do what?" said Nick Cotton. "Go where? If he makes it out of the swamp, he's finished anyway."

Dickie Nyles grinned at Kelly, taking a long second to look at her, before he slid behind the wheel of his car and picked up the mike.

Marilyn and Larry Voight crowded close to Nick and insisted on putting their arms around him. Marilyn kissed him a couple of times. Nick was getting embarrassed before they stepped back. Had he not been feeling so bad, he might have enjoyed those kisses.

"Can you believe this guy?" Marilyn said, nodding at and indicating her husband. "He comes down here to save me, willing to take on Martin Ruhle."

"Quite a man," Nick agreed.

"I'd do anything for you," Voight told his wife.

"And Mark," she said.

"And Mark."

Mark had moved in close to them. His face looked agonized as he cradled his hand. Marilyn saw the broken middle finger and gasped.

"Son, we better not touch it," Larry Voight said. He called to the deputy, "Dickie, we need medical attention here."

Nyles, holding the mike and sitting half out of his car, waved him off and nodded. The deputy's lips moved as he talked into the mike.

"I'm sorry, Dad," Mark said to his father.

Voight put his arms around his son's shoulders. "Hey, by God, we're okay. I mean it. We're really okay."

Nick gathered himself and limped away to let them have their time alone. Every move he made sent a shot of pain through him somewhere.

"Coach," Kelly called to him. "We all look like shit, don't we?"

"We sure do," Nick said. "Wait till the medics get hold of us. I hope you don't mind taking needles and pills, Kelly. How will I explain to your folks if you get malaria?"

"Not to worry, Coach." She stepped closer and whispered, "You won't tell Mark I climbed in bed with you this morning, will you?"

"Kelly, I didn't even know you were there. I won't say a word."

"Thanks," she breathed.

Nick smiled at her. "So you're gonna forgive Mark?"

"I don't know yet."

"You will," Nick said. "After all, you care enough that you risked your life for him."

"Well, don't tell him that," Kelly cautioned. "I don't want him to know it yet. He's got to suffer awhile."

Nick made his slow way over beside the van and slipped down to sit on the ground. His legs had gotten immensely heavy, and his shoulders, neck, and head felt like there was a great weight bearing down on him. He touched his scalp, and the wound had crusted or dirtied over. With his head down, he had a rush of thoughts.

He thought of Martin Ruhle, alias Frank Carr, and of Clarence Bettis. Of Hector and Paulo Garcia. Even Kenny Neeves. Then he thought of Gus Dick, private eye, and smiled a little.

After a moment, Nick straightened his legs, leaned shoulders and head back against the fender, folded his arms on his chest, and shut his eyes. He didn't even care about the dammed mosquitoes.

It couldn't have been more than a few seconds before he slipped into a dark cavern of uneasy sleep.

About the Author

Thomas Cox is the author of 3 books (2 sports books and 1 novel) plus a number of short stories and articles that have appeared in *Manhunt Mystery Magazine*, *The Saturday Evening Post*, and *The Country Gentleman*. The author has also produced a children's book for young readers, *Wolf's Night*, with 1stBooks.

Printed in the United States
21026LVS00001B/13